LOVE AT THE FLUFF AND FOLD

THE STRAYS OF LOON LAKE, BOOK 1

KITTY BUCHOLTZ

Daydreamer
Entertainment

Love at the Fluff and Fold

Published by Daydreamer Entertainment

Copyright © 2017 by Kathleen Bucholtz

ISBN: 978-1-937719-19-7
ISBN: 978-1-937719-18-0 (ebook)

Library of Congress Control Number: 2022903348

Cover Design: John Bucholtz and Stephanie Shackelford
Cover Images: Romantic couple © Monkey Business - Fotolia.com; Border collie puppy © Viktoria Makarova - Fotolia.com

Edited by Marcy Weydemuller

For Mom,
Thanks for always encouraging me to write down my stories.
You said you liked them all, but I think you might've liked this
one best.
Love you!!

Love at the Fluff and Fold

Kitty Bucholtz

CHAPTER 1

*W*ilfred Larson buttoned his shirt and glanced up at his doctor. "So? What's the verdict, Dill?"

Dr. Bob Dillon, Dill to his friends, wrote a few notes on Willie's chart and said, "Clean bill of health. As always. Should have plenty of fishing in your future."

"Wanna take the boat out tonight?" If there was one activity Willie loved most, it was fishing. Trout, bass, walleye, smelt — he loved them all. He and Dill had been fishing together since they were just out of diapers. He had the photo evidence to prove it.

"Let me ask the boss and I'll text you."

Willie nodded. He and Dill were quite proud of their texting skills these days. Not many of their retired friends had gotten on board with that particular method of communication, but Willie found that his nieces all stayed in touch more frequently if he texted them rather than called or emailed. No one wrote letters anymore since his wife, Velma, died.

Dill laid the chart down and leaned back against the counter in the small examination room at Loon Lake Hospital. "How's Cassie these days? I haven't seen her much."

Willie slid off the exam table and tucked his shirt into his trousers. "She's busy with her final papers and exams. Graduation's coming up in a month or so and she wants to have perfect scores. You know how she is."

Dill ran a hand through his snowy white hair. "Oh, yeah. Beth's the same."

Willie's youngest niece, Cassie, had been driving back and forth to Northwestern Michigan College in Traverse City, about forty miles away, often carpooling with Dill's granddaughter, Beth.

"How's Cassie doing with, uh, you know." Dill waved his hand vaguely through the air.

Willie shook his head. "Single and determined to stay that way, I guess. I wouldn't say that Fletcher fella broke her heart as much as he humiliated her. Makin' like you're gonna ask a woman to marry you, and then high-tailing it outta town soon as the grass gets greener...that's no kind of man for my Cassie."

"If this were the Wild West, we could chase after him with shotguns."

"If we're chasing after folks with shotguns, seems like we shoulda started with Danny. But that ship's sailed and I haven't been able to turn it around for anything."

Danny Kessler was like a son to Willie, just like Cassie was like a daughter. The two kids had grown up together in Loon Lake, had been all but joined at the hip since kindergarten. He'd thought for sure they'd wind up together. But just about the time the two of them had started noticing that their best friend was a little more interesting, a new girl had sailed into town and ruined everything. Danny had fallen hard for Bright Shiny, the not-so-secret nickname his friend Jax had given Lily.

"He still downstate doing construction?"

Willie nodded. "He's been working his way up in that big construction company near Lansing. Getting promoted, doing more than they ask, getting noticed." He didn't try to keep the pride out of his voice. He'd been the one to give Danny his first hammer.

"Maybe you should drop a hint that Cassie's available."

Willie snorted. "Oh, he knows. He pretends he doesn't care, but he's been asking about her more since I mentioned it a few months ago. But if I can't get the boy to come up and visit for anything but holidays, I don't see how I can get them together again. Too bad I'm not dying," he said as an afterthought. "That would put a fire under his behind for a visit."

Dill chuckled. "Yeah, well, we're all dying, aren't we?"

"Sooner or later," Willie agreed. Sooner or later...hmm. "You know," he said slowly, his brow furrowing in thought, "it wouldn't be a lie. You just said it yourself."

Dill took a step toward the door and held up his hands as if warding off Willie's words. He was used to Willie's crazy ideas after sixty-odd years of friendship, but he didn't like to hear them at first. "Hold on, where you going with this?"

Willie feigned an innocent expression. "I'm just repeating what my doctor told me. I'm dying. The kids should know so they can help me make my final plans. I'll need both of them to help get my affairs in order. Right?"

Willie waited and was soon rewarded. Dill grinned and

dropped his hands to his hips. His friend couldn't resist the cockamamie plans they cooked up together.

"It just might work," Dill said.

"We can make our plans tonight on the lake. Bring a notebook."

Dill waggled his phone in the air. "We can use the notes app on our phones, remember?"

"Right, right," Willie agreed. The two men were determined to be the most tech-savvy senior citizens in Loon Lake. Willie walked to the door and slapped Dill on the shoulder. "This'll be fun. I've always liked Christmas weddings."

CASSIE WALKED AS FAST AS SHE COULD TO THE administration building at Northwestern Michigan College. She needed to pick up her cap and gown before the office closed. Two more weeks and she'd be free of school. Finally.

She enjoyed taking classes, but she'd been working on her associate's degree in hospitality management, and then her bachelor's degree in business administration for seven long years. Thank goodness NMC had the University Center. She could get her bachelor's degree from Ferris State University without having to move away from home. She'd thanked God for that innumerable times over the years.

While most of her classmates were locals, hardly anyone lived as far away from Traverse City as she did. And none of them planned on living in a town the size of little Loon Lake after graduation. She didn't care what other people thought, though. She loved her hometown and planned to stay there. It had character.

And characters. Life was never dull, even on days she wanted it to be.

She turned in her paperwork a few minutes before five o'clock, breathed a sigh of relief, and headed for her car. During the forty-five minute drive back to Loon Lake, she thought of all the things she could do this summer since she wasn't taking classes. She could relax. Go to the beach more. Go fishing with Uncle Willie more. Hang out with Tabitha and her kids more. Maybe she'd even get a dog.

On impulse, she pulled into Sonny's Restaurant a mile from home to see what kind of pie they had today. The fruit pies were made with canned or frozen fruit this early in the year, but they had a banana cream, Uncle Willie's favorite, and a chocolate silk, her Achilles heel.

Pulling into her parking space at the Loon Lake Fluff and Fold, she gathered her backpack, her purse, and the bag with the two pieces of pie, and headed upstairs to the apartment she'd shared with Uncle Willie since her mom died when she was fifteen.

Now that she was graduating, she'd need to decide the rest of her future. Like maybe getting her own place to live. Her uncle had been adamant about not taking out student loans, which was why it had taken forever to get her degrees. Earning the money to pay cash made college a part-time pursuit. But now she would start this next phase of her life debt-free. The pie was too small a thank-you for everything Uncle Willie had done for her, but he knew how much she loved and appreciated him. She really was blessed.

Which was something she needed to remind herself of now and then. Her mom was dead, she hadn't seen her dad in years, her almost-fiancé had dumped her, her once-best-friend wouldn't talk to her, and she was twenty-five years old still living at home. But that was the empty portion of a very full glass.

Very full.

Upstairs, she dropped her bags in her room, found a place for the pie in the fridge, set out some ground beef to thaw, and wandered across the street to see if her uncle was in The Laughing Loon.

Uncle Willie was quite the businessman, and he'd taught her at least as much as she'd learned in college. He owned three businesses on this corner of Loon Lake — the Loon Lake Fluff and Fold, The Laughing Loon convenience store and gas station, and the Idle-Awhile Cabins. He'd sold the Cup and Cone Ice Cream Parlor before her mom died to help pay for Cassie's and her sisters' college tuition.

Since then, he'd worked with the Alexanders, local goat farmers, to sell small containers of goat's milk ice cream and goat's milk cheese at The Laughing Loon. It was a big hit with tourists and locals alike, and Uncle Willie got to continue feeding his ice cream habit.

A bell tinkled overhead as she walked into the store. She waved to a few customers she knew and stepped behind the counter to bag groceries while Uncle Willie rang up the items.

"Hello, darlin'," he said with a smile in her direction. He pulled things out of the hand basket in front of him. "Oh, Nancy, I see you're trying the new coconut passion fruit ice cream from Crooked Creek. This is a good one. Just came in yesterday."

"You've tried it? I just love passion fruit." Nancy Franklin was the history teacher at Loon Lake High, one of

Cassie's former teachers. She traveled every summer and brought back pictures and videos to show the kids what the rest of the world looked like. Cassie had loved that class. None of her college teachers had made learning as fun as wacky Mrs. Franklin.

"He thinks it's his job to try all the ice cream before he sells it," Cassie said, grinning at her uncle.

"It's good business to make sure you're selling quality products," Uncle Willie insisted. "Kids these days." He shook his head at Mrs. Franklin, who laughed with him.

Cassie helped him with two more customers, then gave him a hug hello in the lull.

"How was school today?"

"Good. Organizational Management is still kicking my butt. I'll be glad when I never have to think about that again. Everything else is good."

"I can't tell you how proud I am. Graduating with honors. Your mother would be thrilled, but not surprised."

Cassie leaned in and kissed his cheek. "Thanks, Uncle Willie. I couldn't have done it without you."

"Well, that's true," he said, making Cassie giggle. "Kevin will be here in a few minutes, then we can go have supper together. Pick out a movie. You don't mind staying in with an old man, do you?"

Cassie rolled her eyes. "Old Mrs. G is old. You're just…"

Her uncle raised his eyebrows.

"Old-fashioned?" Cassie asked.

Uncle Willie grunted. But his eyes twinkled in fun.

Looking through the DVD rentals, Cassie picked an oldie-but-goodie that they both loved, *RED*, a spy comedy with Bruce Willis, Morgan Freeman, and Helen Mirren. She checked it out behind the counter, told her uncle she'd meet him at home, and left to make dinner.

Before heading upstairs, she walked through the laundromat to make sure nothing needed attention. She'd been working for her uncle since she was ten, along with her once-best-friend, Danny Kessler, and she'd learned that providing good service in a clean and friendly atmosphere was key to bringing customers back time and again. She tended to check things anytime she passed to make sure their customers were getting what they deserved.

As it turned out, one of the washers was half full of dirty water. A handwritten note from CW Emerson, the town dog catcher and an EMT, explained "I swear I didn't do anything to break it."

Cassie laughed. This was the third time in six months that CW had a problem with a machine. She pulled out her phone and called Edge, Jax Edgerly's older brother — no one called him Leroy. The leather-clad biker was a mechanical wizard who could fix anything with a motor. He promised to stop by the next day.

Sitting on the couch later, watching the movie with her uncle and eating her yummy pie, she thought about her very full glass of life. She still had plenty of friends from high school, and she'd become better friends with some, like Edge, now that they were adults. She and Tabitha had grown even closer as Danny drifted away. Even CW wasn't the turd he was as a high school football quarterback. Of course, that new teacher, Lena Hart, had brought out CW's best qualities lately.

Six months ago, Cassie thought she'd found a man who brought out her best qualities, a man she might fall in love with, maybe marry. But he hadn't understood that when she said Loon Lake was her home, for now and always, she'd meant she wasn't leaving. He'd taken a job in Grand Rapids in January and she hadn't heard from him since.

Not exactly true love.

But that didn't mean she couldn't be happy. Like right this minute. She glanced at her uncle out of the corner of her eye. He'd been a major influence as long as she could remember. When her parents were fighting, he and Aunt Velma brought her and her sisters down to The Cup and Cone, made them laugh, and fed them ice cream.

When Danny's dad drank too much and lost his temper, Uncle Willie and Aunt Velma kissed his bruises and fed him ice cream.

When both of their dads left their families within a year of each other, Uncle Willie and Aunt Velma smothered them in love and gave them stability. And ice cream.

From the time they were ten and eleven, Cassie and Danny had swept the Fluff and Fold's floors, emptied the lint traps, run across to The Laughing Loon to buy quarters for customers, and counted out the money they earned together, imagining all the things they'd do when they got older.

Uncle Willie taught them both how to run a business, how to treat customers, how to level a two-by-four, and how to catch and clean and cook many a fish.

Cassie smiled at the TV. She may not have a husband and kids and a big life in the big city like her two older sisters, but she was genuinely happy.

When the movie ended, Uncle Willie turned to her and laid his hand on her arm. "I need to tell you something."

Cassie felt a tiny frisson of alarm. His voice and expression were more serious than she'd seen in a long time.

"Sure," she said, trying to infuse the word with a calm that was quickly waning.

"I went to see Dill today for my annual checkup."

Cassie felt a tremor in her stomach. *Please, nothing bad.* She'd lost too many people she loved.

"And?" she prompted when he didn't say anything.

"Well..." He dropped his gaze as if he couldn't tell her whatever it was if he were looking in her eyes. "I'm...I might be dying, honey. So there are some things we need to do."

Cassie felt herself gasp, her hands suddenly covering her mouth. *No, not this. Not yet.*

Her uncle finally raised his gaze to hers, looking determined. "I need you and Danny to help me get my affairs in order. Can you do that? Will you work together and do what needs to be done? For me?"

"Of course!" Cassie threw her arms around his neck, trying to hide her tears from him. "Whatever you need. Anything at all. I promise."

Uncle Willie held her tight for a moment, then pushed her away. "I called Danny earlier today. He'll be here in the morning. Then I'll explain what I know to both of you. Okay?"

Cassie nodded. She had a hundred questions, and she wanted to press Willie with questions now, not wait. But he rose from the couch and moved toward his room.

"I'm tired. I'm going to bed. I'll see you in the morning, darlin', okay?"

Cassie nodded again, not trusting her voice to work properly. He didn't look well, couldn't meet her eyes. Just how bad was it?

Lord, please don't take him yet. I'm not ready.

DANNY KESSLER TRIED NOT TO THINK AS HE SHOVED clothes in a suitcase. What did he need? How long would he be gone? He threw in T-shirts and jeans, a couple rougher pieces in case Uncle Willie needed some work done on one of the buildings, a couple nice shirts and khaki pants just in case of...

He shut down that line of thinking. He wasn't going to die this week. They wouldn't be planning a funeral. They just wouldn't. But if he went to church with Cassie and Uncle Willie, he didn't want to wear torn jeans and a T-shirt. He wasn't in high school anymore.

He packed his computer bag with his laptop, a Wi-Fi device, his backup hard drive, and shoved his Kindle and a couple paperbacks into the space that was left.

What else?

He wanted to call Cassie. He desperately wanted to call Cassie. But Uncle Willie had said not to because he hadn't told her yet.

His poor girl. She'd be all alone in the world. Well, she had her sisters, but she'd be all alone in Loon Lake. Who would look out for her?

Once again, a pain sliced through his gut. He used to be her hero, her knight, her best friend. He used to be the one who looked out for her, brought her wildflowers, shared her favorite pizza on the hood of his car while they watched the stars move across the sky.

And then he'd ruined everything.

Which was why coming home was so painful. The people he loved most were in Loon Lake. The ones he hadn't hurt whispered behind his back. They must. That's what small town folk do. And then there were the people who were just disgusted and disappointed in him, like his mother and his ex-wife's family. Going home was simply not an option for him.

But if Uncle Willie needed him, he'd face the dragons for as long as necessary. When the crisis was over, of course, he'd flee back to Lansing where he'd tried to make a life for himself.

He looked around his one-bedroom apartment, trying to think of what else he might need. He threw in a load of laundry, putting everything he wanted to take in one load, hearing Cassie's voice, as he always did, about separating whites and darks. Then he washed all his dishes, dumped a quart of milk down the sink, and pulled out his Igloo cooler to take the other perishables with him in the morning.

Working with his hands eased his mind. For a whole forty minutes, he didn't have to think about what he would hear when Uncle Willie told him and Cassie what was wrong with his health — he wouldn't say over the phone. When Danny was done, nothing else he could think of to do, he sat on the couch and let his mind wander.

Cancer? It was probably cancer. That's what everyone died of nowadays. Would it be slow or fast? Would he suffer? Danny squeezed his eyes shut and tried to think of something else.

Maybe it was his heart. That would be better, right? Less pain? But death would come suddenly. Maybe he shouldn't wait until tomorrow morning to drive up. If he left now, he could be there by midnight.

Danny pulled out his phone and texted Jax Edgerly, his best friend.

> Can I sleep on your couch tomorrow night?
> Don't know for how long. A week or two?

A minute later, Jax replied.

> Sure. What's up?

> I'll explain tomorrow. Thanks, brother.

He leaned his head back against the couch. *God, please don't let him die. Not yet. I'm not ready.*

His phone rang, startling him. He felt his heart stumble in his chest when he saw the name on the screen. *Sunshine.* It was Cassie.

He should've changed the name in his phone's address book. She hadn't called him in two years, but the effect of seeing her nickname hadn't dimmed. His chest squeezed just the same. Uncle Willie must've told her his news.

He held his phone tight, immobile with regrets. He'd messed up, then messed up again. Trying to minimize future damage, he'd said something stupid to hurt her so she wouldn't contact him again. Unfortunately, it had worked. Three strikes.

But he couldn't leave her hanging, alone, not when she must be hurting. He slid his thumb over the screen to answer.

"Hey," he said, hearing the catch in his voice and hoping she hadn't.

"Oh, Danny." She cried into the phone without speaking for a minute. He squeezed the bridge of his nose and felt tears slipping out. Whether they were for her or for Willie, he wasn't sure.

Finally, she spoke. "What are we going to do?"

He shook his head. He used to pride himself on having all

the answers to her questions. But he'd been lost and without answers himself lately. Today in particular. "I'll be there in the morning. We'll figure it out."

She didn't say anything and he imagined she was trying to stop crying. "I wish you were here now," she whispered.

Danny leaned forward over his knees, squeezing his eyes shut, trying to keep everything inside. He didn't say anything. He wanted her, needed her, felt desperate to find comfort in her arms. But he was bad news, a disappointment, a screwup. She deserved far more.

"Will you be here for breakfast? I'll make pancakes. I'll go to the store and get some strawberries and Redi-Whip."

His favorite. He felt a tug on his lips that would've been a smile if things weren't so grim. "Maybe," he finally said.

The silence grew, but it was the peaceful silence they used to share. There was a measure of comfort in the quiet.

Finally, she said, "Be safe, don't drive too fast. I'll have breakfast ready at eight, or whenever you get here. Be careful, Danny."

"I will," he managed.

Then she was gone.

How would he sleep now? He'd pushed her out of his head as best he could, tried to at least lock that door in his heart. He'd never be rid of her, but now he'd have to share her space, breath the air she breathed, feel the sunshine of her presence.

It just might kill him...if Uncle Willie didn't die first.

CHAPTER 2

*D*anny made it until about three o'clock in the morning before the siren call of the road pulled him out of his bed and onto U.S. 127 heading north. He drove too fast, despite Cassie's plea, only slowing down when he turned off the freeway in Grayling. The deer on M-72 kept smart people from going too fast. He'd counted eleven deer feeding on the side of the road or bounding across in front of him by the time he hit the outskirts of Loon Lake. He thanked God he hadn't hit number nine. That one was too close.

As he passed Loon Lake Lumber and Logs — what was it with this town and its new predilection toward wacky business names? — he looked to see if he recognized any of the trucks outside. It was good weather for late April, and anyone doing any building or remodeling needed to start early to take advantage of it. He slowed and stared, trying to determine if the blue Ford was Jax's truck, but he couldn't tell and he didn't want to stop.

Cassie needed him.

His dashboard clock read 6:47, but he wasn't afraid of

waking her up. She'd be sitting on the top of the stairs to her apartment, watching the morning sun glisten on the lake. From the top landing, you could see little bits of blue water where The Laughing Loon's boat gas pump stood, and around the curve where the lake widened. She'd be sitting there, watching the sunrise, watching for him.

He slowed around the curve, careful because the road wasn't banked well and impatient folks tended to skid into the Wallace's yard. But his caution had as much to do with his reprieve coming to an end as it did with safe driving. He'd managed to find excuses not to come back for Christmas this last year, his first Christmas away from home. It had been a full eleven months since he'd set eyes on her.

He took a deep breath and turned left into the parking lot of the Loon Lake Fluff and Fold. Cassie wouldn't be able to see him or his truck yet. He needed a minute.

Ten seconds later, he opened the door. He'd never be prepared. Might as well go in.

His steps slowed as he came around the corner of the building and looked up the stairwell. She'd heard him coming. Her feet flew down the steps and she jumped the last two to land in his arms.

There wasn't anything he could do but crush her to him, pulling her back into his heart where she belonged.

A voice in his head told him that was a mistake. If it wasn't for Uncle Willie, this would be the Worst. Idea. Ever.

But for now...

He held her close, turning as his weight shifted until he found his back leaning against the side of the building, his face buried in her hair, her face buried in his neck. She didn't say a word or make a sound but he could feel her tears dripping down his neck and into his T-shirt.

A thought skittered through his mind that he hoped no one was around to see them, but it was gone before it gained a foothold.

For now, he reveled in the feel of her body, the smell of her shampoo, the...sound of her laughter?

He pulled back enough to look down at her face. Yes, that was laughter as well as tears. She used one hand to wipe her eyes but didn't move away or let go of his neck with the other.

"Our ESP's still working," she said, gazing up with sparkling eyes. "I only came outside a few minutes ago. I knew you'd be here soon. I just knew it."

Danny snorted gently and raised a hand to wipe the rest of her tears. "Like always." He ran his fingers over her cheeks, glad for the excuse to touch her. He'd have to let go of her soon enough.

He thought about all the times they'd been able to find each other, knowing where the other would be for no more reason than years of experience. She had a favorite tree in the woods behind the Fluff and Fold. He favored Uncle Willie's private dock at The Hole. He knew she'd be waiting here on the steps. She knew he'd arrive much sooner than he'd promised.

They belonged together.

No.

He shut that thought down. Not anymore. He'd ruined everything by falling for Lily's superficial glow and marrying her. Lily had made it clear a hundred times that he'd ruined her life as well, despite that fact that she'd married the son of a Congressman not eighteen months after their divorce. No way would Danny risk ruining Cassie's life, too. She deserved more than he could ever give her.

He forced himself to loosen his grip and push her away. "Where's Uncle Willie?"

"In the shower. He hasn't said anything to me since he went to bed last night. He said he wanted to wait until you got here. Hungry?"

She turned and headed up the stairs.

Early morning temperatures in mid-April weren't warm, but when you'd been cooped up in the snow for four to six months, folks took advantage of any excuse to get some fresh air. Cassie wore a thick hoodie with the zipper pulled all the way up, but she also wore denim shorts. Right now, watching her walk up the stairs was kick-starting his libido.

Dangerous. He looked away.

And looked back.

At the top of the stairs she turned suddenly. She pulled up the wrist of her sweatshirt and wiped it across her face. "All good?" she asked.

He nodded. Very good. Beautiful.

"Can't tell I've been crying?"

He shrugged. "Maybe he'll think it was me."

Something passed between them, a look Danny couldn't interpret. But his gut told him he'd been right to stay away from her all this time. The longer he was away, the more he wanted her back.

No, once he did whatever Uncle Willie needed, he'd have to hightail it back downstate. It was the only way to protect her.

WILLIE COMBED HIS WET HAIR AND TUCKED IN HIS SHIRT. HE paused, listening. Voices in the kitchen, plural.

He smiled. He'd half expected Danny to bang down the door at midnight. Maybe he'd even driven up and slept in his truck last night. In any case, he was here. Finally. Now it was time for Willie to put on a show.

He practiced a couple different expressions in the mirror. Too maudlin. Too fake sad. Too sickly. He took a deep breath and tried to relax. He'd just be himself. He wasn't lying, after all, just...stretching the truth. As soon as he got the two kids back together, he'd explain.

He'd been thinking about it last night when he went to bed...long before he was tired. What had made those two kids friends, what kept them friends? All he could think of was that they'd done everything together for as long as he could remember. So he needed to make them do everything together again. Then they'd remember how much they enjoyed each other's company.

How much they loved each other.

He nodded to his mirror image. Yup. Just remind them how much they love each other and, after they make amends, explain that while he would eventually die, he didn't have any expectations about it happening soon. They'd be mad, sure. But by then it would be two against one and he'd take whatever punishment they brought.

He opened the door and walked to the kitchen. Before they noticed him, he saw the kids moving around the small space in sync, Cassie stirring pancake batter, Danny cutting strawberries. Just as it should be. His heart squeezed a little. It was his job to take care of them, and doggone it, if they couldn't find the right road on their own, he would drive them to it.

His foot hit the creaky floorboard near the couch and both kids looked up. Danny put down the knife and wiped his hands on a towel as he strode over. He was tall, lean, strong, with a kind face and an easy laugh. The kind of man anyone would be proud to call his son.

They embraced in a gorilla-like hug, slapping each other's backs, and hanging on for another few moments. When Danny pulled back, Willie said, "It's good to see you, son."

Danny nodded and forced a smile. "Good to see you, Uncle Willie."

Willie had known Cassie would be upset with his death announcement. She was a woman. But he hadn't realized how strongly it would affect Danny. The young man was trying not to cry. For a moment, Willie considered telling them both the truth now. He didn't want to hurt them; he wanted them to be happy.

Nope. He forced himself to ignore their heartbroken expressions and allowed Danny to seat him at the table as if he were an old man. Sixty-nine was definitely not old. But he needed to make sure his plan worked before he caved.

This was going to be harder than he thought.

The two young people finished making breakfast, trying to maintain an upbeat conversation as they worked. Danny told them about the new office building he was working on, about the guy he worked with who brought onion sandwiches to work — "Just bread and sliced onions, I kid you not" — and how the trees downstate already had full leaves on them.

Cassie talked about her upcoming final exams, how that border collie Chip had knocked up Ted's dog again right before he'd been fixed and she'd gone down to the Feed and

Seed to see the puppies, and that one of the rental cabins might have a leaky roof.

"I'll check out that roof for you today," Danny told Willie.

Willie nodded. "I'd appreciate that, son. Cassie, take him down and show him where, will you?"

Willie watched as the two exchanged a quick glance and looked away.

"Of course," Cassie replied. "Now it's time for you to explain what Dr. Dillon told you. What's going on?"

Willie braced himself and dove into his story. "I was down there a few days ago getting my annual checkup, and Dill told me that even though I look good, he found some problems. Big problems. He thinks I'm dying."

"What problems?" Danny asked.

"How are you dying?" Cassie exclaimed.

Had he overplayed it? Too much? "Well, he's gotta run some tests," Willie said, sticking to the story he'd concocted but trying to backpedal a bit. "I'll know more when the results come back."

"But what's wrong? Why does Dr. Dillon think you're dying?" Cassie asked again. She wiped her hand under one eye, obviously trying to keep her tears from falling.

Willie cringed inside. He didn't want to hurt them, but this was for their own good. He reached over and squeezed Cassie's hand. "We all die, darlin'," he said as gently as he could. Watching her try not to cry nagged at his conscience. "And who knows? Maybe Dill's wrong. I'm sure it's a possibility."

"How long until you hear back about the tests?" Danny asked.

"It's Saturday, so nothing's going to happen today. Dill

will need to decide which tests, and then we'll have to schedule them, wait for the results…" He was making this up as he went along. Good thing he'd been friends with a doctor for so long. It sounded pretty reasonable to him. "It's going to take some time."

The best lies were the ones that were closest to the truth. Didn't he hear that in a movie?

"I don't know much more than you do at this point, but I wanted to get you both together so we can figure out what to do about all the legal stuff. Whatever happens, we should be ready. I'd like to make you joint executors of my estate. Can you work together on that?"

That was the big question. Would they take this crisis as a reason to fight or make up?

They both nodded. "Of course. Sure," they said. Cassie rested her free hand on Danny's and he threaded his fingers through hers.

Willie smiled. Okay, good, it was working. He felt a lot better. This really was a great idea. "Until we know more, I hate to ask, but I could use your help with other things around here. Danny, I appreciate you taking a look at that roof. I know you took a leave of absence at your job, so I'm going to put you on the payroll here—"

"No, Uncle Wil—"

"Don't argue with me, son. I need the help, and I'd rather pay you than a stranger."

"Yes, sir." Danny backed down as Willie had hoped.

"I hope you'll be okay with doing a lot of different things, not just repairs but managing the business, too." The perfect scenario included them co-running his business as he eased into retirement. Danny would be a great manager if he just had more confidence. Cassie had found her confidence in the degrees she'd worked so hard for. "Cassie has finals coming up and I don't want anything taking her away from—"

"Uncle Willie, you are more important than school."

She looked like she was going to cry again. If this kept up, maybe the hurting look on his little girl's face would kill him first.

He donned his stern fatherly expression. "We have spent far too much time and money not to finish well. You *are* going to focus on your studies until graduation is over. End of discussion. I'm sure we won't know much before then anyway, so try not to worry"—he almost winced as he said it —"and study hard. Danny here will cover your shifts until you're done with school. It's only two more weeks."

"Of course," Danny said, giving Cassie a little smile and squeezing her hand.

Willie watched her brave attempt to smile back. Okay, he'd made headway with his plan. Now he needed to get away from this emotional tumult he'd created.

"I hope you don't think I'm slacking in my duties, but I'd like to get a little more fishing in while I still can." The words were barely out of his mouth before both kids jumped in, pushing him to go fishing, relax, enjoy the day, they'd figure things out.

Willie would've smiled at how easily his plan was working, but he didn't want to jinx it. Meanwhile, he really did need to get away on the lake for a while.

This scheming business was exhausting.

CHAPTER 3

*C*assie and Danny offered to help Uncle Willie get his fishing pole and tackle box, offered to go fishing with him since it was Saturday, offered to call one of his friends to go fishing, offered every helpful thing they could think of, but he kept waving them away. They finally let him go with an admonishment to be careful, receiving a grumpy reply in return.

Cassie heaved a sigh when the door closed. Back in the kitchen, she started cleaning up just to have something to do. Her emotions were a wild mix of the fear of death and the hope that her uncle wasn't really dying, the fear and the hope that his small town doctor was wrong. Fear and hope that Danny might somehow be convinced to stay here in Loon Lake since the man he loved like a father needed him.

Danny brought dishes in from the dining nook and the two filled the dishwasher in tense silence. They worked well together, Cassie noted, like they always had, having done this dance hundreds of times before.

After Cassie had moved in with Uncle Willie, Danny

used to eat with them at least a couple times a week. Even after he started dating Bright Shiny, he was over here working on some project or another with her uncle. Cassie had taught him to cook, and insisted that a real man helps clean up. That's what Aunt Velma had always said to Uncle Willie.

She sighed again, missing her aunt and her mother acutely for a moment. Aunt Velma had died two years before Mom. She'd caught pneumonia one winter, and left for her heavenly home on the first day of spring. Mom's cancer had taken her from her family in the spring, too.

Cassie always wondered if better medical help sooner would have saved either of them. She wondered it again now. Dr. Dillon was a good doctor. She knew lots of people he'd sent over to Munson Medical Center in Traverse City when they needed more than he could give them. But what if Uncle Willie shouldn't wait for his friend's tests to be done? What if he went to Munson right now? They could find whatever was the problem and maybe even fix it.

"I think we should—"

"I've been thinking—"

She and Danny spoke at the same time. "Go ahead," she said.

"I've been thinking about the fact that Dr. Dillon doesn't know what's wrong, but he thinks it's serious enough to tell Uncle Willie he's dying. I think we should encourage him to see a doctor at Munson."

The corner of her mouth tipped up. "That's what I was about to say."

"The thing is," Danny hesitated. "I know I haven't been here for a while, but does he look any different to you? Have you noticed any changes in his health?"

"No," Cassie turned to fully face him, the towel in her hand forgotten. "That's what I've been wondering. How can a dying person look and sound and act as healthy as ever and suddenly find out they're that sick?"

Danny flicked his gaze around the kitchen, not looking at her. "I can only think of one thing."

Cassie sagged against the counter. "Cancer."

Danny closed the dishwasher and moved closer, offering his embrace but allowing her to decide if she wanted it.

Of course she did. She had managed to live without him just fine. So long as there was nothing extraordinary to celebrate, nothing confusing to talk over, nothing frightening to need comfort from, and nothing beautiful to share. The rest of the time she barely thought of him.

She moved into his arms and closed her eyes as the two of them soaked up each other's warmth. "What are we going to do?"

Danny was quiet for a while. Cassie waited. She'd learned long ago that he wasn't ignoring her, he just needed time to think. "We do everything he asks. We make life easy on him. We give him nothing to worry about. And we pray."

Cassie nodded against his chest. That sounded like a good idea.

Danny pulled away, and Cassie heard an involuntary grunt of protest from her throat. He gave her a look that seemed to say, *don't*, and took another step back. "So," he said, rubbing his hands together in a nervous gesture, "why don't you show me that leaky roof."

Despite the rocky start, the rest of the day was rather wonderful. The weather was perfect — low 70s, sunny, a light breeze — and the company was the best. She showed Danny the cabin with the leak and helped him make a list of materials he needed. She sat on the log fence, swinging her legs while he spoke to Jax on the phone, arranging a time they could work on the roof together. And she tried to pretend she wasn't staring when he took off his flannel overshirt, his T-shirt revealing a lot of muscles she hadn't forgotten.

Just before Danny hung up with Jax, Cassie's friend Tabitha drove by, turned around, and pulled into the cabins' parking area.

Tabitha Martin gave lie to the young single mom stereotype. Although she was a teenager when she gave birth to Summer, she'd been married for a year by then. Her husband hadn't left like Cassie's and Danny's dads had. He'd decided to join the Army in an attempt to provide a better future for his family. Sadly, he'd been killed overseas a year after Chas was born.

Tabitha was a tough cookie. She didn't take kindly to people feeling sorry for her. She'd created two home-based businesses and still managed to do the soccer mom thing, even teaching Sunday School twice a month. She was like one of those nuns you see on a BBC show — tough and strong and incredibly kind.

Cassie jumped down from the fence, trying to decide what to do if Tabitha said something embarrassing about Danny suddenly appearing out of the blue.

"Should I be yelling 'stranger danger'?" Tabitha teased as she got out of her car and gave them both a hug.

"Yeah, it's Tabitha," Danny said into the phone. "Wanna talk to her?" He held out the phone even as Tabitha started to back away. Danny just stood there and grinned. Finally, she sighed and rolled her eyes and took the phone.

Cassie stepped closer to Danny and smiled. He winked at

her. Jax and Tabitha should've gotten married ages ago, but both of them fought their attraction every step of the way, insisting there was no way they'd be right together, the playboy and the single mom. That didn't stop Cassie and Danny from pushing them together, though.

"Fine, sure, but you better help," Tabitha said into the phone. "I'm not doing everything myself." She hung up without saying goodbye and handed Danny his phone.

"So where you been? What're you doing here?" she asked. She slid a sly look over to Cassie, and said, "Miss all the good things you left behind?" She raised her eyebrows like she'd caught them together behind the bleachers.

Another stereotypical small town event, which had never happened.

Unfortunately.

Cassie changed the subject. "Where are the kids? I figured you'd be Ms. Soccer Mom today."

"Summer's at a birthday party, and Chas is at a play date with Shelley Thompson's son. And now back to you. Whatcha doing?"

"I miss you, too, Tabs." Tabitha scowled at the nickname and Danny laughed.

Cassie heard her phone beep and checked the screen. "Uncle Willie says Edge is done fixing the washer, and that he's going night fishing with Dill tonight so we should make our own plans."

"Perfect," Tabitha said, "because I was just going to invite you both over to dinner. Why don't we make it early so we can catch up? Five o'clock? Jax'll be off work at four."

Cassie looked to Danny and raised her eyebrows. He nodded. "Sure, great. Sounds good."

"What should we bring?" Cassie asked.

"How about dessert and a bottle of wine?" Tabitha waved her hand vaguely toward the other end of town. "You know that mixed red we found at The Triple L? Bring that one."

Danny snickered. "You've got Jax drinking wine?"

Tabitha rolled her eyes. "He's such a Neanderthal. He pours beer into a wine glass if I force him into polite company."

Cassie laughed. "I've seen him. It's funny."

"To you, maybe," Tabitha muttered. "Anyway, come over at five. Earlier is fine. Bring beer if you have to," she said to Danny.

"Want me to wear a suit?" he asked. Tabitha slugged him in the arm and he danced away.

"I can't believe this is the best we can do when it comes to men," she said in a stage whisper aimed at Cassie.

Danny stuck his tongue out at her as Tabitha got back in her car.

Cassie shook her head at him. "You're so not a grownup."

Danny licked his finger and stuck it in her ear. "You're right," he said with a laugh as Cassie screeched and wiped furiously at her wet ear.

"You're so disgusting," she said, shoving him.

He put his arm around her neck in a head lock and kissed her hair, laughing as she struggled.

Oh, man. That was nice. She leaned into him. Really nice.

She missed him so much. She thought she'd done a good job of forgetting what it was like to hang out with him, laughing and teasing.

But in one magic moment, it all came rushing back.

DANNY FELT A FLOOD OF EMOTION AS HE HORSED AROUND with Cassie. It was like they were sixteen again. She playfully struggled to get away for a second and then leaned into him like she always had. It felt good to have his arm around her, laughing with her. Kissing the top of her head made him feel like he was her protector once again.

If only he knew how to protect her from the many causes of a broken heart. He sighed and let her go, walking back to where he'd dropped a few tools.

He needed to be careful while he was here. She'd made overtures to him a couple times since he and Lily had gotten divorced, but he'd pushed her away. It would be so easy to fall into old habits and spend all his time with her. But one of his old habits seemed to be hurting the people he loved most, and that was one thing he would not allow to happen again with Cassie. He had to keep her at arm's length without hurting her feelings.

"Are you going to work on the roof now?" she asked.

"Nah, Jax'll help me later. We'll get it done before the next rain." He glanced at his watch. "You hungry yet?"

Cassie shrugged. "I could eat. Want me to make us something?"

"I'm jonesing for Jimmy's," he said, cocking his head in the direction of Jimmy's Pizza. "Wanna go?"

She grinned. "Sure. I just have to get my purse. Walk or drive?"

"My treat, and let's walk. I could use the exercise."

Danny put his tools back in the locked compartment of his truck, and they walked the half mile or so to Jimmy's. The lake faded behind them, the woods crowding up against the road. The chirps of chickadees and the calls of robins filled the air.

He had forgotten how much he loved the sounds of Loon Lake. There weren't any loons any more since the area had gotten so populated, but there were plenty of mallards, black ducks, wood ducks, some bufflehead, and a lot of Canada geese making their way back to their northern homes. When cars weren't driving by, the sound of the woods felt comforting. It was good to be home.

Sort of.

As they came up to Sandy Beach Drive, he felt the tension rise in his shoulders. Cassie looked over at him and gave his hand a quick squeeze.

"She doesn't know you're here? Want me to come?"

He shook his head and straightened his gaze back to the road in front of them. If only he didn't have to face this dragon every time he came up here. "No, it'll be better if I go by myself. Three years and she's still angry Lily's not her daughter-in-law anymore. She won't be happy to see you."

He was pretty sure his mom wouldn't be happy to see him either. Regardless of the fact that she considered him more of a loser than his incarcerated older brother, he still had to stop and see her when he was in town. She'd make a bad situation worse if she heard he was here from someone else.

Cassie briefly touched his hand again, but didn't say anything as they passed the road. It wasn't news to her that his mom didn't like her. He had no idea why, but she never had.

After a tense moment of quiet, Cassie started chattering about school, about new goings-on in Loon Lake, about the puppies she'd seen and how she was thinking about getting a dog after graduation — a whole slew of upbeat topics that required no response but restored his good mood. By the time he opened the door for her at Jimmy's, she had him laughing again.

Inside the pizzeria, more than half the tables were full of people eating or waiting for take-out. The scents of warm cheese, hot bread, and fried chicken filled the air. Danny tried to lead Cassie to an empty table near the front windows, but one old friend after another saw them and called out.

"Hey, Danny! Look, Danny's back."

"Look who's finally come home."

And then, "Are you two finally together? It's about time."

Danny saw Cassie smile and shake her head...and blush. He needed to put an end to that line of questioning before it spread.

"No, I'm just up here helping Uncle Willie with some repairs. Just a visit." He winced inside, hoping his carefree-sounding words weren't hurting Cassie. She was his oldest friend, after all.

They finally sat down and looked at the menu, choosing an old favorite they both loved. Danny took a deep breath and smiled at Cassie. Now that the questioning was over, maybe they could go back to just chilling together.

"Well, my word, if it isn't a blast from the past. Daniel Kessler, as I live and breathe."

Danny looked up at the waitress. Oh no. Connie Templeton. She'd chased him all through high school. Relentlessly. She was one scary chick. He forced himself to speak. "Connie. Hi."

She gave him a calculating look then looked at Cassie. "Still trying to catch the one that got away, huh?" She made a tsk-ing sound and shook her head.

Cassie's eyes widened and she opened her mouth to speak, but Connie turned her back on her.

"So," she said to Danny, "how long you home for?" She looked down at his left hand. "Wanna catch a movie? Have dinner? Do the horizontal mambo?" She laughed and hit his shoulder with her order pad. "I'm just teasing you."

Danny forced a "ha-ha" from his throat and looked down at the menu. "Yeah. So we'll have a large mushroom and pepperoni pizza, and two Cherry Cokes. You still serve them as fountain drinks?"

"Only place in town that does," Connie said in a sing-song voice. "I'll get that right out to you." She leaned closer to Danny and said in a low voice, "I'll grab you some breadsticks, too, even though you didn't order them. Shh," she whispered near his ear.

Danny pulled back, trying not to let her get too close. "Oh, that's all right," he said, but Connie was already sashaying away. He felt heat rising in his own face now and didn't want to look at Cassie. Public embarrassment — the joys of small town life.

He heard something and raised his head. Cassie looked like she was choking to death. She caught his gaze and burst out laughing, nearly hysterical. She finally caught her breath enough to say, "Welcome home. Loon Lake, where everyone knows your name and your underwear size."

Danny swatted her hands with the menu and put it back in the stand. He shook his head at her, but he couldn't keep from smiling. "It's not like this in Lansing," he said. "I can go weeks without running into someone I know. You should try it sometime."

"When I drive to T.C. for class, I don't usually see anyone I know, so I feel like I'm getting a little alone time even though I'm surrounded by fifteen thousand people. I kinda like it."

Danny looked around Jimmy's as they talked. Nothing had changed. Same menu. Many of the same employees — except Connie was new. He tried not to shudder. He may have to find a new favorite restaurant if she acted like this every time he came in.

He saw a table of older men in a corner drinking coffee and looking over their shoulders toward him. He nodded and looked away. They did the same. One of them knew his mom. He'd have to go straight to her house after lunch to avoid a lecture later.

He recognized several other people, many of whom stared at him and Cassie for a moment and then turned away talking. Were they talking about him? The guy who'd screwed up his marriage so quickly and fled downstate? It's not like he was the only guy who'd ever gotten married right out of high school and gotten divorced a couple years later. But he knew how people talked. He'd lived here his whole life. Boy, did he know how people talked.

Cassie tapped his hand. "Just pretend you don't see them. It's better that way. They don't mean any harm."

Danny focused on the pretty girl in front of him and tried to take her advice. She was right. And she was way more appealing to look at and talk to than a bunch of old men in plaid flannel.

"Tell me more about what's been going on in your life," he said. He remembered in the old days when the sound of her voice had calmed him. When his dad had run out of the house yelling and cursing them all and had never come back. When his mom had constantly lectured him about not becoming like his father. When his big brother went to jail the first time, the second time, the last time.

He'd had a lot of time to think about his life since he and

Lily had finally signed the paperwork and made their divorce final. He understood a little more about what "poor white trash" meant now that he'd lived in the city awhile. He understood how young men without a positive male role model struggled to make a decent, respectable life for themselves. But he'd had Uncle Willie. So if he was a screwup even with a positive male role model, maybe that's what he was born to be.

The sermons he'd heard told him that wasn't true. That at any time he could start over, try again, be forgiven and move on. But he wasn't so sure.

Cassie laid her hand over his and didn't pull it away. He realized she'd stopped talking. She gave him a smile that seemed to say, you're going to be okay.

Without thinking, he brought her hand to his lips and kissed her knuckles, his eyes on hers. Then the noise of the pizzeria intruded and he quickly lay her hand back on the table, patted it, and pulled away.

He needed her.

He made a decision. He would renew their friendship, see if things could go back to the way they once were. She was his balm of Gilead, and if he could heal their relationship somehow, he was determined to do it. Maybe he was being selfish, but they would need each other more than ever to get through Uncle Willie's health crisis.

He wouldn't say "death" any more often than necessary. After all, the tests hadn't been done. Who knew what was really going on with his health?

For the next hour, he laughed at Cassie's stories, told a few of his own that had her clutching her stomach and wiping her eyes with laughter, and in general tried to soothe the hurts between them. He walked her back to the Fluff and Fold, then he braced himself to drive over to his mom's and let her know he was in town.

"You can do this," Cassie said, a warm and solemn strength infusing her words. "You're a good man. You can do the right thing even when it hurts."

He tightened his lips and nodded.

"And then we'll open a bottle of wine and spend the night laughing with our best friends."

"Yup, all right, see you soon." He got in his truck and drove off trying not to wonder why he'd married a girl who pointed out all his flaws instead of one who gave him courage.

CHAPTER 4

*D*riving around Sandy Beach Park, Danny felt so many conflicting emotions. He had a lot of good memories here. He and Cassie had learned to swim in the shallows of the boat ramp when they were six or seven. The big Loon Lake festival, Loony Days, set up booths and contests and food tents in the center of the small park under the maples, and all kinds of water races were held in the lake in front of the park.

And over by the tree with the drooping limb, that's where he'd stood the first time his dad hit him.

Definitely mixed feelings.

He drove out of the park and down the wooded lane, around the curves, watching for dogs and squirrels, braking for children playing baseball on the dirt road, waving to whomever waved at him.

If he could delete the bad memories like an unnecessary file on his computer, if he could erase his family and keep his memories of growing up with Cassie and Uncle Willie and Aunt Velma, he'd be living in one of those Hallmark movies.

Loon Lake was a pretty wonderful place if he could forget the bad times.

By the time he saw his old house, he hadn't decided if he hoped his mom would be home so he could get it over with, or gone so he wouldn't have to do this today. But there was her car. He pulled in next to it. Grass sprouted up thick enough to hide most of the gravel that had once delineated driveway from yard. The additional roof built over the mobile home sagged in the middle. One of the windows had a crack in it.

All things he could fix. But she hadn't wanted him to. She wanted the work done by a professional. Of course, she could never see him as a professional no matter what license he got or what company hired him.

He got out, tried to say a prayer for help but didn't know what to say, and trudged up to the front door. He rang the bell and waited. The pizza lurched in his stomach, threatening to come up.

The wooden inside door shook as someone tried to open it. He could hear the wood squeak, the door stuck in its frame. The shaking intensified, causing the metal screen door to rattle in its frame as well. He heard some low cursing, and the door burst open.

He tried to smile. "Hi, Mom."

His mother stood stock still, staring at him. She was dressed in going-out clothes as she called them, colorful polyester prints and comfortable nurse's shoes. Her hair needed to be colored again, an inch of gray showing at the roots. She looked a decade older than she was.

"Well. Hello." She stood unmoving another moment and then pushed at the screen door, almost hitting him in the nose. "Come in."

Inside, Danny stood awkwardly, unsure of whether she wanted him to sit down or not. She moved toward the kitchen area to the right. "Want a drink?"

He cleared his throat. "Sure."

With her back to him, she motioned for him to sit at the kitchen table. It was new since the last time he'd been home. As he sat, he saw her pull out a bottle of whiskey and two glasses. The pizza pushed upward.

"Uh, no, water, please. Water would be fine."

She grunted and put one glass under the tap to fill it. She poured a finger of whiskey into the other glass and sat down across from him.

They both took a sip, uncomfortable.

"You visitin' or you back?" She didn't quite meet his eyes.

"Just a visit. I'm not sure how long I'll be here."

She nodded. "You look good. Been eatin' well?"

"Trying," he said. He tried to think of something else to say. "Nice table. New?"

"Rod bought it for me." She met his questioning look with a defiant half-glare. "He's my boyfriend. He's good to me."

Danny nodded, his hand moving in a placating gesture. "That's good." He didn't really want to know, and he didn't want to fight.

He looked toward the front window with the crack in it. He didn't want to ask, but it was the right thing to do. "You need me to fix the window for you?"

She shook her head and sipped her whiskey. "Rod'll do it." They sat quietly, then she said, "He'll be here any minute. We're going to O'Bannon's in Cadillac, meet some friends for dinner." She looked up, unease lighting her eyes. "You weren't planning on staying here, were you?"

Gosh, thanks, Mom. I wouldn't want to put you out. He gritted his teeth. "No, I'm sleeping on Jax's couch."

"Don't get sassy with me," she said and downed the rest of her whiskey. "Just makin' sure there's no misunderstanding."

Danny felt a lifetime of bottled up anger, disappointment, and hurt rising up with the pizza. He stood to leave before he let any of it out. "There's no misunderstanding. I just wanted to let you know I'm in town. I'll be busy working, but you have my number if you need anything."

His mother stood as well, shaky on her feet. He wondered how much she'd already been drinking today. He clamped his mouth shut and walked the three steps back to the door. He half-turned enough to wave a hand and say, "See ya," then he left, letting the screen door slam behind him.

He was in his truck a mile down the road before he realized...those were tears on his mother's face.

CASSIE PULLED ON HER YELLOW SUNDRESS WITH THE BIG coral and pink flowers, then put her hair up in a clip. She looked in the mirror to make sure she looked okay. It was one of her favorite casual dresses. And because she wore it a lot, no one should notice and say anything about her trying to impress Danny.

She'd tried to renew their friendship a couple times since she'd heard he and Lily had divorced, but he didn't want to talk back then. Not about anything, which was really weird.

In the past, if there were times one of them didn't want to talk about what was bothering them, they'd still talk about other things. But after her second call about a year after the divorce, asking him when he was coming home, if he wanted to go to a movie, go fishing, anything, he'd stopped answering her calls.

She'd texted him near the holidays to tell him when meals would be served, and he texted short replies about that. But then he stopped coming home, too. The last she'd seen him was nearly a year ago, and he had been standoffish.

Then this morning...

She held onto the counter, feeling a little dizzy. He'd held her so tight, and he felt so good in her arms. He'd gotten bigger since last summer, surely, his arms and shoulders and chest hard with muscle.

But more than that, it seemed like her old Danny had resurfaced. He laughed easily again, though he had more quiet, serious moments as well. She wasn't quite sure what to do with him.

I want to keep him.

She turned away from her reflection. That kind of thinking needed to stop. He didn't want her. He'd made that clear. But maybe he was finally ready to be friends again. If that's all she could have, she'd take it. She missed him. Even more so now that he was back and smiling at her again.

She came down the steps with a bottle of wine and a pie from Sonny's as Danny drove up. She smiled and waved and got in the passenger side. The smell of aftershave and shampoo hit her and made her woozy. She forced herself to think about something else.

She looked around the inside of his new truck. It was

much nicer than his last one. He must be doing well down in Lansing. "Nice truck," she said.

"Thanks." He waited for a car to drive by before pulling onto the road.

Poor guy. She'd braced herself for a bad mood after the visit with his mom. She tried to think of something else to say as he drove.

Tabitha lived on the other side of the main part of town. A little two-bedroom house that she'd made into a warm, safe haven for her children. It only took a few silent minutes to get there. Danny parked behind Jax's truck, and Cassie started to get out.

Danny caught her arm and stopped her. He took a deep breath. "I'm sorry."

Cassie thought he'd go on, but he didn't. She weighed several options before she decided what to say. "I'm your friend, Danny. I'll always be your friend. You don't have to apologize about how you feel when people are mean to you. I want to smack her every time she hurts you." She moved her arm so she could squeeze his hand.

He winced but didn't pull away.

Cassie's eyes widened as she looked down at the palm of his right hand. It was red with blisters. One had already popped. She gasped. "What happened? What'd she do?" Her voice rose an octave above normal, anger boiling up to cloud her vision.

He shook his head, looking at his hand. "She didn't. I went over to Jax's and split wood for an hour."

Cassie stared at him in disbelief.

"I know, I should've put gloves on. I thought my callouses would be enough, but...I was a little upset." He turned back to her with a glint in his eye. "Jax has got a lot of firewood now."

Cassie pursed her lips and sighed deeply. She hated the never-ending pain Danny's family brought him, brought each other. She wished she could make them all disappear so Danny could relax and heal and find some peace.

She let go of his hand and climbed down the step to the ground. She looked back into the truck where Danny still sat. "Well, come on, I'm going to take care of that hand." She slammed the door and walked to the front of the truck, wishing she could throw something at Mrs. Kessler.

"It's fine, Cass, don't worry about—" Danny shut up when he saw her glare.

"It'll be fine when I'm done with it. Don't you even think about ignoring it until it gets infected."

"It won't get in—"

"I know you, Danny Kessler, and your cuts get infected every time you don't take care of them. I've seen them hundreds of times and you know it." Cassie fought back unexpected tears as her anger grew. "Uncle Willie needs you to help him with that roof, so the least you can do is make sure your hands are strong and well for the task."

She tried to calm down, get her breathing under control. A part of her recognized her outburst wasn't entirely about Danny's hand or his mom, but she couldn't think about all that right now.

Danny wanted to argue, she could see it in his face. But all he said was, "You are bossier than ever, you know that?"

She raised her eyebrows at him and turned toward the house. Then she stopped and planted her hands on her hips. "Darn it, you got me all upset and I forgot the pie."

He sighed with some male drama and turned back. "I got it."

"And the wine," she called.

"Yup," he said from inside the truck.

When he caught up, she took the bottle of wine, saying, "Don't carry anything with that hand until I fix it up."

"Woman," he said warningly.

She turned, challenging him. "Man," she said, mimicking his tone.

A long moment passed, then Danny looked away, but not before Cassie saw his lips curve upward. She bumped his shoulder with hers, a gesture they'd both always used to push the other out of a mood.

"You are so annoying, you know that?"

She smiled up at him. "So are you. Good thing we're both okay with that."

Tabitha answered their knock and took the pie before two little bodies charged through the door. "Uncle Danny! Uncle Danny's here," Summer and Chas screamed, jumping at him.

"Hey, what am I," Cassie exclaimed, "chopped liver?" Jax came to the door and took the bottle of wine from her so she could squat down and get cuddles and kisses.

"All right, you little cookie monsters, inside," Jax said as he herded the kids back into the house.

Cassie hugged Tabitha and Jax, and they engaged in small talk for a couple minutes while Cassie cleaned and bandaged Danny's hand at the kitchen sink. Jax handed Danny a pair of tongs and a package of hot dogs, then he grabbed a plate of raw hamburger patties and a package of American cheese slices.

"We're outta here," he said, heading for the back door. "Don't talk about us while we're gone."

Cassie chuckled and Tabitha shook her head. "Boys," Tabitha said under her breath.

Cassie smiled at her friend, wanting to say a lot more about Tabitha's determination to pretend there was nothing between her and Jax but a grudging friendship. Instead, she said, "What can I do?"

She helped her friend prepare a green salad and finish topping the strawberry jello salad in the fridge. They decided to eat indoors since the lovely May day was already getting chilly. Then they also wouldn't have to deal with mosquitos if any were out. Just before the men came in with the burgers, Tabitha and Cassie set up two TV trays in the living room, put on a Sponge Bob DVD, and cut up the hot dogs on plastic plates for the kids.

"Everyone hungry?" Jax asked as he and Danny brought in the burgers. "We've got hot meat and lots of it." He waggled his eyebrows at Tabitha and everyone laughed.

"You are so bad," she said, pouring wine into two wine glasses. "Danny, you want wine or beer?"

"I am a man of sophistication and taste, unlike my friend here, so I will try the wine, thank you." He gave a little bow.

"City slicker," Jax said. "Don't tell me you lost your good taste down there."

"*Au contraire*," Danny said with an attempt at a highbrow accent.

Everyone laughed. Ahh, Cassie gave an inward sigh of pleasure, it was good to be together again. She'd always had the most fun when the four of them were together.

The adults finally settled at the kitchen table, wine in three wine glasses and beer in Jax's wine glass. After a big bite of cheeseburger, Jax said to Danny, "So spill."

Danny looked at Cassie while he finished chewing. She

nodded her head. In Loon Lake, something like this would never stay a secret.

"Uncle Willie called me last night." Danny wiped his hands on a napkin and took a drink.

Cassie could feel the tension in the other two. They knew Danny's relationship with her uncle, how he asked Danny to visit more but never pressed. They would figure this out before Danny finished the next sentence.

"This morning, he told us…"

Cassie felt the tears building again.

Danny cleared his throat twice before he could finish.

"Oh no," Tabitha whispered quietly.

"He told us he's dying." Danny cleared his throat again and took a long drink of his wine.

Silence prevailed. In the living room, Cassie heard the kids giggle at Sponge Bob's antics.

She took Danny's hand and he squeezed hers. "He doesn't have any details yet," she said. "Apparently, Dr. Dillon still has some tests to run. Uncle Willie wouldn't say any more. Just that he wanted us to help him set his affairs in order."

Danny looked to Jax. "Can you help me with some repairs? One of the cabins has a leaky roof. I'll have to look around the place, see what all needs to be done."

"Of course," Jax said, "whatever you need, I'm there."

Cassie hadn't seen Jax this subdued…well, ever. Her uncle was a good man, a kind man, and was loved by many people in Loon Lake. She'd forgotten that this might be hard for her friends to hear since they loved him, too.

Tabitha rubbed Cassie's shoulder. "How are you doing, sweetie? This must be a shock. He looks healthy as a horse."

Cassie nodded, blotting a few tears with her napkin. She

took a deep breath. "I almost can't believe it, honestly. It's hard to take in."

"So Willie doesn't know anything? What'd the doc say that came down to 'you're dying'?" Jax asked.

Cassie shrugged and shook her head. "We tried to get more details, but you know Uncle Willie, completely closed mouth when he wants to be. He said he'll tell us when Dr. Dillon runs some tests and the results come back."

"That could be a week or more," Tabitha said. "So you're all just supposed to sit on pins and needles till then? Geez, I hate doctors." She looked over her shoulder to make sure her kids weren't listening. She'd recently spent a week convincing her kids that doctors were heroes with lollipops so they wouldn't cry when they went in for a checkup.

Danny snorted a little laugh. "Actually, Uncle Willie decided to sit in his boat all day instead. Said he wanted to fish while he still could."

Jax laughed. "That sounds like him."

"So how long are you here?" Tabitha asked Danny.

He shook his head, glanced at Cassie out of the corner of his eye, and said to Tabitha, "I don't know, however long I'm needed."

When they couldn't think of much more to ask about Uncle Willie, the conversation turned to other topics, and soon they were all laughing at each other's stories. They took a break while Tabitha put the kids to bed. Jax helped, getting a lagging Chas to follow his sister by agreeing to read them a story.

"So are they dating or what?" Danny whispered as they loaded the dishwasher.

Cassie snorted. "Are you kidding? He's over here all the

time, it seems." She put her fingers up to create air quotes. "Helping."

Danny read the look on her face. "But?"

"You know Tabitha. She's not going to let anyone into her life who's not as serious about life as she is."

This time, Danny snorted. "So Jax is out of the question. What's he doing reading the kids to sleep then?"

Cassie felt a mischievous grin spread across her face. "I think he's ready to be a husband and dad, but he's scared. He just needs a little push." She looked hopefully at Danny.

He didn't let her down. "Challenge accepted." He winked at her and started the dishwasher.

Cassie cut the pie while Danny got out clean forks, both of them trying to listen as Jax's story sent the kids into fits of giggles. Cassie hoped one day it would be her husband and children she heard as she cleaned up. But for now, helping some of her best friends find love and happiness would be good enough.

CHAPTER 5

Sunday morning, Cassie attended church with her uncle as usual. She was pleasantly surprised when Danny slid into the pew next to her just as the service began.

"If we need to ask for a miracle," he whispered close to her ear, "I figured I should be here in person."

Cassie smiled at him and began to sing the opening song. Surrounded by the sound of Danny's singing voice, which she rarely heard, on one side, and her uncle's on the other, she felt well and truly blessed. She determined right then to enjoy every possible moment with Uncle Willie until he was gone. The fewer tears, the better.

Please help me, Lord, to love them well as long as I have them.

She knew she should brace herself for the day Danny left. He had a job and a home and a life somewhere else. But if they could renew their friendship while he was here so they could keep it up after he left, that's all she would ask.

After church, Danny apologized and rushed out to change

and get working on that roof with Jax. Cassie and Uncle Willie dawdled, saying hello to their friends as they usually did. Tabitha found them a few minutes later after she'd picked up her kids from Sunday School.

"Hey, Uncle Willie," she said, giving him a hug. "How are you?" She looked sad and serious.

"Fit as a fiddle," he said. Then he looked from Tabitha to Cassie and back. "Ah, I see. Well, except for that." He coughed a little.

Tabitha put her hand on his shoulder for a moment. "I'll be praying for you. Can I ask other people to pray for you, too?"

Uncle Willie looked uncomfortable. "Well, I'm trying to keep it quiet until I know more. So maybe don't tell everyone yet."

Tabitha nodded. "I understand. Let us know."

Her kids began pulling at Uncle Willie's pant legs. "Uncle Willie, Uncle Willie, do you have any candy?"

"Candy?" he asked. "Why would I have candy?"

"Because you have a whole *store* full of candy," Summer said, laughing.

"Because you always give us candy on Sunday," chimed in Chas.

"Oooh, that's right, I do, don't I? Well, what if I did have candy in my pockets, what would you say?"

"Please, may we have some candy?" they cried in unison. They laughed as Uncle Willie patted all his pockets, a stricken expression on his face.

Then he patted his shirt pocket and looked enormously relieved. "Whew," he said, wiping his brow. "For a minute there, I thought I'd eaten it all myself." He bent down and gave each child a Dum Dum lollipop, not letting go until they'd each kissed him on the cheek.

"You take that outside now," Tabitha said and gave them a little push.

"You're doing a good job, Tabitha, good job," Uncle Willie said and gave her a wink. "You all know where to find me." He waved and left.

"He's going to work?" Tabitha asked, frowning.

Cassie sighed. "I know. I try to tell him to take it easy, but it just makes him mad to be coddled. I figure if he's happy, he's healthier. Don't you think?"

"I guess," Tabitha said. "Well, what are you doing today?"

Cassie faked an excited expression and clapped her hands once. "Today is dryer cleaning day! Doesn't that sound fun?"

Tabitha glanced at her empty wrist. "Oh, wow, look at the time. I've got to go."

Cassie laughed. She caught up with a few more friends, then headed home. It was such a gorgeous day, she and Uncle Willie had walked the mile to church this morning and she was happy to walk it again.

Once home, she changed into her cleaning clothes and grabbed her iPod. She chose a playlist with some of her favorite fast tunes starting with Hollyn's "Alone." The Fluff and Fold was empty for a moment — probably everyone was out enjoying the weather — so she danced and sang while she worked. She was half inside one of the big dryers when she thought she heard a voice.

She backed out and squeaked. She slapped her hand over her mouth and pulled off her headphones. A good-looking young man stood just a few feet away. She giggled in embarrassment.

"I'm sorry," he said, smiling. "I was trying to get your attention without startling you."

"I'm so sorry," Cassie said, "what can I do for you?" She pushed some of the loose strands from her ponytail out of her face and tried to look professional.

The man in front of her wasn't her usual clientele. Not a harried single parent with a broken washer at home and a load of baseball uniforms to wash for today's game. Not a smells-like-the-outdoors fisherman or hunter whose wife wouldn't allow him to wash those grimy clothes at home.

No, this man had a catalogue look to him. Picture perfect, if not a bit too glossy. Wavy blonde hair, a pale blue button-down shirt with the sleeves folded back evenly, pleated trouser shorts, leather loafers. In every way, exactly the kind of man both of her sisters had married. Exactly the kind of man they wanted for her.

He smiled at her, the fluorescent lights reflecting off his perfect teeth and putting a flirtatious twinkle in his sky blue eyes. "I was hoping you could help me," he said in a perfectly modulated voice.

Cassie was glad Caroline and Gretchen weren't here. She'd be married before her pastor could lock up the church.

"The sign here," he pointed to the change machine, "says it only takes ones and fives." He turned on the charm, his eyes and mouth and the tilt of his head saying, *you know you want to give me what I want.* "Can you change a twenty?"

Cassie recognized his type. He was a city slicker just like Terry, her sister Caroline's husband. Nice as can be, but determined to get his way.

She nodded toward The Laughing Loon. "They can help you across the street." She smiled because he was a customer, but turned back to the dryer she was working on.

"Can I buy you a Coke?" he asked.

Cassie held in her sigh. She smiled over her shoulder and said, "No, thank you," and resumed cleaning. When she heard the bell over the door tinkle, she turned the volume back up on her iPod. Beyoncé started singing "Single Ladies" and Cassie tried not to think of Danny putting a ring on her finger.

A few minutes later Mr. Downstate was back with a roll of quarters and two cans of pop. "In case you changed your mind," he said, offering one to her with his "charming" setting dialed up a few notches.

Definitely like Terry, willing to buy his way into people's affections, if necessary.

"I'm good, thanks," she said. She took a deep breath and told herself to calm down. Her emotions were all in a tangle. She shouldn't take it out on some poor stranger.

Finished with the larger dryers, she began cleaning the smaller ones near the washing machine Mr. Downstate had chosen. High-quality clothes, she noticed. She was surprised he hadn't taken them to the dry cleaner in town. "Detroit or Chicago?" she asked.

"Excuse me?" He paused in sorting the clothes into two washers. Proper sorting. And the washer setting was on permanent press. Danny threw everything into the same machine on the regular cycle, didn't matter how often Cassie tried to explain why it mattered to separate them.

"Most of our tourists come up from the Detroit or Chicago areas," she explained. "Where are you from?" Might as well make polite conversation if they were going to be standing ten feet from each other in an otherwise empty room.

"Ann Arbor, actually." Was she being too hard on him, or did he shine an "ain't I something special?" smile her way?

Cassie wondered if Caroline had sent one of Terry's friends up here to sweep her off her feet and out of Loon Lake. Before she could pursue that line of paranoia, the bell jingled again.

Danny walked in and Cassie felt her chest inflate with joy. She knew she needed to stop that from happening, but it would take practice to look at him and not think of everything she used to wish for. Hopefully, he'd be around long enough that she'd get lots and lots of practice.

He strode toward her, an old soft T-shirt hugging his chest, stained jeans with a rip in the knee making his legs look long and strong. Just looking at him made her weak in the knees. She leaned against a dryer as she watched him approach.

"Hey, Sunshine. Do you know where Uncle Willie keeps the roofing nails? I looked in the shed but I don't see them." He glanced at Mr. Downstate and nodded politely, then ignored him.

"Um," Cassie tried to think. She needed to focus on not letting Danny distract her, but he looked like a warm summer evening and smelled like sunshine. "He did some organizing last fall. Maybe he moved them to the store's storeroom." Was she stuttering? She felt like it. She had Danny's undivided attention, and it was making her brain soft. "Where's Uncle Willie? Ask him."

"Alex at the store said he went out for something. I'll try the storeroom." Danny glanced over his shoulder at the customer quietly loading the washers. "You good in here? Still bringing us lunch?"

Was that a territorial look in his eye? She felt her heart pick up speed. "Yup, anyone over there besides you and Jax? I'm going to fill the wheelie cooler and leave it over there so you have enough in case anyone joins you."

"You're the best," Danny said with a quick smile. He kissed her forehead, nodded at Mr. Downstate, and hurried across the street.

Cassie watched him for a moment while she folded her cleaning cloth. *God, is there any way...*

That was as much as she was willing to pray on the subject. Honestly, if she could only have him back in her life as a friend, she'd take it. Whatever weirdness had been between them the last few years seemed to be dissolving. That was more than enough to thank God for.

"I'm Paul, by the way. Paul Brighton."

Cassie tried not to be annoyed that her customer had interrupted her happy daydreams. She shook his proffered hand. "Cassie."

"You're from around here?" he asked.

She grinned. "Upstairs."

"Oh." He blinked.

Cassie couldn't tell what he was thinking. They got all kinds in Loon Lake. Some tourists thought the small town and country people were as much an attraction as the fishing and snowmobiling, and treated them as something to be stared at. Others were normal, nice people who happened to be on vacation.

But some city folks, like Paul here apparently, had preconceived notions about what they would find living in such a rural area, and got confused when you weren't what they expected.

She bet he didn't expect to find successful business people up here. "My uncle owns the laundromat, the store across the street, and the Idle-Awhile Cabins across the way."

"Oh," he breathed, nodding.

Yup, he thought she was just an uneducated hick working for minimum wage.

"I'm in the hospitality business myself. My dad owns the Brighton Hotel chain. We're based in Ann Arbor, but we've expanded into three other states now."

"Nice," she said politely. She caught herself judging him as a little full of himself and realized they both had preconceived notions about life outside their own little worlds. She decided to start over. "What do you do there?"

While the washers ran, they talked about how large hotels compared to the seasonal cabins side of the lodging business. Then one of the machines beeped that it was finished and Cassie excused herself to go upstairs and make the boys' lunch.

While she made chicken salad sandwiches, she thought about the differences between men like Paul and men like Danny. Part of the reason she'd had such a hard time finding someone to share a long-term relationship with was that she hadn't met any men who wanted to live in Loon Lake. Even Danny had left.

And she wasn't going to marry someone like Petey Turner just because she knew he'd live here until he died. He was a nice enough guy, but definitely not her type. She wanted to talk about more than fish for the next fifty years. As usual, thinking about it got her nowhere. She didn't see herself as single for the rest of her life either, but many single women didn't. So where did that leave her?

"I guess this is just one more thing I have to trust you with, Lord," she said aloud as she packed the cooler.

Meanwhile, she was beginning to think that the best decision she could make about Danny was to focus on their renewed friendship. She'd have to put all those other feelings for him in a box with old photographs and journals and stick it under her bed. Any other path would be paved with more heartbreak. If she let herself fall in love with him again and he left, it just might kill her...if Uncle Willie didn't die first.

WILLIE ADMITTED TO HIMSELF THAT HE'D BEEN AVOIDING THE kids as much as possible. He told himself it was because they needed to be alone together for his plan to work. Sunday dinner was the first meal the three of them ate as a family since breakfast the day before when he announced his impending death. Danny and Cassie were handling the news well, all things considered. Willie knew they were both good in a crisis, which was why creating a crisis seemed like such a good idea.

But he didn't want them moping about, worrying about him. So he decided that he'd make planning his funeral as much of a fun family activity as he could make it.

After he and Danny washed up from the day's work, they helped set the table. Cassie had made one of his favorite meals — Italian sausage lasagne and cheesy garlic bread. Come to think of it, it was one of Danny's favorites, too.

Willie watched the two of them out of the corner of his eye, pretending to make some notes on a pad. They worked easily together, whether in the kitchen or in the store. The tension of the last few years had mostly drained away, but Willie could see their laughter wasn't as quick and easy, and they made a point not to accidentally touch each other. That last one was easy to see in his postage-stamp-sized kitchen.

Still, they had chemistry. He could tell. He and Velma had chemistry for over forty years before she went on to her reward. He knew what it looked like.

That other fella Cassie had dated last year wasn't a bit like Danny. He was nice enough, but there were no sparks. The few times he'd come to dinner, Willie hadn't felt any need to be cleaning a shotgun or staying awake to make sure there was no hanky-panky. He hurt for Cassie because she'd been hurting when what's-his-name moved away, but Willie was relieved the relationship hadn't gone further.

But now, if he played his cards right, he could be a great uncle again in a year or two. That would make him about the happiest man on earth to have babies nearby. Caroline and Gretchen lived so far away, he only got to see Caroline's kids once a year, and Gretchen had decided to wait until she finished her PhD.

Danny moved Cassie aside and took the hot lasagne pan and set it on two of Velma's old trivets on the table. Cassie brought over the bread and a jug of iced tea.

"Everything smells wonderful, darlin'," Willie said with a warm smile. He had to keep remembering to try to lift their spirits. "You sure are a good cook."

He kicked Danny under the table.

"It smells amazing," he said. "I'm starving."

Willie held out his hands to them and said grace, then he motioned for Danny to cut the lasagne. He had his foot ready to give the boy's shin another kick if he didn't serve Cassie first. So long as he was going to play matchmaker, he might as well get them off on the right foot.

Danny cut a medium-sized piece from the corner and nodded to Cassie. "Here, I know you like the corners."

She smiled at him and held up her plate. She murmured her thanks and smiled at him again when he wasn't looking.

Good. They were getting along today.

Danny cut two massive pieces and served Willie and then himself.

"That's my boy," Willie said with a chuckle.

He let them both take a few bites as the conversation warmed up, then he started on tonight's plan.

"So I've decided to plan my funeral," he announced.

Danny choked and coughed. Cassie gasped, her eyes wide.

"Lots of people don't have time," he said, "but I do, so I want to do it right. And I want you both to help."

Cassie poured Danny more iced tea and started to pound his back, then pulled her hand away.

"Okay?" she asked Danny.

He nodded and put down his fork. He folded his hands with his elbows on the table and Willie thought the boy was taking a few deep breaths.

"It's not that big a deal," Willie said. "It's not like I'm dying this minute. Just doing a little legwork, choosing a coffin, the music, planning the after-party."

Cassie made a little noise in the back of her throat. Danny looked at her, concern in his eyes, and took her hand. She held on tightly, still not saying anything.

Okay, so shock and awe work to bring them together. Noted. Need more of that.

He tried to think of some more shocking things to say.

"I'm meeting with Bud at The Comfy Casket coffin factory to look at caskets." He didn't need to say the entire name of the place, but saying "casket" and "coffin" in the same sentence seemed like a shocking combination.

Cassie visibly paled. Danny pulled her hand closer. Good.

"I'm going to have Edge Edgerly paint mine special," he continued. He hadn't really thought of that, but now that he had, he let his imagination take over. "I'm going to give him some of my old photos and have him paint the biggest fish I ever caught — you remember that walleye back when you were in high school? — as well as my first car."

He looked at Danny. "Did I ever show you pictures of that car? It was a '57 Ford Fairlane 500, two-tone black and white." His eyes lost focus as some of his best memories came back to him. "I took Velma out in that car. Got married a year later."

He wondered if that car had had any real magic or if it just seemed like it when Velma was with him. "I wish I still had it. I'd give it to you."

Danny's lips twitched in a small smile. "I'd love to see the pictures."

Willie noticed the kids had stopped eating. He shooed his hand at him. "Eat, eat, we're just talking here."

He beamed at them when he noticed how reluctantly they let go of each other. If he played his cards right, this was going to be his best idea ever.

"Anyway, I want that fish, and my car, and...I don't know." Willie thought about what else Edge could paint on the casket. Edge and a friend of his painted custom motorcycle parts, so he assumed he'd painted a lot of flames on bikes.

"Flames, I think." He chuckled. "That'd be something,

huh? I bet no one at Christ Community Church has ever been buried in a coffin covered in flames."

"Uncle Willie," Cassie protested. She coughed and took a drink and finally laughed. "What are you doing?"

He grinned at her. "I'm trying to make an awful thing that will happen to all of us eventually, not as awful. I don't know why I didn't think of it earlier. We can't plan our hellos into the world. Why not make our goodbyes something to remember?"

Again, he hadn't really thought about it until he'd said it out loud. He remembered saying goodbye to Velma, how hard it had been, how many of these housekeeping chores they'd had to do in those two weeks when he'd rather have spent all of his time at her side, making her laugh, kissing her beautiful smile.

He sighed. Making all these plans now would make things so much easier on the kids at whatever point in the hopefully distant future that he kicked the bucket.

"Maybe we can come up with a game to make all this more fun, Kick the Bucket instead of Pin the Tail on the Donkey."

Laughs burst forth from all three of them.

There, that was better. He didn't want them sad. Maybe he hadn't needed to go to such extreme measures. Maybe Danny had finally been ready to come home on his own.

"How long can you stay?" he asked.

Danny gave him a direct look. "However long you need me, sir. I mean it. Whatever you need."

Willie swallowed thick emotion. He patted Danny on the shoulder. "You're a good man, Danny. I hope you know that."

Danny looked embarrassed and went back to eating, mumbling something under his breath.

"And when it's all over?" Willie prodded. This was what he really needed to know.

Danny finished chewing and swallowing. "Well," he hesitated, not looking at either of them. "I've got a job and an apartment in Lansing."

Willie hoped he wasn't reading too much into that non-answer, but it didn't sound like the boy had any real ties down there.

"I've got plenty of work around here for you." Willie tried not to sound too enthusiastic while still being clear that Danny could make a living in Loon Lake as easy as he could in the city. "And if you finish it all, I'm sure Jax can help you find more projects. You know how it is, only a few good months for building before the snow hits again."

That didn't sound good, almost like he was saying it was okay to leave then. "Besides, Cassie will need your help to run everything. She's perfectly capable," he said, sending her a smile, not wanting her to think he didn't believe she could manage it, "but I've found it to be too much work for one person. When she inherits, I don't want her to feel overwhelmed and alone."

That part was true. He was trying not to outright lie to them about anything, but he didn't see the harm in stretching the truth. He knew he'd have to answer to lies when he met his Maker in person, but surely there was grace for white lies in service to a greater good.

He thought about asking Pastor Nick about that. No, better to ask for forgiveness than permission. Heaven knew he was quite experienced in asking forgiveness already.

"Now about that party," he began. "I want a band. Good

music, my kind of music. No DJs." He looked from one to the other. "What's the name of that friend of yours who has a band? The one you went to school with?"

"Jason Struthers?" Cassie asked. "The guy who did Melissa Bricker's wedding?"

"Jason still has a band?" Danny asked Cassie. "He played at my—"

Willie kicked the boy in the shins, hard this time.

Danny tried to recover. "Is it still called Jason and the Strummers?"

Cassie shook her head, ignoring Danny's blunder. "No, it's been Cold Northern Lights for a couple years. They're surprisingly good. Though I'm not sure he's done a funeral before."

Danny chuckled. "I'd think not."

"All right," Willie said, "Cassie you call him up, find out what he charges, what kind of music he knows how to play. I'll make up a list of songs I want him to learn." He pointed at each of them in turn. "And I want you two to dance together. I want lots of dancing and singing. I'll be *home*, after all. I want people celebrating and happy for me."

"It's your funeral," Danny said with a laugh.

"That's right, so promise me."

The kids looked to each other again and nodded.

"Now," Willie paused as another idea formed, another way to throw them together. "I don't want you to think I'm selfish, but I'd like to enjoy my last days and maybe work a little less."

"Of course." The kids spoke on top of each other in their rush to agree. Boy, he had a good family here. What a lucky, lucky man he was.

"I already told you that Cassie's education is priority one—"

"It'll be fine, I'm not leaving you any more than—"

He turned on his serious-father voice. "Don't argue with me, young lady. I need to stay calm and focus on my health, so you'll do what I say." Velma would've smacked his hand for speaking like that to their niece, but she wasn't here to help him with his scheme so he had to use the tools he had.

"Yes, sir," she said, obviously unhappy.

"So, Danny, I'll need you to pick up a few shifts at the store when you can. I put you on the payroll today. Cassie will show you—"

"No, sir, I am not taking your money. You and Cassie—"

Willie pounded his fist on the table once. It startled all three of them, actually. This was not his normal way of handling discussions, but he needed to stay in control so he could keep his plan on track.

"I'm not trying to be a tyrant here," he said, the closest to an apology he was willing to go right now, "but we need to pull together as a family. If either of you were in charge of the business and you needed Jax's help, would you make him work for free?"

"No, sir," Danny said, looking at his plate.

Cassie shook her head.

"And if you needed Tabitha's help a few weeks before school was out, would you insist she forget her children's educational needs, or would you work around her schedule?"

"We'd work around it," Cassie said, "but this isn't the same."

Willie sat back in his chair. He looked from one to the other. "You're both good, kind, intelligent people. I couldn't be prouder of who you've become. But you can't have your own way all the time, not even if you think you're trying to help. You need — *we* need — to work together. Right?"

"Yes, sir," they said in unison.

For a moment, Willie wanted to smile benevolently and get a ring for them to kiss. He felt like Al Pacino in *The Godfather*. Only his story would be called *The Uncle Who Loved Them So Much He Deceived Them*. He bit back a chuckle.

"All right, then," he said. "Let's finish this fine meal and clean up. Who picked up a movie?"

CHAPTER 6

*D*anny and Jax spent Monday morning ripping shingles off the roof of one of the cabins. This one was scheduled to be rented on Friday, so Jax had rearranged his schedule to help.

It was good, hard work in beautiful weather. Danny took a moment as he stood on top of the roof to look over at the lake shimmering blue in a light breeze. Dark green pines covered most of the shoreline. Lighter green leaves were nearly full on most of the maples and weeping willows. The birch, beech, elm, and other trees were unfolding more new leaves every day.

Jax threw a shingle off the roof and turned to look at the lake. "Gorgeous view. Miss it?"

Danny nodded. There were dozens of great things about living in Lansing and southern Michigan, but nothing compared to Loon Lake.

"So stay," Jax said.

Danny turned back to the roof and pried up another shingle. "It's complicated."

"No, it's not. It's simple, but you want it to be complicated because that makes you feel like you have more options." Jax started pulling shingles again. "Trust me, I understand that particular self-delusion."

"I'm here for Uncle Willie. I don't know what's going to happen when he's gone, but..." It scared him a little. He'd never given any thought to Uncle Willie dying, now or later. The man had always been a friend and a mentor, but more than that, he'd been a father. He blinked his eyes a couple times.

"You are such a doughnut-brain," Jax muttered.

"What?"

"Your brain has a hole in the middle," his best friend exclaimed, his voice heated. "Look at everything you have here. Friends and family who love you, a girl who's still mad about you even though you don't deserve her, a beautiful place to live and work—"

"Sure, if you have two jobs, sometimes three," Danny interrupted.

"Life is hard, don't be a baby," Jax said, kicking at a stuck shingle. "If you're not willing to work a little harder to have what you want, then go back to Lansing. I don't care."

Danny looked over at his friend fighting the stubborn piece of roofing. "Yes, you do. That's why you're being a pain in my—"

A long whistle rang out from the road. A green Chevy Malibu, two-toned with rust, had pulled onto the gravel shoulder of the road. "Hey, boys," a woman's voice called out, "looking good!"

"Who's that?" Danny asked. "One of your many admirers?"

Jax grinned and waved. "Just wave."

Danny smiled and waved, still unable to see inside the car. A female arm waved out the window, then the car eased back onto the road. A truck coming around the curve from behind hit its brakes to avoid a collision.

"That was Connie Templeton," Jax said, laughing. "I heard you two were an item now. You just waved at her, so it must be the truth. At least, in her head."

Danny groaned. "Thanks, Jax, thanks a lot, buddy."

Jax hooted with laughter at Danny's pained expression.

"You don't understand. When I was at Jimmy's, I felt like prey sighted by a predator."

Jax snorted. "Oh, I do understand, trust me. You haven't had to live in the same town as Connie all this time. I've been the prey more than once. Luckily, my little bunny legs were faster than the fox."

Danny laughed.

"So what are you going to do about Cassie?"

Danny whacked his thumb with the hammer and swore. "I'm going to help her get Uncle Willie's affairs in order. That's why he asked me up here."

"Doughnut-brain," Jax sing-songed. "He asked you up here because Cassie almost got married at Christmas. He's tired of waiting for you to fix your mistake."

"She what? I knew she was dating, but no one said anything about marriage." Danny pinned Jax with a glare. "What happened?"

"Some guy she went to college with in Traverse. Everyone expected she'd get an engagement ring for Christmas."

"So he broke her heart?" Danny wanted to punch the guy.

"Nope, you're still the only guy who's done that," Jax said with a pointed glare. "I think she was more embarrassed than heartbroken. You know how this town is. Let people know anything about your life and when things don't come to pass..." He shrugged.

"It's humiliating." Danny knew that feeling well. It was why he couldn't come back. No one would ever forget what he'd done, how he'd messed up.

Jax walked a few steps closer and lowered his voice. "Listen, brother, I don't blame you. I was with you the first time you saw Bright Shiny. I get it. She's gorgeous. You wanted to date her and I supported you — pretty much making both of us idiots. You wanted to marry her, I stood up for you as your best man. You got divorced, I couldn't have been sadder *or* happier for you. But it's time to come home. Cassie loves you, I know she does. Or why wouldn't she have gotten married by now? And I know you've never stopped loving her. I think"—Jax jabbed Danny in his chest with his hammer—"that's the reason you won't come back, because you still love her and you're scared."

Danny stared out at the lake again. "You get that speech out of a Cracker Jack box?"

Jax grinned. "I've been staying up nights writing it for you. It's better than my best man speech."

Danny cocked his head. "Almost anything would be better than your best man speech."

"You marry Cassie, and I'll give you the best congratulations speech in the history of weddings."

"I'm not marrying her." Danny climbed down the ladder, pulled off his shirt, and slung it over the pole fence that separated the parking area. He grabbed two icy cold water bottles from the Igloo cooler in his truck and tossed them up to Jax, then headed back to the roof.

He'd been thinking about this moving-back-to-Loon-

Lake idea the last few days. Heck, the last few months. He missed his friends, especially his two best friends. He wanted to make amends for the stupid things he'd done. He just had to figure out how.

"I'm not marrying her," he reiterated, "but I am going to try to be her friend again. I know I've been lousy — to you, too — and I hope you'll both forgive me. But I'm not marrying either of you."

Jax put his hand over his heart. "I'm hurt." He laughed and took a long pull on the cold water. He pulled off his shirt and tossed it over the side, not even trying to keep it out of the dirt.

"You sure?" Jax asked. "Absolutely positive you don't want to date her?"

"Absolutely sure," Danny said. He felt a sense of the world finally tipping back into place. He'd renew his old friendships, learn to laugh like he used to, get his life together again. Yeah, it was definitely the right decision. He felt his load lighten. "Just friends."

"Great," Jax said with a grin. "I'm finally going to ask her out."

The wet plastic bottle slipped from Danny's grasp and rolled off the roof. "What…what about Tabitha?"

Jax shrugged. "She'll understand." He set down his water bottle and went back to pulling shingles.

Danny stared at his best friend, the one he'd just now said he wanted to make amends with. Probably tossing him off the roof wouldn't be a good start.

Too bad.

CASSIE HANDED MR. MEYERS HIS CHANGE ALONG WITH A warm smile and a hello for Mrs. Meyers when he got home. She rang up a tourist for gas out front, and flipped the switch for Petey Turner to use the gas pump out at The Hole, the lagoon where boaters tied up for gas or to come in to get bait or snacks. Petey was a local, so he wasn't a pump-n-jump flight risk, as Uncle Willie would say. The only people who had to prepay gas were boaters they didn't know since The Hole was out of sight of the store.

Cassie ambled closer to Artie King, a high school sophomore, to give him some encouragement. The kid was a nervous wreck, but he was better than when he started a couple weeks ago.

"These people are your friends, remember," she murmured near the 16-year-old's ear. "They know you're learning. They'll be patient. Just smile and take a deep breath."

Mrs. Hoag, the new librarian, stood across the counter looking at the batteries on the wall. She was a beautiful widow not much older than Cassie and as nice as a summer day was long. "I'll take the Duracell double-As, please."

Artie swallowed audibly. He was as smitten with the librarian as any of the men around. The library had received double the visitors since the widow had arrived. He turned and grabbed a ten-pack and thrust it toward his customer.

Cassie smiled at Mrs. Hoag and whispered to Artie, "Ask her how many she needs." She saw Old Mrs. G walk in and they waved at each other.

Artie, red-faced, stuttered the question, and the librarian smiled and asked for the four-pack. A few minutes later, after he'd rung her up and she'd left the store, Artie wilted against the counter. "Sorry," he said.

"You're doing fine." Cassie patted his shoulder. "Better every day." She reminded Artie how to ring up gas from The Hole, smiled at Petey, and walked over to greet her old kindergarten teacher. Old Mrs. G stood reading the ingredients on a can of soup. She read the ingredients on every item she put in her basket, every time she came in. For some reason, it made Cassie smile.

"Hello, Mrs. G, how are you?" She leaned in and they gave each other a warm hug. Edith Garraghan and her husband Bert — now known as Dead Bert to differentiate him from Bert Coster, Live Bert — had lived in the Loon Lake area their whole lives. She'd been a kindergarten teacher at Loon Lake Elementary for forty years before she retired, asking her charges to call her Mrs. G from day one. Every child adored her, and the town considered her one of its beloved icons.

"I'm blessed, my dear, truly blessed," the old woman said with a warm smile. "How about you?"

Cassie had decided yesterday to pretend Uncle Willie was as fit as ever so she wouldn't hesitate in answering this question all day. People would pick up on it and the gossip would buzz.

"The same," she said, then added, "whether I realize it or not."

Old Mrs. G was short to begin with, but a bit tipped over with age. She often used a cane, though she was without it today, and she'd worn glasses as long as Cassie had known her. She had beautiful pale skin that looked as soft as a rose petal and she always smelled like vanilla. In every way, she appeared a frail old woman.

But get her talking about her faith and she grew two inches and became as animated as the Energizer Bunny.

She leaned forward now, her eyes sparking with interest, and clasped one of Cassie's hands in both of hers. "That is so true, dear. You're very wise if you see that already. The good Lord knows what He's doing in our lives, even if we don't."

"It can be hard to remember," Cassie said honestly, "but I'm trying." If there was anyone she would be tempted to spill the secret to — Uncle Willie didn't want them talking about it yet, though they'd told Jax and Tabitha — it would be her old teacher. She had one of those personalities that made you want to unburden yourself with her. She made people feel better about whatever life — or God — threw at them.

Cassie restrained herself and stepped back before her eyes got watery. "Let me know if you need anything. Artie will take your groceries to your car when you're ready."

"He's a good boy, that one. I had both his parents in my class." Mrs. G smiled affectionately toward the teen.

Cassie turned to the door as the bell tinkled. CW Emerson and Billy Marlowe walked in and headed for the Pepsi cooler. "Hey, Cass. Hey, Cassie," they called. She smiled and waved. They'd been part of the football team in high school, with C-Dubb as quarterback his junior and senior years. They were both in the class ahead of her with Danny and Jax. Rowdy and loud, but mostly good-natured.

She went behind the counter and rang up their Pepsi's and Cheetos.

"You know where Danny is?" C-Dubb asked. "I heard he was in town, wanted to say hi." His name was really Charles Walter, but somehow he'd become CW in junior high, then C-Dubb in high school. As an adult, he went by CW again… unless he was with old classmates.

"He and Jax are fixing the roof on one of the cabins." She

looked at the clock. She needed to bring their lunch over soon.

"Your cabins?" C-Dubb asked, with a hint of alarm.

She nodded.

Billy frowned. "We didn't know it was them. It looked like one of 'em might be hurt. Maybe you should see if everything's okay."

Cassie tried to tamp down any panic about construction accidents. If either of them had fallen off the roof or cut off a leg, the other one would've called 911 already. And C-Dubb was an EMT. He wouldn't have passed by a seriously injured person without investigating, without helping. But she knew Danny had a tendency to let smaller things go until they became bigger problems. Maybe his arm hadn't fallen all the way off yet and he was still working.

She hurried out the front door and around the corner to the first of the cabins' two parking areas. She raised her hand to shield her eyes from the midday sun and drew in a sudden breath. Danny stood outlined against the blue sky, his uncovered chest and arms glistening with sweat. He held a hammer in one hand and rested the other on one hip.

He looked ridiculously masculine standing there, shirtless, muscles gleaming in the sun.

She covered her mouth with her free hand. Her heart beat in her ears and her vision narrowed until she saw only Danny. She hadn't seen him without his shirt in years. My, how he'd grown from boy to man. She was still staring when she heard C-Dubb and Billy howl with laughter.

Cassie felt her face heat up. She turned to see them leaning against each other, laughing so hard Billy nearly fell over.

Great. Just great.

She turned back to catch one last glimpse of Danny and saw him wave at her. She forced herself to wave back. Embarrassment made her movements jerky.

She sent the other two a withering look as she stepped around them and walked back to the store.

"I told you she still liked him," C-Dubb said to his friend. "You owe me ten bucks."

"I don't know, she might've been looking at Jax," Billy said. As she got closer to the door, he called out, "Did you even notice Jax had his shirt off, too, Cassie? I bet you didn't even notice. Maybe you should sell shirts at the Loon."

"Put it in the suggestion box, Billy," Cassie called, and escaped into the store.

"But you don't have a suggestion box," he yelled.

CHAPTER 7

*T*he next morning, Cassie tried not to think about Jax and Danny working outside. She made a point not to check the temperature to see if it would be warm again today. She even considered having Kevin deliver their lunch later.

But, no, she was tougher than that. Sure, they were both handsome, well-built young men, but they were both her friends, not models or celebrities to be mooned over. Despite that, delivering their lunch yesterday had been a test of her will. If only she could've willed herself not to blush and stutter. She'd escaped before they even got down the ladder.

Today was a new day. She would calmly deliver their meal and not let herself be bothered by their attire.

Or lack thereof.

The image of Danny standing on that roof backlit by the sun filled her mind.

She shook her head and tried to focus on her work.

"Hey, Cassie."

She looked up from the accounting printouts she studied at the end of the counter.

"I was hoping I'd find you here," said Paul, the Ann Arbor customer from the Fluff and Fold on Sunday. He grinned and leaned his forearms on the counter, getting closer. "Had lunch yet?"

She snorted a little laugh. "It's 10:30 in the morning."

"So that's a no."

Cassie laughed outright. "Yes." She went back to studying the weekly records. She had an appointment with Oscar Wallace, Uncle Willie's accountant, in a few minutes.

"Yes, you'll have lunch with me?"

She looked up in surprise. Paul raised his eyebrows expectantly, turning on the charm with his smile and his eyes and leaning into her space a little more. Was he flirting with her?

"I'm working," she said. She was about to add a sassier comment, but decided she didn't know him well enough to tease. At this point he was still a customer who needed to be treated professionally, if kindly.

"Doesn't your boss give you a lunch break?" He looked around. "Maybe I could ask him. We can call it a business lunch and discuss the hospitality business."

That piqued her interest. She'd never really talked about business ideas with anyone but Uncle Willie and her classmates.

Her open-book expression cued him in and he pushed. "Maybe I can give you some ideas about how to promote your cabins, things you can do to set yourself apart. It's how my dad made his hotels into the boutique chain they are today. I'd love to help, if I can."

Cassie looked at the time on her fitness tracker bracelet

and gathered up her files. "I have to meet my accountant. I don't know how long I'll be." She realized it wasn't a yes or a no as the words came out of her mouth, but she couldn't help wondering how nice it might be to talk to someone else in a similar business. Had to be more helpful than doing group projects with the other students at school, right? Paul had real life experience.

"I'll drive you to your appointment, and then we'll have lunch when you're done. I don't mind waiting." He stood and pulled out his key fob.

Cassie looked out the window to see a black BMW in the parking area. It looked out of place sitting alongside Ted Grainger's rusted old station wagon and Petey Turner's monster truck with the big winch attached to the front.

"Our accountant is just across the street," she said. "I suppose I could go out after I deliver lunch to the guys on the roof. But not for long, maybe an hour or so."

"Done," he said with a satisfied grin. "I'll meet you back here about…?"

"Maybe 12:30 or 12:45?" It felt so weird saying yes. She didn't feel attracted to him, so she didn't want to give the wrong impression. "A business lunch," she reiterated.

"Absolutely," he nodded, his expression more serious. "I'll see you then."

Cassie's appointment with Oscar took less time than expected and she was back home by 11:30. She pulled out ingredients for lunch for Danny and Jax, and thought about what questions she might ask Paul. She stacked piles of sliced ham and Swiss cheese on rye bread, Danny's favorite, covering one slice with mayonnaise and the other with mustard, thinking about how she could help Uncle Willie reduce the vacancy rate on the cabins in the off season.

When she had lunch ready, she glanced at her watch. She still had a few minutes to freshen up a little. She took her hair out of the ponytail and pulled it back in her silver butterfly clip. She'd put on a sundress today, so she didn't feel the need to change, but she grabbed the little shrug sweater she loved in case the restaurant was cool.

Satisfied with her appearance, she hooked her purse over her shoulder and pulled the wheeled cooler over to the cabin where Danny and Jax were working. "You fellas hungry?" she called up to them.

Jax popped his head over from the other side of the roof and whistled. "Well, don't you look fine, Cassie Lane," he drawled.

Cassie couldn't help but laugh at him. He was a terrible flirt — and terribly good at it — but in her mind he belonged to Tabitha, whether he knew it or not.

He climbed down the ladder, and Cassie saw Danny approach the edge of the roof. She was relieved to see he was still fully dressed. He waved at her and started down. She accidentally found herself watching his backside until Jax interrupted her thoughts.

"You wear that just for me?" His eyes moved over her with appreciation, pausing noticeably at her cleavage.

She slapped his arm and laughed. "No, I did not, Jax Edgerly." She motioned to the cooler. "I put some extra water in there today since I noticed you drank everything I brought yesterday. I don't want you to get dehydrated." Her eyes slipped to Danny for a second.

"Any beer?" Jax asked.

Cassie tilted her head and raised her eyebrows to say, *As if*. She turned to Danny. "How do you put up with him all day?"

"It ain't easy," Danny replied with a mock sigh. "You know he's always been trouble."

Cassie laughed. "You've *both* always been trouble. But I love you anyway." She made sure to look at both of them when she said that. No mixed messages, she told herself, she just wanted to have her old friend back. Honestly, she did love her friends and she wasn't afraid to let them know.

"Stay and eat with us," Danny said suddenly.

Cassie was surprised and pleased at the invitation, and it probably showed on her face before she remembered she was trying to be nonchalant. "Oh! I'd like to, but I can't today. Maybe tomorrow?"

Jax turned his Broken Hearts Unlimited smile on her. "I think you should let me take you to lunch tomorrow. I'm more fun."

"You're also more trouble," Cassie said. "Every woman in Loon Lake knows that. Besides, Jax," she sighed heavily, "you're just too much man for me to handle."

Jax puffed up his chest. "Well," he said, looking mollified, "in that case, I release you to Danny's care. Just do me a favor and don't break his heart."

Danny shook his head. "You're such a drama queen."

Jax reached into the cooler and pulled out a sandwich, a bag of chips, and a Mountain Dew. "Someone needs to entertain the masses." He sat down on a nearby log to eat.

Cassie heard a car pull into the driveway behind them. She turned to see a black BMW headed their way.

Jax whistled.

"You expecting anyone to check in today?" Danny asked.

"Uh, no," Cassie said, uneasiness creeping down her neck. Paul was supposed to meet her at the store. She didn't really want to explain her lunch plans to Danny. But now she'd have to. "I have a business lunch."

Paul opened his door and got out, tall and lean and completely put together.

"I'll be right there," Cassie called. In a low voice to Danny and Jax, she said, "His name is Paul Brighton. His dad owns some big hotel chain in Ann Arbor. We're going to discuss ideas for improvements I could make to the cabins."

Jax snorted and stood. "No, you're not."

Cassie's eyes widened. "Yes, I—"

"Where'd you meet him?" Danny asked. "What do you know about him?"

"He's a tourist," Jax said, folding his arms and moving closer to Cassie. "Family's got a cabin on East Shore Drive. I've done some work for his father."

"He was talking to me, Jax," Cassie grumbled.

"And?" Danny asked his friend.

Jax shrugged. "Seems like good enough people but I don't know them well. Never met the son." He nodded toward the BMW.

"It'll be fine," Cassie said quietly, trying not to let Paul know they were talking about him. Probably impossible the way Danny and Jax were staring in his direction. "It's just a business lunch and—"

"No, Cassie," Jax turned to her, his teasing look gone, replaced by a big brother look she rarely saw. "That's just an excuse to have lunch with a beautiful woman. Trust me. I'd know."

"Where are you going?" Danny asked.

"I don't know, we didn't decide—"

"You're not going off in a strange car with a strange man

and no one knows where you are," Danny said tightly. His big brother look was even tougher than Jax's.

A voice in Cassie's heart wondered if "big brother" was an accurate description. Before she knew what he was doing, Danny pulled out his phone and took a picture of Paul and his car. He walked over to take a picture of the license plate, Cassie hurrying behind, tugging at his arm to stop him. He was embarrassing her.

"Everything okay?" Paul asked, standing up straighter and eyeballing Danny and Jax.

"Hi," Danny said, reaching over to shake Paul's hand. "Danny Kessler. And you are?"

"Paul Brighton. Nice to meet you." He joined in the staring contest.

Cassie tried to squeeze between the men but Danny and Jax stepped in front of her.

"Jax Edgerly," Jax said, shaking Paul's hand. "I've done some work for your dad. Nice guy."

Paul paused, and then said, "Yes, he is."

Cassie looked from one man to another, surprised at the tension, unsure of what to do. She'd only had one other experience like this in her sheltered life. In seventh grade. Again with Danny and Jax. That day had ended with the other boy getting a bloody nose.

Her mother told Cassie later that she needed to be aware of the power she held and to be very careful with it. Cassie didn't understand, told her mother she didn't do anything. But her mom had said, "When you find yourself the woman in the middle of a wolf pack, you need to know how to tame them back into men again."

Her mother's words filled her mind now. She waited quietly to see what the men would do.

Danny held up his phone. "I know this is safe little Loon Lake, but it's the twenty-first century. We'd want to know where to find someone if she went missing." His voice was strong, tough, but not threatening.

Paul stared at Danny for a moment, then nodded and took out his wallet. "Here's my card. All my information is there." He nodded down the road to the Lakeview Inn. "We'll be at the Lakeview for an hour, then I'll bring her back to the store."

Jax said in a voice that was matter-of-fact steel, "You can drop her off here."

The three men seemed to have a short, silent conversation staring at each other. Cassie tried not to move, afraid to scare the wolves, knowing she'd have to get between them if they went for each other's throats.

"Have a nice lunch," Danny said. "The trout is excellent there." Then he put his arm around Cassie's shoulder, walked her to the passenger side of the car, helped her in, and closed her door without saying a word.

Cassie sat there numbly, unsure of what to think or do.

Wolves, indeed.

She should've asked her mom more questions.

CASSIE SMOOTHED HER DRESS OVER HER LAP FOR THE TENTH time. In her mind, she was confident and friendly with sound questions about the hotel industry. She had a few questions prepared that showcased both her book knowledge at NMC as well as her thirteen-plus years of experience working in Uncle Willie's businesses.

That was her mind. Her body was something else. She was fidgety and nervous and not sure how to act after Danny and Jax's he-man display. Should she apologize for them? Should she pretend it didn't happen? Wait until Paul brought it up?

The last idea seemed wise, and it allowed her to pretend it hadn't happened as well.

Though a tiny part of her rejoiced to be at the center of such devotion.

She tried to put the last few minutes out of her mind and focus. She felt nervous as a wild rabbit, and "nervous" for her always translated into "food spilled all over."

For heaven's sake, he was just a man. Good-looking and perfectly groomed and city-slick perhaps, but just a man. If he laughed at her ideas or scoffed at what she'd learned in school, she'd never have to see him again. Except for when he did his laundry or got gas or needed some chips. But at some point he'd go home.

She focused on that. Talk to him for a bit, and he'd probably be gone in a few days.

"So what's good here?" Paul asked, looking over his menu.

"Well, Danny was right, the trout here is the best in the county." She glanced over the other menu items. "The potato leek soup is excellent, and the Asian salad is big enough for three people if you're hungry."

She cleared her throat, then smiled nervously at him. She reached for her water glass. It tipped before she grabbed it with more force than necessary, sloshing some of the contents over the white tablecloth. At least she hadn't spilled it down her dress.

Paul closed his menu. "Trout it is." He leaned forward

and lowered his voice. "Don't worry about it. It's a guy thing. Just relax and forget about it."

Cassie sent him a shaky, relieved smile and took a deep breath. It was still an embarrassing way to start a business lunch.

Paul waved to the waitress. Cassie hoped she wouldn't spill the soup and salad she ordered. She needed to relax. When the waitress left, Paul led the conversation in the usual getting-to-know-you small talk.

By the time their meal arrived, Cassie was back to her old self. Time to change the subject back to business. "So, the reason I agreed to have lunch with you—"

"Was that you found my charm irresistible?"

Cassie stopped mid-sentence, unsure what to say. She laughed and said, "Well, that, and I'm intrigued by what your father did to make his hotels stand out. Can you tell me more?"

He chuckled and touched her hand. "I'm teasing you."

She blinked and tried to continue. Was he flirting with her? If so, was he doing it just because Danny and Jax had been so pushy? Uncertainty clouded her thoughts for a moment.

"You were saying?" Paul motioned with his fork for her to continue. "Wow, you're right, this fish is excellent."

Cassie stirred her soup, helping it cool before she ate it. She burned her mouth on almost everything when it first came from the kitchen. Danny used to tease her and say she should wait until he was halfway done eating, then her food would be the perfect temperature. He was usually right.

She plied Paul with questions, listening intently to his answers, and asking more. She'd forgotten about her soup, and when she glanced down she noticed that she'd spilled it over the sides of the bowl while stirring. She hoped Paul hadn't noticed. Better the tablecloth than her dress.

"Have you ever done an internship?" Paul asked.

Cassie nodded and swallowed. "I worked at one of the big hotels in Traverse City for a few months."

"You should come to Ann Arbor, intern at my hotel. I can arrange it. And in your free time, I can show you around. Do you like theatre? Sports? I can take you anywhere."

Cassie smiled and tried not to sigh audibly. "That's very kind, but my business is here. My uncle needs me." Her own sisters didn't understand her affinity for Loon Lake, so why would a stranger get it? He probably thought her home was quaint, a lovely vacation spot, but not a place to grow roots.

"Besides," she said, "I didn't get a lot out of my TC internship that I could apply to our businesses here. It would probably be the same with your dad's hotel, even though I'm sure it's lovely," she hurried to add.

"We could detail out what would be helpful and create an internship that would be tailored to you specifically." Paul sounded like this would be no problem whatsoever. How much sway did he have at his dad's hotel?

If she were interested in the hospitality business in general, this would be a great opportunity. But it would take her away from home when Uncle Willie needed her most, and she still didn't believe it would help. Their businesses and clientele were so different.

Paul leaned closer, his charming smile flashing. "And as your friend, I would set aside time for us to discuss business as much as you want, almost-owner to almost-owner."

Cassie batted down a twinge of uneasiness. Did he really want to help or was he just flirting? Doing both at the same time confused her. A few meals and discussions, some brainstorming, that was fine. Moving away and not knowing if she was being trained or wooed, that was out of the question.

"I appreciate it," she said, settling back into professional mode, "but this isn't a good time to be away. We're about to start our busy season." She finished her salad and pushed her plate away.

Paul moved his empty plate aside and reached for her hand. "Understood. Then let's talk more while I'm up here. How about dinner in Traverse City next time? See a movie afterward or walk on the beach. Plenty of time to talk on the drive."

It wasn't that Cassie hadn't dated much. And Danny hadn't scared her into not wanting to drive away with someone she barely knew. Paul seemed like a good guy, though he was a bit pushier than she liked.

So what was it? Why did a pleasant evening away sound so unappealing?

She thought about the last couple weeks of hanging out with Danny, laughing and horsing around with their friends. Watching movies with him and Uncle Willie, all three of them crowded onto the couch together. His unexpected visit to church. Danny was home, but she didn't know for how long. She didn't want to miss any time with him, especially if he ended up leaving again.

She pulled her hand away and picked up her purse and sweater. "I'll think about it," she said. "We better get back."

A quiet voice in her head finished her sentence.

To Danny.

PAUL DROPPED HER OFF AT THE CABINS BUT DIDN'T GET OUT
of the car. Jax and Danny popped their heads over the side of
the roof and gave Paul a wave. Cassie stood there as he
pulled away, wondering about men.

She was about to head for home when she saw Danny
coming down the ladder. When he got to the bottom, he
pulled off his shirt and draped it neatly over the fence. Cassie
felt herself tense. She swallowed nervously. Before she could
think of something to say, Danny spoke.

"How was lunch?" His voice sounded tense, more like it
used to when she tried to talk to him on the phone. Not like
the last few days.

"Good," she said. "I just had soup and salad."

His lips twitched. "I can see that," he said, looking at her
breasts.

She gasped when she saw salad dressing on her dress.
She wet her thumb and tried to wipe it off, scrubbing at the
stain with her thumbnail. "Oh, for heaven's sake," she said,
"now I'll have to go change."

Danny cleared his throat.

Cassie glanced up to see him shifting from one foot to the
other, looking everywhere but at her. She heard laughter and
looked up just as Jax threw his own shirt down. It landed
squarely on Danny's head.

"Having problems down there?" Jax asked, laughing
more.

"It's not funny, Jax," Cassie complained. "I can't seem to
go anywhere without spilling food on myself. It's
embarrassing."

"That's not what I was—"

Danny tossed the other shirt on the fence and glared up at
the roof. "Go back to work!"

Jax disappeared, his laughter trailing in the air behind him.

"What—" Cassie began.

"Don't worry about it," Danny said, cutting her off. "You know how he is."

Cassie didn't know what was up with them today so she changed the subject. "So how's the roof going?"

"Good, should be done tomorrow." Hands on his hips, he turned toward the lake, something apparently having captured his attention.

While he looked the other way, Cassie let herself stare. He was just her friend, of course, but that didn't make him any less amazing to look at. The muscles in his chest were large and hard, and they curved around to connect to his neck and shoulders and arms, and down to a tight abdomen. Golden hair shone in the sunlight and sweat.

She remembered the first time she'd noticed hair on his chest. She'd teased him mercilessly until he chased her around the grass near The Hole and tackled her, threatening to throw her in the lake. Normally she wouldn't have cared, but the water near the gas pump sometimes smelled of gas when customers weren't as careful filling their tanks. She'd screamed and held onto him for dear life.

Thinking back on it, Cassie wondered if that was exactly what Danny had wanted. A year older than her, maybe he'd realized where their relationship was headed before she had. But then...why did he pursue Lily the moment she arrived? Maybe she'd never know.

"You look hungry, Cassie, didn't you get enough to eat?" Jax's voice carried in the still air.

She turned away, forcing herself not to look up, not to look at Danny, not to acknowledge the comment at all.

She felt Danny staring at her. Blood rushed to her head so fast she felt a little dizzy.

"I better get changed and get back to work," Cassie said as she headed toward the Fluff and Fold.

Danny grabbed her arm, bringing them closer. Cassie could smell his deodorant and sweat and that unique scent of sunshine-warmed skin. She breathed shallowly as she tried not to react. But she couldn't last. She looked up into his warm, brown eyes.

Danny didn't speak for a moment, just stared at her like he was trying to decide how to proceed. Finally, he said, "Some friends are coming over to watch movies at Jax's house tonight. Wanna join us? We'll probably get pizza. You know Jax and pizza."

Danny's voice had lost the edge it had when Paul was around, and it wasn't as tense as it had been, but…Cassie couldn't put her finger on it. They'd been apart for too long. The boy she'd known inside and out was now a man with a troubled past. She wasn't sure how to act around him anymore.

She smiled, content in her old role of putting Danny at ease, making him feel better. "What time should I come over?"

"I'll pick you up."

"You don't have to. I do own a car, you know."

"I'll pick you up," he said, giving her his old I'm-older-and-know-better look.

She laughed, and part of it came out as a snort, which made her laugh more. Danny grinned. Which made everything better again — the male tension, the weird lunch, the spilled food.

The naked chest.

He reached over and ruffled her hair. She squealed and swatted his hand away.

"Hey! Stop messing up my hair."

He pushed her away and slapped her bottom. "Don't worry, I'll bring you a bib tonight."

And things were back to normal for a minute.

She turned and stuck her tongue out at him and headed for home. A moment later, she turned back, hoping for another glance of him climbing the ladder. But he stood in the same spot, arms crossed, looking serious and a little confused.

Cassie faced forward again, her face heating up. She'd wanted things to be back the way they'd been before he got married and moved away.

But maybe things were too much the same.

CHAPTER 8

*D*anny focused on not falling off the roof the rest of the afternoon, and only hit his thumb once while hammering. Jax baited him, but he did his best to ignore all the remarks about Cassie's many virtues.

He'd made his decision. He was going to fix the relationships that mattered most, and he wouldn't risk screwing them up again. Since he'd been downstate, he'd come to realize how much he'd taken for granted in Loon Lake. He hadn't made any close friends in Lansing. No one would miss him while he was gone.

But just in the last few days, he'd fallen back into several relationships up here as if no time had passed. Tabitha's kids were a lot bigger. He was surprised they'd remembered him, in fact. But mostly things were almost the same. He'd lain awake on Jax's couch last night, unable to sleep, counting his blessings. The count had gone surprisingly high before he'd fallen asleep.

He wasn't upset with Cassie going out with someone, he was upset that she'd chosen a stranger and was getting into his car with him. If she watched the news more, at least where he'd been living, she'd have driven her own car. Or walked. He'd have been able to see her get safely to the restaurant from the roof.

He wondered how serious Jax was about dating her. Probably not at all. But what if they did? What if they got serious, got married, had sex? That's when his hammer missed the nail and hit his thumb. He swore and shook his hand, annoyed with his clumsiness.

"Hello, up there!"

Danny walked over the roof to see Uncle Willie at the top of the ladder. "Should you be climbing ladders?" he asked, hearing the alarm in his voice.

The older man ignored his question. "How's it going? Jax still here?"

Jax came over the top. "Hey, Willie."

"We should be done tomorrow," Danny said. "Looks like this unit was the only one that needed a roof, but there are some minor repairs I need to make to the other buildings."

The three of them talked about the other work to be done. Then Uncle Willie asked, "You seen Cassie today?"

"She's at the store, isn't she?" She wouldn't have run off with that guy again, would she? He tried to tamp down his concern. If he worried about Cassie and Uncle Willie every day he was here, he'd have an ulcer before long.

"I suppose she is," Uncle Willie said with a shrug, "just wondering if you talked to her today."

"Don't worry, we scared off her new suitor," Jax said with a grin.

"Beg your pardon?"

Danny told him about Paul, the "business lunch," and that

he'd seen Cassie walk back to the Fluff and Fold so he knew she was safe.

"Huh," Uncle Willie said, staring off into the distance. "What'd you think of him? Is he right for our girl?"

Danny clamped his jaw shut against the first two or three responses that came to mind. He finally went with, "I guess I wouldn't know."

Jax snorted. "Of course he's not right for Cassie. Everyone knows she has no intention of ever leaving Loon Lake. Mr. Beamer would never move here. End of story."

Danny looked over his shoulder at his friend. Jax didn't have a moment's doubt about Cassie not ending up with Paul. He relaxed a bit.

"What are you fellas doing tonight?" Uncle Willie asked. "I was going to go out, but I don't want Cass sitting at home alone and bored. Can you take her wherever you're going?"

The question felt so normal. Uncle Willie had asked it of him a thousand times over Danny's life. And just like the other thousand times, Danny didn't mind saying, "Yes, sir." He continued, "We're all going to watch movies at Jax's house. Does it matter what time I bring her home?"

Uncle Willie waved a hand. "Naw, stay out all night if you want so long as all three of you get to work on time in the morning." He winked and waved and headed back down the ladder.

"Hey, uh," Danny called down, then lowered his voice so it wouldn't carry. "Have you talked to Dr. Dillon? When are you getting those tests done?"

"Next week," Uncle Willie said, not pausing in his descent. "Don't worry, I'll tell you when I know more."

Danny wanted to ask more questions, but the older man

jumped the last two steps to the ground and hurried away. Danny sighed and turned back to work.

"He sure doesn't look like he's dying, does he?" Jax asked, keeping his voice down. "Doesn't act like it either."

"He says he's not in any pain," Danny said, watching him walk away. "Thank God for that."

The two of them worked in harmony for a couple more hours, then called it a day. Back at the house, Jax told Danny to shower first so he could pick up Cassie and the pizza while Jax showered.

Danny pulled on a clean pair of jeans and an old Marvel Avengers T-shirt since they planned on watching a couple Marvel movies tonight. At the Fluff and Fold, he took the stairs two at a time, knocked hard on the door, and opened it halfway. "Hello?"

He couldn't tell if Cassie had called "Come in" or "Coming," but he figured it was six of one, half a dozen of the other, so he went inside. She hurried out of her bedroom still buttoning up the front of her dress. Lightly tanned skin was being squeezed back behind pale blue cotton as he watched.

Earlier today, he'd done his best to act the gentleman and turn away, but he was too surprised to think about it this time. As her hands fiddled with the buttons, her breasts moved, calling his attention. She looked beautiful and smelled wonderful. Her hair was still damp from the shower.

The thought shot through some part of his brain that if Lily waltzed into town today, he'd never notice her. His old best friend was more than enough for him.

"Oh! I didn't hear you come in," Cassie said, turning away a little to finish the buttons. "I was just coming to answer the door."

Danny looked down at the floor and rubbed the back of his neck, embarrassed. "Sorry, sorry, I should've waited," he said. He peeked up to see if she was done. He cleared his throat and put his hands in his pockets, not sure what to do with himself. He wondered if there were new rules now that they were adults.

"Maybe I shouldn't just walk in like that, huh?"

Cassie smiled her sunny smile. "My fault. I shouldn't walk out of my room half-dressed." She shook out her damp hair and finger-combed it.

Danny could hear the thought coming — *I wouldn't mind seeing you half-dressed* — and pushed it away before it could gain a foothold. He remembered a verse he'd memorized in Sunday School, "take every thought captive... something, something." He couldn't remember the whole thing, but it seemed sound advice to keep him out of trouble.

He pulled himself together and picked up her purse and sweater on the kitchen table. "This everything?"

"Almost," she said and hurried to the refrigerator. She pulled out a big bowl covered in plastic wrap. "I made chocolate chip cookie dough so we can have hot cookies while we watch the movie." She held up the bowl with a big grin.

Danny put his hand over his heart and groaned. "When was the last time I told you how wonderful you are?"

She cocked her head, pretending to think. "It's been awhile." She walked toward the door. "But go ahead, you can say it now."

He opened the door for her and chuckled. "You're the best, Cassie Lane."

They picked up the pizzas at Jimmy's — thankfully, no

Connie in sight — and Jax hit "play" as soon as they walked in.

"Don't you want to wait for the others?" Cassie asked. "Who else is coming?"

Jax grabbed two slices of pizza and sent Danny a look that said he wasn't going to bail him out.

Danny grabbed a paper plate and piled slices on it. Speaking into the pizza box, he said, "Yeah, I guess no one else could make it. Just the three of us tonight." He looked up and winked at her. "More cookie dough for me."

Cassie giggled.

He'd forgotten how much he loved that sound. The reason they'd suddenly been thrown together was not one that implied levity. She still smiled a lot, and he'd heard her laugh, but he hadn't noticed her giggling until now. It soothed a scarred place in his soul. He wanted to make her giggle again.

Jax brought tall plastic cups from the kitchen while the movie trailers continued to roll and poured everyone some pop. Then he poked Cassie in the shoulder. "Get over on the couch with Danny. This is my favorite chair." When she hesitated, he said, "Mine. Up, up."

She shook her head at him and took her plate and cup over to the couch. "Men," she said. "You're like Sheldon. *That's my spot.*"

"Bazinga!" Jax mumbled through a mouthful of cheese and pepperoni.

Danny tried to give Jax a warning look, but his friend wouldn't meet his gaze.

Cassie got settled a few inches away, took a big bite of hot pizza, and dripped cheese down her chin. She started giggling again.

The melted mozzarella hung two inches off the bottom of her chin, dangling in the air. She tried to get her cup onto the coffee table without spilling it and without moving so much that the cheese would drip onto her clothes. She was about to get pop and cheese all over.

He shook his head at her. "Who takes care of you?" he said as he took her cup and set it safely on the table. Then he helped her with the dangling cheese, making her laugh as he swept it up on his finger and stuffed it between her lips.

He heard a camera sound and looked up to see Jax pointing his phone at them. "Smile," he called.

Tomato paste and a little cheese still spattered Cassie's chin, so Danny grabbed a couple napkins and mopped at her face, making her giggle even harder.

He laughed at her. "Chew, woman. Swallow before you choke."

She finally managed to swallow the bite of pizza. She wiped at one of her eyes where tears were forming.

"Goofball," he said. He opened one napkin all the way and spread it out across her chest, trying to let it hang from her shoulders. It kept falling.

"I think you should get one of my beach towels," Jax said, laughing from his chair.

"No," Cassie cried, still laughing.

"I told you you need a bib," Danny insisted. He fiddled with the napkin but there wasn't much he could do unless he touched her skin. He reminded himself she was one of his friends who needed a helping hand, no big deal, and he tucked the napkin under the edges of the neckline of her dress. Her skin felt soft and warm on his fingertips.

He grabbed one more napkin and spread it over her lap

without touching her. "There," he said, "think you can manage now, or do you need to be spoon-fed?"

Cassie took a swallow of pop and wiped her chin and neck one more time. "No, I'm good, really." She giggled again. "I can't believe you said I'd need a bib tonight and then I did before I even swallowed the first bite. Honestly, I'm not usually this bad."

Danny gave her a look that said he didn't believe her for one minute. She elbowed him in the arm. He winced and pulled away.

She looked from his expression to his arm and got closer to squint at it. "Oh, Danny, you've got a sunburn. Why aren't you putting on sunscreen?"

He shrugged. "Movie's starting." He pointed to the big flat screen.

She looked over at Jax. "You're sunburned, too. For heaven's sake, guys, you're going to get skin cancer if you're not careful. Do you have aloe here, Jax?"

He nodded, staring at the screen.

"After we're done eating, I'm putting aloe on both of you." She had that same expression she had when she'd bandaged his hand Saturday at Tabitha's.

"Fine, in between movies," he said just to mollify her. "Now shush."

It was a good night, Danny thought later. Good food, good company, a good movie. He'd had to pretend he found Cassie's ministrations annoying when she insisted he take his shirt off, and then she gave him what-for when she saw his red skin. He winced a little in a few places, but mostly he enjoyed feeling her hands rubbing the cool aloe onto his arms and back and chest.

Jax, of course, went the other direction, calling Cassie an

angel with a sinner's hands and trying to either make her laugh or embarrass her — Danny wasn't sure which — and succeeding in doing both.

She made cookies while Jax switched DVDs. Then she and Danny ate spoonfuls of dough while Jax inhaled the hot cookies. He grimaced at them. "You two are sick. You're going to get food poisoning."

Cassie teased him, moaning and closing her eyes in pleasure. "Oh, this is so good, wow, yum."

Danny joined in and they kept it up until Jax laughed and said, "Shut up, you two, the movie's on."

Cassie had started nodding off about the time J.A.R.V.I.S. became Vision, and she'd fallen asleep completely, her head on his shoulder, by the time Scarlet Witch agreed to help the Avengers fight Ultron.

Danny looked down at her peaceful face. How could she sleep with her neck twisted like that? He moved so his shoulder more fully supported her, hoping it would help her to not get an awful crick in the neck. She murmured something unintelligible and snuggled into him.

He didn't move. Was this appropriate for friends, even the friends they used to be? Should he wake her up and take her home? He was feeling tense and unsure until Jax looked over and smiled.

"Don't worry, dude, when she falls asleep at Tabitha's, she's really out," he said quietly. "Might as well finish the movie. She won't notice." And he went back to watching.

Well, there you had it from someone who knew her better.

Danny took a breath and relaxed, letting his friend sleep against his side. He did make one small move he probably shouldn't have. Making sure Jax was facing the TV, he leaned over and put his nose near her hair, inhaling the scent of flowery shampoo and beautiful woman.

Yeah, that was really nice, a terrible idea. He didn't do it again. But he didn't forget it.

When the movie was over, he and Jax finished off the cookies while talking about the work they'd do tomorrow. He leaned forward a little to take a few cookies from the plate Jax held out. Cassie didn't move.

"Trust me," Jax said, "that girl is out. It'll take you a few minutes to wake her up, too, if you want her to walk under her own power."

Sure enough, when Danny tried to rouse her, she mumbled and curled back into sleep. He snorted softly as he watched her. He'd never met a girl like her.

"Grab her purse and sweater, will you?" he asked Jax. "I'll wash out the bowl and bring it over to her tomorrow."

"You can let her sleep here if you want," Jax said.

Danny looked at his friend to gauge if he was suggesting something Uncle Willie would find highly inappropriate.

"You'd have to sleep on the floor, of course."

"She'll be more comfortable in her own bed," Danny said, knowing that was true after sleeping on Jax's couch the last few nights. He picked her up as gently as he could, but she still barely stirred.

Jax helped him get her belted into the front seat, but by the time they were done, they were both giggling like little girls. It was ridiculous that she still hadn't woken up yet.

Thankfully, Uncle Willie rarely locked his door, so Danny opened it as quietly as he could and made his way to Cassie's bedroom. He hoped Uncle Willie didn't still have that shotgun lying around. He didn't want it pointed at his back during a misunderstanding.

He got her onto the bed, dropped her purse and sweater on the floor, and took off her sandals. He tugged the top blanket out from under her to lay it over her sleeping form. Once finished, he stood there for a moment wondering about this girl he'd known his whole life. He had a thousand memories with her, maybe ten thousand, but she was still a mystery to him.

He leaned down and brushed her hair away from her face. He realized that big barrette thing was still pinned to the back of her head. That had to be uncomfortable to sleep on. He managed to unpin it without pulling her hair hard enough to wake her. Then he kissed her forehead and tiptoed from the room.

"She sleeps like the dead, doesn't she?" Uncle Willie's voice came from the hall by Cassie's door.

Danny just about jumped out of his skin. "You about gave me a heart attack," he whispered. He joined Willie in the hall.

"She's been that way since the day she was born. Maybe that's why she's so sunny all the time — she gets more sleep than the rest of us." He chuckled and turned back toward his room.

He stopped and turned to face Danny, looking him in the eye with an unexpected intensity. "I rarely think about the fact that she's not really my daughter. She's the daughter of my heart. I'd do anything, take any risk, to give her what I thought would be best for her."

Danny nodded. "I understand," he said. But he didn't understand the underlying meaning of the words. And Uncle Willie's intense expression said there was an underlying meaning.

Uncle Willie put a hand on Danny's shoulder and gripped it hard. "I feel the same about you. I don't call you 'son' for nothing. Whatever it takes for your happiness and well-being, I'd do it."

Danny was glad for the dark. It was hard for him to tell the people he loved how he felt about them. He wanted to tell Uncle Willie now that he was the best father a man could want. But all he could do was clear his throat a couple times, give up on speaking, and nod at the man.

Uncle Willie smiled, gave his shoulder another squeeze, and headed for his bedroom. In his regular, casual voice, he called out, "G'night, son," and closed his bedroom door behind him.

Danny stood for a moment looking from the closed door to the sleeping woman, asking God what he was supposed to do to deserve them. Then he forced his feet to move and drove back to Jax's, a man without answers.

CHAPTER 9

On the surface, the rest of the week continued with the semi-routine that Uncle Willie's businesses had always had. Shifts were assigned to work around employees' schedules when possible, which would be crazy-making someplace else. But Uncle Willie always managed to work things out, even if he and Cassie took extra shifts to make sure Artie could study for exams, or Betsy could go visit her new grandbaby, or Kevin could have the first day of every hunting season off.

A new woman Danny had never met, Lindy Bricker, worked at the Fluff and Fold part-time now. She'd only been in Loon Lake for almost a year, apparently getting away from an abusive husband somewhere. She was quiet but seemed nice, and everyone who used the fluff 'n' fold service rather than the self-service machines loved how she handled their laundry.

The cabins wouldn't have full-time staff assigned until late May when the summer rush began. Meanwhile, Uncle

Willie assigned this person or that person to help Danny with whatever maintenance and painting needed to be done.

In less than a week, Danny felt he knew more about the management of the Laughing Loon, the Fluff and Fold, and Idle-Awhile Cabins than he'd known about any business he'd ever worked in. By far.

He knew his presence was particularly helpful right now because every time he offered to take a shift for Cassie, she thanked him four or five times and rushed home to study. Finals for her last two classes (*"ever,"* she'd said, but he didn't believe her) were next week, with graduation the following Saturday. He felt enormously proud of her for sticking with it so long and finishing, but he didn't know how to say that so he didn't say anything. He just tried to help her get enough study time.

The two of them had asked Uncle Willie every day that week if Dr. Dillon had scheduled any tests yet, if there was any news at all. This morning, Danny had joined them for breakfast, and when they asked, Uncle Willie finally lost his cool.

"I told you I'd tell you when I know. Stop hounding me!" And he stormed out.

Danny looked over at Cassie. "That's new."

She bit her lip. "Yeah. I don't know what to do. Should I ask Dr. Dillon if temperament changes are one of the symptoms?"

Danny rubbed his chin. "Maybe we should give him what he wants, at least for a while. If he doesn't tell us anything in another week or two, we can talk to Dr. Dillon then."

"I feel uncomfortable keeping such a big secret from my sisters," Cassie said. She fiddled with her napkin. "I know we don't get along as well as we should, and maybe that's my fault, but this seems like something they should know."

"It's not our secret to tell," Danny insisted. "I understand how you feel, but we should be glad he told us, at least, so we can jump in if things get out of hand."

"I don't want to think about what would've happened if he hadn't told us, Danny," she said, tears in her eyes. "He could've just dropped dead and I'd be here alone and..."

"Don't think about it." Danny had been trying not to cross the friendship line and mislead Cassie about his intentions, but she obviously needed comforting. His chest hurt when he saw her cry. Watching her wipe her eyes, he had to do something. He took one of her hands and squeezed it.

"You go study and I'll clean up," he said. "You need to stay out of the kitchen and focus on school. Uncle Willie and I can fend for ourselves for a week."

"I don't mind," Cassie said, taking her plate and juice glass to the sink. "I like having someone to spoil."

Danny set his dishes in the sink and patted his stomach. "I'm going to have to start buying clothes at the big-and-tall store if you keep it up."

He noticed her glance appreciatively at his stomach, watched her gaze wander up and down his body. He felt it in his nerve endings as if she'd touched him.

He mentally shook himself. Just friends. Don't do something stupid.

He grabbed her shoulders and pushed her out of the kitchen. "Go. I don't want to be responsible for you not graduating with honors."

She paused on the way to her room. "Are you coming to graduation?"

Danny tried to read her look. Was she inviting him?

Would he be intruding? "Um," he stalled, "I haven't looked at the schedule. Maybe Uncle Willie needs me to watch the store so he can go cheer you on."

Danny would like to be there, yelling and cheering for her, but he'd left. Now that he was back, and unsure how long he'd be around, he didn't know where he fit in anymore. He tried not to look like he was waiting for an invitation, so he turned back to the sink and started loading the dishwasher.

A moment later, she was at his side, her hand softly touching his arm. He glanced at her, startled.

She took a deep breath and said, "I'd really like it if you'd come, Danny. You're my family. It would mean a lot to me."

She looked nervous. Was she afraid he'd say no? Silly girl.

"I would be honored," he said, infusing the words with the pride he felt.

Her sunshine smile hit him full in the face, like it so often did. "Thanks," she said. She stood on her toes to kiss his cheek. Then she twirled away to her room to study.

Danny watched her go, uncertainty battling joy. For that moment, joy won. He had a family who loved him and wanted him around, even if he wasn't a blood relative.

He smiled the rest of the day, trying to figure out what he could do to return the feeling to Uncle Willie and Cassie. Then he remembered, he should get Cassie a graduation present, something that spoke all the things he couldn't.

Customers came and went all day and Danny didn't have much time to look for gift ideas online in between customers. Jewelry seemed too intimate, or not personal enough, depending on what website he looked at. Plaques and photo frames didn't seem right. She didn't have enough space in her room above the Fluff and Fold for new furniture. He'd have to ask Uncle Willie for ideas — if he ever came back from wherever he was hiding.

"Hey, Danny." Ted Grainger spoke up from the cash register.

"Hey, Ted, sorry," Danny said, hurrying over to ring up the live bait and potato chips on the counter. "How's it going?"

"Right as rain," Ted said, his mouth tipping up halfway on one side, the equivalent to a full grin for Ted. "Even better when I find three more people who want a puppy."

Danny nodded. "I heard something about puppies over at your place. What kind?"

"Half golden retriever, half Chip." Ted grimaced.

Danny laughed. "I think I've heard of Chip."

Ted nodded. "I'm sure glad his new owner got him fixed. 'Course, I guess she'd have to since she's dating the animal control officer."

"C-Dubb has a girlfriend?"

"Yup. Teacher at the elementary school. They met when Chip adopted her son."

"Sounds like a story."

"Unfortunately, it apparently took a few months for anyone to realize the dog wasn't neutered. He's smart as a whip and escaped their yard a dozen times. Got into mine at least once. Ole Chip strikes again, huh? We should make him the Loon Lake mascot. Half the dogs in town are related to him." Ted shook his head. "I said something to Jax a few months ago that Chip is the Jax Edgerly of the dog world here. He didn't think it was funny."

Danny winced and laughed. "No, I wouldn't think he would. Jax is a better man than he lets on. Pups must be cute, though. I hear Chip is a gorgeous dog. Border collie, right?"

"They're cute as a button, the wife likes to say. But I need to get rid of them before she convinces me to keep the rest. Between her and the kids…" He shook his head again.

Danny laughed. He was about to say, I'll let you know if I hear of anyone, but his brain spit out a new idea. "Any of the pups look like Chip?"

"Two of the ones left do. One's already actin' like his spittin' image. Gets out of the pen every time I turn my back."

Would it be too much? A puppy would certainly be a memorable gift. He'd have to get Uncle Willie's take on it.

"You know, I might know someone, after all," Danny said. "When do you suppose I could stop by and look at them?"

SATURDAY MORNING, DANNY PULLED HIS TRUCK INTO THE dirt parking lot of Grainger's Feed and Seed across the street from the lumber yard. The bright red barn-shaped building had been one of his favorite places as a kid. The smell of hay and straw and corn seed had made him feel happy on days when his mom drank too much. He'd ride his bike down here, play with any new puppies or kittens or rabbits people were trying to find homes for, help load trucks in return for an ice cream bar, and sit and listen to old men tell tall tales.

He felt a smile build as he walked in and smelled the hay and seeds. The scent of pleasant memories. He wandered around while employees helped other customers. At one point, Ted noticed him and pointed toward the far corner of the barn.

Danny pulled a dog biscuit from an old pickle jar that had been on the counter as long as he could remember, and went looking for Chip's progeny.

No one knew how the black and white border collie had ended up in Loon Lake. Danny had never seen the dog himself. He hadn't been back since Chip arrived. But he'd heard stories. Apparently, he was a great dog.

Danny walked softly as he approached the corner where Ted's dog had her litter. He broke the dog biscuit in half and spoke a quiet hello to her, giving her the treat. She got up, wagging her tail, and hopped over the low fence keeping the pups in one place.

She sat, looked at the other biscuit half, and raised her paw to shake. Danny laughed. "It's good to see you again, too, Ginger," he said, and gave her the treat. She took it gently and ate like a lady. Danny scratched her head and gave her some attention for a minute. Then he said, "Mind if I take a look at your kids?"

She walked over to the fence with him, still wagging her tail. She looked from the puppies to Danny as if to say, *what do you think?*

Danny stepped over the fence and sat down in the hay. Three pups raced over, two black and white, and one a brownish color who looked nothing like Ginger or what Danny imagined Chip looked like. He laughed as they vied for his attention, licking his hands like he was ice cream.

One of the black and whites climbed up Danny's knee and put his paws on Danny's chest, begging for more attention. The brown pup followed suit. The other black and white, this one with a black eye patch, not to be outdone, used his siblings like a ladder and tried to get on top of Danny's shoulder. His foot caught in Danny's shirt pocket and he started to slide down.

Danny laughed and held the pup's bottom. Using Danny's hand as a stepping stool, the squirming ball of fur crawled onto his shoulder, a puppy with a purpose. He put one paw on Danny's ear to brace himself and looked down at his siblings as if to say, *King of the mountain, you can't push me down*.

"You're a little bit of trouble in the making, aren't you?" Danny said.

The pup swiveled his head around like he'd forgotten he was sitting on a human. Immediately, his little tongue started licking Danny's ear and cheek and hair as fast as he could.

"Enough, enough!" Danny said, laughing harder.

The other two pups barked their squeaky barks, begging to be played with as well. Danny used one hand to pet both of them while still holding and scratching the patch-eyed pup with his other hand.

How to choose? They were all adorable. The brown one looked like he or she would be a quieter companion. The other black and white was more yippy than the other two.

Would Cassie prefer a quiet dog? Would she be annoyed if she had a dog that got into everything? Danny noticed Mr. Trouble seemed happy and quiet up here against his chest. Maybe he'd calm down as he grew. Of course, early and consistent training would produce a good dog. He'd do it for Cassie, if she wanted.

Of course, that would mean he'd be in Loon Lake for quite a while. Right now, holding the pup, that didn't bother him. He'd think about it later.

He turned the pup onto his — he checked, yup, *his* —

back in Danny's left hand, tickling his stomach while the pup played "catch the hand" with all four paws and his tongue.

Absolutely adorable. Cassie would love him. Danny could picture her face when he gave her the pup as her graduation present. He couldn't wait.

He went to find Ted. "I'll take the trouble-maker," he said with a grin. "But I can't pick him up until next weekend."

He was still smiling as he put his truck into gear. If the pup was for anyone else, he might have to consider keeping him and gifting one of the other two instead. But this was for Cassie.

Nothing was too good for her.

CHAPTER 10

*M*uch as Willie had missed having Danny around, much as he'd put this plan in action to get Danny and Cassie to see what everyone else could see, he was relieved they were both busy today. Cassie was studying and Danny was out running errands and shopping for a graduation gift for Cassie.

This last week he'd often found them surreptitiously assessing him for imaginary symptoms of his impending death, and they'd constantly asked him when he'd see Dill until he yelled at them yesterday. Neither one let him carry or lift anything heavy, and Cassie cooked more meals now, even with all her studies, forcing "healthy" food down his throat whether he wanted it or not.

It was annoying and exhausting and endearing.

Thankfully, both the store and the laundry were busy today, and their first summer guest had checked into the cabins yesterday. So he could lose himself in work without interference. And without anyone treating him like a sickly old man.

He waved at Jax and Tabitha as they entered the store. Another couple who should've been together years ago. Kids. He shook his head.

"That's not the correct amount?" asked Shelley Thompson. "I'm sorry, I have such baby brain."

"Sorry, no, it's right," Willie said with a smile at the massively pregnant woman. "I was thinking about something else."

Shelley laughed. "I know what you mean." She patted her belly. Any day now, the population of Loon Lake would increase by two. Folks were looking forward to having a set of twins around. Always lots of pranks with twins.

She waddled out, greeting Jax and Tabitha as they approached the counter with two pop bottles.

"Hey, Willie," Jax said, pulling out his wallet. "How you doing today?"

Tabitha leaned closer and lowered her voice. "We know you haven't told anyone yet, so we wanted to be sure we didn't mention it in front of anyone. But we're worried about you. How are you?"

Oh great. They knew. He'd forgotten. Just when he was having a peaceful day. "Oh, you know," he coughed a little, feeling ridiculous, "I'm okay."

Tabitha put her hand on his arm. "What can we do for you? How can we help?"

The bell tinkled as two more customers walked in. Willie wanted to roll his eyes. If anyone heard them talking, things would get out of hand real fast.

"Bryan," he called to the other employee working today, "can you take the counter for a few minutes?" He walked around the side and hooked a finger toward the back storeroom. "You two, follow me."

He heard his voice and knew Velma would tell him to stop it with the grumpy tone. But Velma wasn't here to help him so he was going to be as grumpy as he wanted.

He opened the door to the storeroom and motioned Jax and Tabitha in ahead of him. They looked worried and confused. The door had barely shut when Jax said, "What's going on?"

Willie put his hands on his hips. "I know the kids told you I was dying," he said as the door clicked shut and they had complete privacy. "But the fact is I'm healthy as a horse. Danny, however, has been worrying me for quite some time. And I'm not feeling confident about Cassie's plans for the future either. So I figured out a way to help them along."

The young people looked more confused, if anything.

He rubbed his nose and looked at his shoes as he explained. "Dill gave me the idea and I ran with it. I'll tell them — I don't know, something — once they're back together and I can see grandkids in my near future. But until then I need your help."

Tabitha stared at him with her hands over her mouth. Jax finally started laughing. A moment later, Tabitha joined him.

"You told them you were *dying* to force them together?" Tabitha sounded shocked. And delighted.

Willie chuckled. "I know, I know, it's a little crazy, but how long are we supposed to wait for them to come to their senses? And look how quickly things have progressed already."

Jax snorted. "You might die of old age before they give in to the obvious."

"Exactly!" Good, Jax understood at least. "So will you help me give them a little push? I've got a few other tricks up my sleeve. I've talked to my attorney and he's drawing up papers to make them both executors of my estate, and leave them each half of everything. That should help. They'll have to work together. We just need to remind Danny how much he used to like living here."

"And how much he used to love Cassie," Tabitha added, still looking sad. "I don't know if we can do that. He's one of the most stubborn men I know."

"No, he still loves Cassie," Jax said. "That's part of the problem. I think he thinks he doesn't deserve her after what happened with Bright Shiny."

Tabitha rolled her eyes. "That is so in the past."

"Try telling him that."

Willie nodded, thinking. "Well, you two are their best friends. You must have some ideas for getting them together. Will you help? As soon as they get together for keeps, I'll tell them I'm fine."

Tabitha gave him a look that reminded him of Velma. "Do you have a plan for how to get them to forgive you when they find out? I haven't seen Cassie cry this much since her mom died."

Willie's chest tightened. He knew they were concerned — he'd be upset if they weren't — but he maybe hadn't realized how worried they really were. "Well...then we need to do this fast and save them some heartache."

Jax and Tabitha shared a look. Then they both grinned at Willie.

"We're in," Tabitha declared.

"We're so in," Jax said, rubbing his hands together. "I'm going to make his life miserable until he does the right thing. Operation Death Match begins."

Willie laughed. He should've asked these two for help in

the beginning. Danny and Cassie should be engaged by the end of the month.

CHAPTER 11

*C*assie picked up a four-hour shift at The Laughing Loon Tuesday to clear her mind. Her final exam the night before had been for the hated Operations Management class. Now that that was behind her, she felt like she could breathe again. She felt totally prepared for tomorrow's Human Resource Management final, so today she needed to think about something besides school.

She walked into the store at two o'clock and checked in with Kevin to see what needed to be done. In front of the long front counter with the two cash registers, there were three shelves for candy and gum. No one had re-stocked it since the weekend rush ended Sunday afternoon, so she worked on it now.

She eyeballed which candy needed to be filled or replaced and went to the storeroom to get more. When she brought a stack of boxes out and put them on the counter, she noticed a beautifully decorated box sitting to one side. A fancy hand-lettered sign on the front read, *Suggestion Box*.

Her brow furrowed as she tried to remember any

discussion about this with Uncle Willie. Nearly every conversation they'd had over the last week and a half had been about his health, and whether he was eating right or getting enough sleep. Had they talked about giving a suggestion box a try? Not that she was against it. It could prove useful as tourist season warmed up. Plus, it was pretty cool-looking.

She turned to look for Kevin. "Hey, Kev, do you know how long this has been here?" She pointed to the colorful box.

He shrugged. "Don't know. It was here when I came in this morning. I didn't work yesterday."

Cassie made a mental note to ask Uncle Willie about it later. She relaxed into the easy work of restocking shelves, letting her brain take a break from any heavy thinking. Less than a week and she'd finally have her degree. Then she'd only have to think about work.

And Uncle Willie's health.

And her friendship with Danny.

Figuring out what to do about the two most important men in her life was proving to be even more difficult than her Operations Management homework. She let her mind wander across various scenarios while she worked. The best case scenario would be that Dr. Dillon was somehow wrong about his diagnosis. Danny might return to Lansing, but at least they'd have their friendship back.

Worst case scenario...no, she wouldn't borrow trouble and consider how she would live her life here without either of them.

She looked up as a customer entered. Dr. Dillon! The tall white-haired man looked around the store, then turned to ask Kevin where Uncle Willie was. Cassie hurried up to him.

She'd promised not to go to his office and ask questions, but here he was. She didn't feel at all guilty about taking advantage of the situation.

"Dr. Dillon, hello, how are you?" she asked.

The older man turned and gave a start when he saw Cassie. He took a couple steps back, but she stopped him with a hand on his arm.

"I'm just looking for Willie," he said. "I'll catch him later." He took another step toward the door.

"Dr. Dillon, I just want to ask you a question or two about—"

He shook his head. "I'm sorry, sweetheart, doctor-patient confidentiality. I can't tell you anything." He patted her shoulder, another step closer to the door.

Cassie followed him, frustrated even as she understood. "Well, can you at least tell me when you'll be running the other tests? How long it will take to get the results back?"

Dr. Dillon frowned. "Other tests?" Then his eyes widened and he nodded, saying, "Oh, right, the other tests. Well, there are so many to choose from, you know, to find the one that could give us answers, and they all take a different amount of time to get results back. You know, it depends on so many factors, but I'll make sure Willie talks to you about them soon."

He walked as he spoke, hurrying out the door before Cassie could ask another question. It almost sounded like he muttered, "Willie Larson, you scamp," as he rushed to his green SUV.

Cassie stood staring after him, feeling heart-heavy. She sighed for the seventeenth time and wandered back into the store. She'd get through this last week of school and graduation, and then her new project would be protecting

Uncle Willie and his health from a lack of adequate information. When someone tells you they're dying, "don't worry" was impossible advice.

She tried to stay busy the rest of her shift but it was a slow day at The Laughing Loon. Plus, Kevin was acting weird, looking like he wanted to say something and then clamping his mouth shut and shaking his head when she asked what was up.

She decided she'd do some laundry and look over her notes for tomorrow's last test. The Fluff and Fold was nearly empty, thank goodness, so Cassie filled several machines with Uncle Willie's and her dirty laundry. The thought skittered through her head that it would be weird to only do her own laundry some day when Uncle Willie was gone. She kicked the idea away and tried to empty her mind. What could she think about that was peaceful and soothing?

The bell tinkled and she turned, trying not to let her disappointment show that her solitude was being interrupted. She felt her eyes widen and her mouth form a smile before she could form a thought.

Danny. His presence always seemed to light up her day, no matter how she felt.

"Hey, Sunshine," he said, striding toward her. "Have you seen Uncle Willie?" He picked up a lingerie bag lying to the side of a washing machine and examined her lacy bras inside. He looked at her and raised his eyebrows.

Cassie snatched the bag back and tried not to let herself blush. "Not since this morning," she said.

Feeling the heat rise. Trying to think cold thoughts.

She tucked the bag under a dirty towel and turned her back on it, hoping Danny wouldn't say anything.

"Nice," he said with a grin.

She slapped his arm, her face getting hotter. She didn't know how she felt about Danny knowing what she wore under her clothes. But she couldn't help being glad she didn't wear plain white cotton.

"Listen, I saw Dr. Dillon earlier." Thank goodness she had a reason to change the subject.

Danny's expression turned serious. "We promised we would back off."

"I didn't go see him," she rushed to explain. "He came in the store looking for Uncle Willie. I asked him when he'd know which tests he wanted to run and how long they would take. He didn't know, said it depended, talked about doctor-patient confidentiality and left."

Danny huffed out a frustrated breath. Cassie understood. She'd been doing a lot of that herself.

"I think we need to get more information," she said, "do more research. It's the twenty-first century, there's all sorts of things being discovered to help people live longer. We need to—"

"You promised him you'd focus on finishing school first," Danny admonished sternly.

"I will, I am," Cassie said, moving closer, "but after graduation we should — I don't want to wait any longer. He told us for a reason, and now he won't talk about it. What does that mean? Is it something that affects his mind? Maybe he's in denial. Maybe he's losing his understanding of what is happening to him. Maybe—"

"Cassie, stop." Danny gripped her shoulders. "Enough with the maybes. They don't help. Let's deal in facts. First — uh oh." He ducked down toward the floor.

Cassie was so surprised, she ducked down, too. "What? What's wrong?"

Danny put his finger over her lips. "Shh. Connie Templeton is headed this way. She was looking for me earlier. I've managed to dodge her so far, but I'm trapped in here. With all these windows, she'll be able to see me."

He swung his head around, looking for a way out. His expression looked almost like a deer on the road, trying to decide which way to run to avoid being hit by oncoming traffic.

It was such an abrupt change of topic, Cassie giggled.

"It's not funny," Danny said, "I remember how she was in high school and she's worse now."

Cassie laughed again and stood up, glancing casually over her shoulder. Connie waited for a car to pass. She probably couldn't see inside the laundromat yet.

"If you stay down, you can make it to the storage closet before she gets here," she said, loading the last of her laundry into the machines, her back to the front door.

Danny spun around and duck-walked to the end of the row of machines, bent down and looked toward the door, then dashed the six feet to the storage closet and rushed inside. He closed the door quietly behind him.

Cassie let out another laugh. Goofy man. The bell tinkled and Cassie heard a woman's heeled shoes on the linoleum and concrete floor. She closed her eyes and tried to wipe away her laughter, then turned. "Oh, hi, Connie."

She put the rest of her gentle cycle clothes, including the lingerie bag, into a washer and closed the lid. Connie wouldn't think there was anything abnormal about Cassie being at the Fluff and Fold. No reason for her to think Cassie was hiding a fugitive.

"Have you seen Danny?" Connie asked. She stood at the

end of the row of machines Cassie was loading, looking around the empty room.

Cassie was about to say no when the other woman added, "Someone said he came this way."

Changing her answer, Cassie replied, "He went out the back. He said something about checking the buildings for any repairs he needs to do."

"I didn't see him," Connie said, frowning. Her straight blonde hair was pulled back in a ponytail, her makeup light, only her lipstick garish. She'd be a very attractive woman with a couple of minor tweaks — one of which would be to stop chasing every available man in the county.

Schooling her features into the professional-at-any-cost look she'd perfected over the years, Cassie said, "That's probably because you came in the front."

"I know that," Connie said defensively. "Sheesh, I'm not as blonde as I look, you know." She turned on her high heel and clicked her way to the door. Outside, she looked to either end of the porch and finally turned right, apparently going around to check the back of the building.

Cassie chuckled and shook her head, leaning back against the washer. "Why you aren't married yet, Connie, is a mystery."

Not.

"Psst!"

She looked toward the storage closet, the door slightly ajar. "I thought I heard something, but it must be the wind," she said aloud.

"Psst!" Danny's verbal cue was longer and more insistent this time.

Cassie wandered toward the closet, stopping in front of it

and pretending to look around. "What is that noise? Do you hear it, Connie?"

The door opened suddenly, an arm shot out, and Cassie felt herself pulled nearly off her feet and into the closet. She fell into something hard and warm and knocked her head against something just hard. The door clicked shut behind her and she was engulfed in darkness.

She reached up to rub her smarting forehead.

"Ow! Fingernails," Danny whispered.

Cassie giggled as she wiped her slightly damp hand on her jeans. "If you hadn't yanked me into a dark closet and hit me in the head, my fingernails wouldn't have scratched you."

A big, calloused hand scraped down her cheek until it found and covered her mouth. "Shh, she could come back any second."

She tried to step away, turning her head to remove his hand, but her foot caught on something and she started to fall. Since Danny now had one arm around her waist and one hand over her mouth, he lost his balance in the dark, too.

Cassie's hand shot out to catch her balance. The mop handle fell as she hit the wall, bouncing down somewhere around them. She realized it was the mop bucket that her foot had tangled in as she struggled to stand up again. Danny grunted as something hit his body, then he gained his feet and pulled her up against his chest. She finally found her footing and burst out laughing.

"Cass!"

"Where's the light switch?" Patting the wall, she tried to stop laughing. She found it just as Danny grabbed that hand. The light flashed on and immediately off again. It reminded her of one of those lights and mirrors shows she'd seen at the fair. The image of Danny's face in that split-second of light seared onto the backs of her eyes.

He looked surprised and half-laughing and worried about being caught, all at the same time.

He looked absolutely adorable.

Crowded into this small, dark space, Cassie remembered the shenanigans the two of them had pulled growing up. Situations like this that ended in belly-busting laughter, and sometimes a little bit of trouble. Then, as now, Danny would clap his hand over her mouth to try to keep her quiet. Then, as now, his hand smelled of sweat and grass and dirt and Danny.

The memory swept through her, easing the tensions of the last week or so, making her feel like time had melted away.

She'd gotten her old friend back, she was sure of it. Maybe a few parts of her wanted more than friendship — her lips tingled, wishing for a kiss — but she'd take this gift and not complain.

Much.

CHAPTER 12

Thursday morning, Cassie made a huge celebratory breakfast. She'd finally finished college. Hurray! She'd texted Danny last night after she finished her final exam and told him to bring Jax over for breakfast in the morning. When he seemed to hesitate, she typed back one word.

> Bacon.

Looking out the front kitchen window now, she saw Danny's truck pull into the parking lot. She smiled. "They're here," she called to her uncle. "You about ready for breakfast?"

Uncle Willie came out of his bedroom with a big manila folder and his usual morning cheerfulness. "That bacon smells like joy on a plate."

Danny and Jax knocked and came in — apparently, Danny wasn't afraid to find her half-dressed this morning —

and commented on the meat-scented air before they even said good morning.

"This is what a man should wake up to every day — the smell of bacon and the sight of a beautiful woman in the kitchen," Jax said loudly. "Isn't that right, Danny?" He came in the kitchen and side-hugged her, kissing her cheek several times.

"Jax Edgerly!" Cassie protested, laughing as she pulled away.

"A beautiful woman anywhere in his home, not just the kitchen. The bedroom would be fine." He waggled his eyebrows at Cassie. "Wouldn't you agree, Danny?"

Cassie tried to focus on flipping the pancakes, but out of the corner of her eye she saw Danny flick a glance her direction before he said to Jax, "Sure, maybe."

Uncle Willie cuffed Jax on the back of the head. "Careful how you talk about my niece."

Jax ducked his head and grinned. "Sorry, sir. Just thinking about how nice it would be to marry a nice girl and have such a great life."

Uncle Willie grunted. "You both should be married by now, all three of you. If Velma were here now she'd be plotting and planning for you. You don't seem to know how to do it for yourselves. She taught me how to pursue her, feeding me every line along the way."

Cassie chuckled with the boys. "I didn't know that, Uncle Willie."

Her uncle dove into the story of his courtship, entertaining them throughout breakfast, singing the praises of a forever love. "Not that it's easy," he said. "If you want to have an easy life, don't get married and don't have kids.

Marriage is tough. But worth every moment, if you do it right."

"I'm surprised to see you touting the virtues of marriage, Jax," Cassie said after another comment from him aimed at Danny.

"He's not," Danny answered. "Jax isn't interested in marriage as much as he likes to rattle people's chains."

"I'll get married someday," Jax said, and Cassie thought he sounded serious. "But right now it's much more fun being single." He looked at his watch. "Sorry to eat and run, but I have to go pick up something. See you guys later."

Jax kissed the top of Cassie's head and murmured "Delicious," then left. Danny frowned at his back.

"Where's he off to so fast?" Uncle Willie asked Danny.

"Tabitha has to take one of the kids to the doctor this morning, so Jax volunteered to take the other one to school." Danny mopped up the last of the maple syrup on his plate with his last piece of pancake. "He just *thinks* he's single. I don't know why he doesn't see what's right in front of him."

Uncle Willie snorted and shook his head. Then he said, "Before you two get off to work, I need your signatures." He pushed his plate aside and opened the manila folder Cassie had seen earlier.

"For what?" Danny and Cassie asked in unison.

"I haven't updated my will in too long," Uncle Willie said matter-of-factly. "I'm making both of you co-executors of my estate, and joint heirs of the businesses I own. Just sign here."

"Wait, wait—"

"Uncle Willie, what are you talking about?"

Again, Cassie and Danny spoke over each other, both on the same wavelength. What was Uncle Willie doing making them joint anything?

"You two know the business best, know how to continue running it after I'm gone. It's the logical way to handle it." He pulled out some more documents. "Here are all the papers my attorney drew up for me. If a miracle happens and I don't die soon," Uncle Willie seemed to choke on the words, "you both still run everything together, but I get to fish to my heart's content until I die."

"You and Cassie are running everything just fine," Danny said. "What do you need me for?"

Uncle Willie looked like he had prepared an answer for that question. "If I take a long time to die, if I'm incapacitated or lose my mind, or even if I fall through the ice and die while ice fishing — which would not be the worst way to go, in my opinion — someone will need to step in and help. It would be wrong of me to burden Cassie with the whole thing and no support. And selfish of either of you not to be willing to help. That's what families do, right, help each other?"

When he said it like that, Cassie didn't think she or Danny had any good arguments. "I guess we do have years of experience working together here," she offered tentatively, still considering Uncle Willie's words.

Danny was silent, thinking before he spoke as he so often did. "I don't see how helpful I could be from Lansing," he said. Uncle Willie and Cassie both waited. Danny clearly wasn't finished. "I'd have to move back here. Get an apartment somewhere. See what other work I could find during the off season."

Uncle Willie frowned slightly. "No, no, I've tried to pay my employees fairly, generously even, when I can. But this is a family business and family has to be able to make a living without juggling multiple jobs. The business is already three jobs in one. No, you'd both get paid a decent enough salary to live modestly."

He gave Cassie a stern look. "I was going to wait until after graduation to tell you, but you're getting a fat raise starting next Monday. Other businesses pay their employees more when they go to school to learn how to do their jobs better, so I'm doing the same. Maybe we'll even have to make that our policy for the kids we've got — graduate from high school, get a raise." He nodded his head once as if making a decision already.

Cassie didn't know what to say. Her uncle had been a kind and generous employer, not only to her, but to everyone who worked for him. What she'd learned about generosity and compassion in the workplace hadn't come from a classroom or a book. She'd learned it every day that she'd worked for Willie Larson since she was ten years old.

"Thank you," she finally said, determined not to cry only because she didn't want to make him uncomfortable. She picked up the pen Uncle Willie had tossed toward her earlier and began to read the papers in front of her.

"Uncle Willie," Danny began slowly, "I'm honored that you put such faith in me, even though I don't deserve it. But this is a big decision. I'd have to quit my job in Lansing, get out of my apartment lease..." He shook his head. "I don't know what that would entail or what the consequences would be. I feel like the wisest course of action is for me to fully understand how this would affect my current obligations first. Then get back to you.

"But you should know," he leaned forward and his voice became more earnest, "I will do whatever is necessary to help and support you and Cassie. You don't have to pay me for it by giving me part of what rightfully belongs to your blood relatives. I won't let Cassie down, any more than I'd let you down. Well," he paused, and Cassie could see a look of pain cross his face, "I've already let you both down too many times in the past, but I'll try never to do so again."

Uncle Willie's face filled with compassion, his eyes and mouth softening as he studied Danny. "Son, you may have to earn my respect — and you've done that — but you don't have to earn my love. These documents are about *my decisions*, my choices as to who I think is most fit to carry out my wishes when I'm gone. If you don't want the responsibility of co-managing the business with Cassie, I understand, and I won't blame you. I don't think the construction work you're doing fulfills you, but if that's the path you want to pursue, I'll support you. I think you're showing wisdom unusual for your age these days to give it all some time and thought before you agree. I admire and respect you for that."

Uncle Willie gathered the papers and put them back in the folder. Cassie hadn't signed them yet, but of course she would.

But what would Danny decide to do?

CASSIE CLEARED THE TABLE AND WIPED DOWN THE KITCHEN. When Uncle Willie left for work, she gave him a hug. They held onto each other for a long moment. Then he pulled back and kissed her forehead and patted her cheek.

"Everything's going to work out," he said.

After he left, Cassie picked up a few more things around the apartment, and turned in a circle looking for anything else she could do to stop thinking and wondering about Danny. He'd always been contemplative, even as a boy, but if anything, he'd grown more inscrutable as a man.

They used to joke that they always knew what each other was thinking. But she wasn't at all sure what he was thinking this morning. Did he want to stay here or return to Lansing? Was she the reason he didn't want to come home? Or could she be what brought him back for good?

She thought about her decision to keep their relationship that of friends only. It was absolutely preferable to not speaking at all, which was what the last few years had turned into. But if he showed her any encouragement at all, she'd jump at the chance to have the relationship she'd always wanted with him.

At loose ends, she flopped down on her bed and called Tabitha. As soon as she picked up, Cassie said, "Help me, I don't know what to do." She explained the highlights of the morning's conversation.

"Of course I admire him for not promising Uncle Willie to do something he'd want to back out of later," Cassie said, "but I can't help wondering if I'm the reason he's not sure. What if I'm the reason he won't come home? What if he says no to Uncle Willie when he wants to say yes just because he'd have to work with me every day for the rest of our lives?"

Cassie fought to keep the tears inside. She didn't want to cry. She wanted answers.

"Aw, hon," Tabitha said in the "mom" voice she used when one of her kids got hurt. "Do you want me to come over? I can reschedule my morning appointments."

Cassie knew Tabitha couldn't afford to miss work, which spoke to how great a friend she was. That kind of love tipped the scale and her tears began to flow. When one rolled into her ear, she turned onto her stomach.

"No, don't do that, just tell me what to do." She sniffled and wiped her eyes with the heel of her hand. "I want to do the right thing. He's my uncle, he's been training me to take over his business since I was twelve, and I've always wanted to." She was glad she didn't have to explain her shifting thoughts to her best friend. "But he loves Danny like a son. If we can't work together, it would be like forcing Uncle Willie to choose between his children, and I can't do that to him."

"You know Danny doesn't want that either," Tabitha said. "But the fact is you don't know what he's thinking, right? Maybe he's just trying to figure out how to leave his old life and rebuild a life here."

Sure, that was a possibility. "It seems unlikely based on how long he's been gone and how infrequent his visits have become."

"But the three of you have reconnected in the last couple weeks. I've seen you together. No one looks uncomfortable, not even Danny. If anything, I'd say he hasn't looked this relaxed in years. That's saying something, Cass, especially considering how much of the last two weeks he's spent with you."

Cassie thought about Tabitha's words. She might be right. Even the last time Danny visited, he'd seemed ill at ease and eager to leave.

"Cass," Tabitha said, the "mom" voice gone and her usual steel backbone sounding through the phone. "You know the saying about doing the same thing over and over and expecting different results? It's time to make a change. Patiently waiting for him to see that you want to marry him and have a hockey team of babies with him hasn't worked. You've been using that tactic for ten years."

"I haven't been—" Cassie began.

"Yes, you have. I've watched you two together for as long as I can remember. I think he loves you but doesn't know how to leave the past in the past. You two need to start over. And it needs to begin with you telling him how you really feel."

Cassie took a long breath, rolling onto her back again and staring at the ceiling. If she told him how she felt — for the first time ever — and he didn't reciprocate...

"What have you got to lose?" Tabitha asked. "You don't have the relationship you want, and he may move back to Lansing if he doesn't know there's a good reason to stay."

"I might've agreed with you a few weeks ago, Tabs, but now we're finally friends again. I don't want to screw it up." Friendship was definitely better than nothing.

"And how long do you think this fun, flirty friendship will last once you both marry someone else and have kids and build lives hundreds of miles apart?"

Cassie didn't answer.

"Go find him, Cass, and tell him. Don't be a coward."

Cassie gasped. "Hey!"

"I know you think you're being the sweet, patient girl you think he wants. But maybe he wants to be pursued enough to know you want him. Trust me, men want to be chased as much as women do."

Cassie chuckled. "Not by everyone. He hid in the storage closet downstairs when Connie came in looking for him. Don't tell anyone."

Tabitha snorted. "See? He wants to be pursued by *you*."

"You don't know that."

"Then go prove me wrong. If you think he might leave again, you have nothing to lose. This might be your only chance."

After they hung up, Cassie lay on her bed a few more minutes. Did she have the courage to tell him how she felt even if it ruined everything?

She thought about her future. There was no one in Loon Lake she was interested in dating. So she'd have to find someone who loved her enough to be willing to move here, or she'd have to settle for marrying someone here who was willing to stay. The latter seemed like a terrible, sad solution. But it might be that or choose to be alone for the rest of her life.

With options like those, taking a risk with the one man she'd always wanted seemed like the obvious and best choice.

She heaved herself up and went to the bathroom to rinse her face and fix her hair. She stared at her reflection. "You can do this. You know what you want, so go get it." She stood there a moment longer, wondering if her reflection might think up a less scary idea. Then she grabbed her jacket and went to find Danny.

His truck was still parked outside the Fluff and Fold, which narrowed the search perimeter. In fact, she knew where to look first. Sure enough, Danny sat at the end of Uncle Willie's private boat dock about twenty yards down the shore from the dock at The Hole.

She slowed her pace as she approached, her hands fisted in her pockets. What should she say?

The two of them had spent a lot of time at the end of this dock. Sometimes staring up at the stars, finding constellations — like the one her father had named her after — and talking about things that were too difficult to talk about in the daylight. Cassie wished it were dark now. It would make it so much easier.

She ambled down the dock and sat cross-legged next to him. Neither acknowledged the other. The sound of birdsong filled the morning air. Cassie closed her eyes and tipped her head back toward the sun. The warm snap they'd enjoyed had been followed by a colder burst of weather coming down from Canada. But the sun still felt warm and kind on her face.

She felt her lips stretch into a peaceful smile as she listened to her favorite bird, the chickadee. One called and called and called, never giving up. And then, there it was, a return call. The first bird paused. Was he surprised to finally get an answer? Then he spoke up again, and the other bird answered again. The two went back and forth until Cassie finally opened her eyes. If that bird could keep trying, she could try at least once.

She blinked in the sun, then turned her head to find Danny watching her. She smiled. He continued to look serious.

Forgetting her own nerves, she sought to comfort him. It had always been this way with them. She reached her hand over and found his. He squeezed it, and looked back to the lake.

She watched as a group of mallards came in for a landing on the water. Beautiful. Soon there would be trails of little yellow chicks following the adults. Her heart squeezed. She kind of wanted that for herself, to have her own little brood. She thought of creating a little family with Danny. The desire pressed in on her heart, squeezing until it was hard to breathe.

She sighed. She needed to take the plunge before she lost her nerve.

"Danny—"

"Cass, I—"

"Sorry."

"No, you go."

She wanted to say, *forget about other people's expectations,* our *past expectations. Your relationships with people are between you and them, not the rest of the world, not even the rest of Loon Lake. You have to believe that if you're going to be happy here. It'll make you crazy to let everyone else tell you what to do or think or feel.*

Maybe that sounded too much like the lectures he expected to hear. How could she encourage him to relax and start his relationships — *their* relationship — fresh? How could she ask for a do-over?

One more deep breath and a prayer for courage. "Danny, I want to talk about us."

She risked a glance at him. His eyes opened wide, his mouth an "o" of surprise.

Uh-oh. Did she already have her answer?

CHAPTER 13

*D*anny stared at Cassie, unsure of what to say or do. He'd expected her to want to talk about the business, her inheritance. He was trying to make sure he wasn't taking anything that was rightfully hers while also giving Uncle Willie what he wanted.

But...he blinked and shook his head a little, trying to clear it. If she wanted to talk about them, it was bad news, right? Cassie wasn't selfish. It wasn't that he thought she'd ask him to remove himself so she could inherit the entire business. But what could she possibly have to say about the two of them that wasn't bad news?

She probably needed to set some boundaries to protect herself, and rightfully so. He'd treated her unkindly the last few years. He knew she'd had a crush on him, maybe more, all through high school. But he'd been blinded by Lily's newness, how different she was from any of the small town kids he'd grown up with. He'd begun to dream of being a different man living in a city with endless possibilities. He'd be successful and respected. No one would know about his brother or his parents. He could make himself as new and as shiny as Lily.

Cassie had continued to be his friend all through high school, listening to him talk about Lily, not calling her Bright Shiny in front of him, struggling to be supportive even when he'd decided to ask Lily to marry him. She'd even continued to be his friend when his marriage fell apart. But by then, he was so embarrassed by how he'd acted, how wrong he'd been about Lily — about everything, how he'd screwed up the lives of everyone around him. He couldn't stand to be around Cassie after awhile because she still didn't blame him.

He deserved the things his mother and his ex-wife said about him. They were all true. He was a screwup, an uneducated loser, a country hick without a future. But Cassie didn't see it that way. She always saw the good in people, even him. And for the last few years, that had hurt more than anything else. Because she was just wrong.

At least, that had been his thinking up until he'd seen her waiting for him on the stairs two weeks ago. Maybe it was the threat of death hanging over them, but in that moment he wanted to accept her constancy and forgiveness and start over. She made all things new again and filled his life with sunshine in a way no one else ever had.

So if she looked at him so seriously and wanted to talk about their relationship now, after what Uncle Willie surprised them with this morning, it couldn't be good. She'd have to tell him that while she believed in him from a distance, she couldn't risk her future by being yoked to him permanently. She was probably going to tell him he was too uneducated to run a business, that he needed to bow out so he didn't ruin Uncle Willie's life's work.

He swallowed and stared at the lake, telling himself to

buck up and take it. She couldn't say anything he didn't deserve.

"Go on," he said, the tension in the silence stretching his nerves.

She cleared her throat. "I'm not sure where to start."

"Say it quick, it'll hurt less," he said, still avoiding her gaze. He saw her nod out of the corner of his eye.

She cleared her throat again. "Okay, quick and painless. Um...I love you. I'm in love with you. With or without what Uncle Willie wants to do with his will, is there..." She swallowed. "Will there ever be a chance for us? I thought maybe it was now or never, ask you before you decided if you're leaving."

When she said, "I'm in love with you," Danny turned to stare at her. Comprehension was slow in coming. He opened his mouth to speak but didn't know what to say so he closed it. Then opened it again. Finally, a short laugh came out.

Cassie started to pull her hand away, but he held it tight.

"I'm sorry," he said, "I'm just having a hard time...you still...even after everything? How?" he choked out. "How can you love such a complete screwup?"

She shook her head at him, her expression hardening. "Danny Kessler! I know people have told you that for years, and you've chosen to believe them." Her voice was hard as nails. "But I have defended you to *anyone* who dared talk like that about you. This is your only warning. Don't you ever talk about yourself that way again, or I'll give you the what-for I've given the others." Her voice was fierce by the time she finished.

He scowled. "Hasn't anyone told you how crazy that makes you look in light of the evidence? Don't you care what people think of you?"

She huffed a little breath and one corner of her mouth tipped up. "I care what God thinks of me," she said. "And He seems pretty adamant about forgiving people and loving them and helping them. How could I do less than that with my best friend? As for the rest, the people who know me know who I am on the inside. And the ones who don't..." She shrugged. "Why should their opinion matter? Do you care that much what people think?"

"I care what people think of you," he said. "You're beautiful and generous and smart and kind, and I don't want anyone to think less of you for pursuing a known loser for a decade."

She slugged him in the arm.

He pulled back, surprised.

"I told you to watch what you say," she said sternly. She looked like a little bulldog growling at him.

He stared at her, not understanding but really enjoying this new-to-him side of Cassie. A snort of laughter burst up from his chest, and he squeezed her hand tighter. He looked out over the lake again, trying to fit all these puzzle pieces together.

Cassie loved him. And she was defending him to *him*. Could this be real?

Cassie took a long breath and waited. He could always count on her to wait for him to think things through. It was one of the things he'd always loved about her. She could chatter like a girl with the best of them, but when he needed quiet, she gave it to him.

He tried to figure out the pros and cons of attempting to start over with her, but his mind couldn't keep one thought in his head long enough to measure it before it jumped to another and another.

She loved him.

Not only as a friend, though he'd always known she'd never stopped loving him that way.

No, she *loved* him. As a man. Still.

It was a miracle.

He raised his eyes to the blue of the sky. Fluffy gray and white clouds skimmed across an invisible surface like dragonflies on the lake. Somewhere up there, God was watching. What was He thinking?

He's probably thinking I'd be a fool to throw this away again.

His stomach felt queasy. If he screwed this up...

No, he wouldn't. He'd do what he hadn't done with Lily. He'd fight for Cassie's heart every day for the rest of his life if that's what it took.

He turned to her, facing her with his whole body, still not letting go of her hand. She looked nervous. How could he dispel her nerves, explain to her how humbled he was by her faith and constancy? He skimmed his free hand down her hair, over her cheek, and rested it against the side of her face, awed by her trust in him.

And still he had no words to say what he wanted to say.

So he kissed her.

He didn't even think, just leaned in, giving her no warning. But apparently she didn't need a warning.

She met his lips with hers, soft and warm. Her free hand curled around his neck, pulling him closer. No other kiss had felt like this one. Years of waiting and wondering and never knowing. He'd forgotten how much he'd once wanted to find out what her kiss tasted like.

Sunshine. She tasted like spring flowers and sunshine. Of course. He should've known.

His heart felt like it was going to burst from his chest. Forgiveness and renewal and new life, right here on a dock in Loon Lake. Perfect.

The magnificent kiss ended and he crushed her against him, her hold on him just as tight.

He decided right then. Now that he had her — her love and faithfulness and laughter and strength — he would never, ever let her go.

CHAPTER 14

*C*assie felt like she was living in a dream, but she didn't want anyone to pinch her. How had this happened? Danny Kessler had kissed her!

She'd been so surprised, her brain had turned off and she hadn't asked him why or what he was thinking or what it meant. She'd have to ask those questions at some point, but right now she was going to enjoy walking on clouds, something she'd always wanted to do.

This was the first day in ages that Cassie didn't want to go to work. She wanted to follow Danny around and hold his hand and kiss him again when no one was looking. But he had to get to work, too. The cabins were almost fully rented this weekend and he had a few more things to do that couldn't wait.

Cassie smiled and sighed as she drove to the supermarket. Danny Kessler had kissed her. The thought kept running through her mind, around and around like a carousel.

In the store, she picked up the groceries she needed, her mind on autopilot. Did this mean he would stay? When was the right time to ask her questions? She stared at the aisle of bread choices, not fully seeing them.

Someone pushed a cart past her, then stopped. "Cassie, I just wanted you to know we're praying for all of you."

Cassie blinked and focused on the familiar face. Mrs. Polanski, one of the high school teachers, smiled kindly and kept walking. "Thank you," Cassie called out.

That was nice of her. Because of her upcoming graduation, maybe? The teacher was too far away to ask now. Anyway, that was very sweet. You couldn't have too many people praying for you.

It wasn't until Cassie was pulling a gallon of milk from the refrigerated unit that the thought struck her: Did Mrs. Polanski know about Uncle Willie?

The lovely fog in her head cleared and she dropped to earth with a thump.

How could she know about Uncle Willie? It was a secret.

Then she remembered where she lived. Secrets in Loon Lake didn't last past noon. Cassie checked her watch. Still only quarter after ten in the morning. Well, maybe her teacher meant something else.

At home, as Cassie unloaded groceries from her car, she heard her name being called. She glanced around and saw Mr. Frederickson waving from the gas pumps at The Laughing Loon. She smiled and nodded, her hands full of groceries.

He put his hands together as if praying and then pointed to her, his expression serious.

Cassie nodded and called out "thank you" before she took her groceries upstairs. Okay, that was not a coincidence. No way would people stop her and say they're praying for her and her family just because she was graduating from college.

Sure, it'd taken forever, it seemed, but it was neither a miracle nor something to be so gravely serious about.

She winced as she put the groceries away. Ouch, wrong word.

She made up a big bowl of egg salad for lunch and texted Danny that he and Jax should come to the apartment to eat since she had a noon-to-four shift at the store. He probably wouldn't check his messages until he and Jax took a break.

Her phone beeped a minute later.

> Wish I was having lunch with you instead.

A smile burst out and Cassie was glad no one could see her grinning like an idiot.

> Me, too, maybe we can have lunch alone together when graduation is over.

She hit send and leaned against the wall, her eyes closed and her phone pressed to her heart. She didn't know how this had happened, but she couldn't stop thanking God.

Her phone beeped against her chest.

> Any chance we can spend Sunday alone together?

Cassie giggled and jumped up and down on her toes.

> 100% chance.

She added several different smiley faces. She almost erased the last one, the kissing smiley, but she hit send before she could change her mind.

Oh, wow, this was unbelievable. Amazing. She knew she

was acting like a lovestruck teenager, but she figured this is who she would've been ten years ago if things hadn't gone off course. Maybe she deserved a little silliness in her love life.

She checked her watch. Gotta go. Reluctantly, she turned off the ringer on her phone before she slid it into her back pocket. She hurried over to the store and tried to get her mind on work.

Lunchtime was a busier time at The Laughing Loon, so that would explain why there were so many people in the store. It didn't explain why there were so many groups of two or three or four people huddled together speaking in hushed tones. She hoped something awful hadn't happened. She didn't like to watch the news much since they only reported bad news, but it did make her too often the last to know when something significant had happened.

"Hey, Bryan," she greeted her co-worker. "Hi, Doris," she said to the woman he was ringing up. Doris Kingston, the city clerk, smiled sadly at her.

Cassie prepped the second cash register, and called to the woman behind Doris, "I can help you over here."

As Doris took her bag from Bryan, she leaned toward Cassie and said, "I'm so sorry," and left.

The customer Cassie was helping, someone she didn't know, leaned forward and whispered, "I've heard an organic vegetable diet with everything cooked in coconut oil makes the body fight twice as hard."

Cassie smiled uncertainly. "Okay, thanks."

There was nothing else it could be. Somehow, people had found out about Uncle Willie. And not just a few people. Cassie rang up a customer paying for gas who thankfully didn't say anything but "thanks."

But the next customer was Mr. Kent, a retired fisherman who fished all day. "We all die," he said. "We have to become worm food so the worms can grow big and then someone else can catch bigger fish." He nodded and left with his two cartons of worms.

Cassie stared after him, her mouth open in surprise.

Then she started laughing. "What?" She asked the air in front of her.

"Is it true?" Bryan asked, in a brief respite from customers.

"What?" Cassie asked carefully. Even as she spoke, she realized it was too late. Uncle Willie's secret was surely out.

"That Willie's dying? Kevin told me he heard Willie say it himself. I couldn't believe it. But then it seemed like everyone was talking about it, so...is it true?"

"I..." Cassie didn't know what to say. Denying it seemed useless at this point. But she'd promised Uncle Willie not to say anything. "Um..."

Bryan took her stumbling as an affirmative and squeezed her shoulder. "I'm so sorry," he said.

Cassie started to speak, but customers came up and required their attention again. She saw several people put folded up papers in the suggestion box. Well, that seemed to be working well, at least. She hoped people were commenting about the specialty ice cream. It would make Uncle Willie happy.

But she couldn't think of a single thing she could do to make them stop talking about his illness. Small towns had big mouths, even in the name of compassion and "I'm praying for you."

On the other hand, she loved Loon Lake because people *did* pull together when they needed each other. You couldn't have one without the other, so…she sighed. She'd just have to grin and bear it. Oh, poor her, being loved by so many people.

She smiled to herself. Just this morning she'd tried to figure out how to help Danny with this problem. People may know everything about you, and may have long memories when it came to your most embarrassing deeds, but in the end, you're family.

As her shift continued, it got easier to take all the comments with the love and good intentions with which they were given. She pocketed two recipes for soups that cured cancer, and thanked old Mr. Grimsby who brought in a huge package of frozen venison. "I carved it myself from a buck last season. I eat venison every day without fail. Willie tries that, he's going to see a difference."

Cassie accepted the hug and the meat and thought she really should bake Mr. Grimsby a cake or something. He kept to himself a lot, so this was a grand gesture for him. After graduation, she'd make him some cookies. He could keep them in the freezer and have one every day after dinner. Of course, the difference he saw might be a tightening of his waistband.

She was on her way home from her shift, wondering if she'd see Danny tonight and whether he'd kiss her in front of Uncle Willie (ack!), when she stopped in her tracks. If the town knew, her sisters would need to know. She'd liked the idea of not having to tell them when Uncle Willie asked her not to. But now someone was going to have to call Gretchen and Caroline.

Crap.

A car came around the curve and Cassie realized she was standing in the middle of the road. She jogged to get out of the way and took the venison to the deep freezer they kept in the back of the Fluff and Fold for their personal food storage. She leaned against the freezer and wondered how awful a person she might be if she tried to get Uncle Willie to make those calls. She considered all the nice things she'd done for her uncle lately.

Yup, she was okay with being awful this one time.

SOME DAYS IT WAS EASY TO BELIEVE IN MURPHY'S LAW.

Cassie had just gotten upstairs when her phone rang. Looking down at the screen, she saw her sister Caroline's name. "Aw, great."

She stared at her phone, counting the rings, trying to decide if she should pick up and, if so, what she should say. Had someone told Caroline? If they hadn't — her sisters usually called once a month or so — what should Cassie tell her?

If she let it go to voice mail, she could put off the conversation another day...or ten.

Then Cassie remembered her sister was probably only calling to wish her well for graduation. If she could keep the conversation short and on topic, she could comply with Uncle Willie's wish to tell her sisters about his health later. After all, she technically didn't know anything concrete yet.

She picked up the call on the last ring.

"Hi, Caroline." She forced herself to sound bright and cheerful. She loved her sister, but it was always easier from a distance. The greater the distance, the better.

"How's everything going? You ready for your big day?"

Caroline sounded like a normal, happy person today, not a bossy big sister. Cassie relaxed. This would be one of the good calls then.

"Yup! I'm wearing the dress you gave me for my birthday last year for the honors society convocation tomorrow night. And Tabitha made me a gorgeous dress I'm probably going to freeze to death in for graduation Saturday."

Caroline laughed. "I heard your weather's been very back and forth up there. I hope it doesn't snow, at least."

Cassie laughed and flopped down on the couch. "As of today, the forecast is for the mid-60s. But who knows what it'll actually be in forty-eight hours." Don't like the weather in Northern Michigan? Give it a few hours and it'll change. A joke she'd heard all her life, but true nonetheless.

"Sorry again that we can't make it," Caroline said. "I don't like taking the kids out of school, especially so close to the end of the year, and—"

Cassie interrupted. "Care, I told you, it's fine. We'll celebrate when you and Gretchen come up this summer."

"I promise we'll have a big party," her sister insisted. "And send me pictures. Does Uncle Willie know how to use the camera function on his phone?"

"Yeah, he's been practicing doing regular pics and selfies." She and her sister laughed together.

"Well, listen, send me your updated résumé, will you?"

Cassie heard the change in tone in her sister's voice. "Why?" She lengthened the word into two long syllables filled with meaning.

"I was talking to a friend whose brother manages a hotel near Lake Michigan. Pretty fancy place. You'd love it. He wants to see your résumé."

"Caroline, I—"

"It doesn't hurt anything. It's not an interview. It's not a job offer. Come on, Cass, you've been down here. Chicago's great. Best pizza ever, remember? You told me—"

"I told you that I'm staying in Loon Lake. I love visiting you, and I love visiting Gretchen, but I am not moving to Chicago or Ann Arbor. Ever."

Okay, that might be a bit of a stretch. Who knew what would happen over the next fifty years of her life? But maybe Caroline could only understand absolutes like *never ever*. Her sister loved her and wanted what was best for her. She just didn't think Cassie was able to decide what "best" was. She would be forever fifteen in her sisters' eyes, the little girl they left behind when they moved away to college.

"You can't stay there scraping by from one tourist season to the next. I can see why, as a teenager, you thought it was an adventure to live over a laundromat—"

Oh, here we go.

"—but you're an adult now with a college education. You need to move on and do what's best for *you*. Uncle Willie doesn't need you. He'll be fine without you. You need your own life, a husband, kids, a career."

I love her. I love her. I love her.

"I have my own life and a career, thank you." She tried not to let her sister hear that her words were forced through gritted teeth.

"And I'm just trying to help you move that career up to the next level. This hotel is beautiful and doing well. It could be a huge step up for you."

"Why can't you just be happy that I'm happy?" Cassie didn't mean to let that slip out. She didn't want to hurt her sister's feelings. As tough as Caroline could be, Cassie was

always surprised at how hurt she could get when Cassie tried
to tell her the truth in a way that she'd listen.

There was a pause. Uh-oh.

Please, God, don't let me have hurt her feelings. Please
help her just listen *to me for once.*

"Cassie, I...I'm proud of you. You finished your degree,
you have no student loans — which Gretchen and I can't say
— and you've helped out Uncle Willie in ways I..." She
hesitated again. Cassie knew she'd never liked living here,
never liked working at the store during high school. "I'm
sorry, I didn't mean to make it sound like I'm not proud of
you and happy for you. I just want to help."

Cassie closed her eyes and tried to find the right words.
"Thank you. Really. I do appreciate it, but I know what I
want to do with my life and I'm doing it."

She thought about Danny and the sudden change in their
relationship. More than ever, she really did have everything
she wanted in life. But as much as it would appease her sister
to hear she was dating, she refused to mention it now. She'd
waited to tell them about Conrad until he'd proposed, and
when he didn't, she was so relieved not to have to deal with
the aftermath with her siblings. For now, she wanted to
treasure her newfound love and keep it to herself.

"All right, well..." Caroline seemed to have run out of
things to say. "Have a great time this weekend. Send
pictures."

Cassie assured her that she would, and they hung up.
Amicably, Cassie hoped, but she couldn't be sure. She let out
a huge sigh. How come families were so difficult? Why was
it so hard to love each other and *not* get on each other's
nerves?

She perked up. On the other hand, with her sister focused

on trying to move Cassie out of Loon Lake, she hadn't asked how Uncle Willie was doing and Cassie hadn't had to lie. Thank goodness. She was a terrible liar.

Her phone rang again. Danny.

She felt her entire body bloom into a grin as she pressed the Accept button. "Hi." She heard the breathy, giggly sound in her voice and didn't care.

He chuckled. "Hi." His voice sounded deep and warm. "How're you?"

"Um, fine now." She smiled as her finger drew patterns on the couch cushion. She hadn't been this way with Conrad, had she? Weird.

"What happened?" Danny asked.

Yeah, not a good liar. But then, Danny knew her like no one else. "Nothing. Caroline called, that's all."

"And?"

"It's fine. She's just unable to turn off 'big sister' mode." She told Danny about the hotel in Chicago. "She does this all the time. It's her way of helping."

"Listening might be a better way of helping," Danny said, hitting that nail on the head.

"Yeah, well…"

"I know, I know, you can't choose your family *or* how they choose to show they care."

They chuckled together, then were quiet.

"So…?" Cassie prompted. "Everything okay at your end?"

"Yeah, I just…"

Cassie grinned. "Missed me? Wanted to hear the sound of my voice?"

His voice came through the line softer. "I wanted to hear you say it again."

Warmth spread from her heart outward, making it feel like the world was glowing. "I love you, Danny."

She heard his sigh. "I can't believe it. I don't deserve it."

"Oh, shush."

"Is that any way to talk to the man you love?" She could hear the grin in his voice.

She giggled. "I don't know. I'm going to go with 'yes.'"

After another couple moments of sweet talk, Cassie interrupted. "Danny, is there anything wrong with wanting to live here at Loon Lake? I mean, of course I know it's small and doesn't have a lot of opportunities, but do you think my sisters are right and I should go see more of the world before I decide?"

"You're old enough to make your own decisions," he said firmly. "Don't let your sisters pressure you into following in their footsteps."

"But you left. Is it better in Lansing? Did you like it better there?"

There was a long silence. "It's different. And yes, I'd say there are more opportunities. But...it's different. I can't see you being happier in the city. You like knowing everyone. You like smiling at everyone and saying hello and knowing they'll say hello back. I think you don't even mind when people get in your business like they do here. I see you put a suggestion box in the store. That's like a sign that says, 'All crazy ideas welcome here.'"

Cassie laughed. "Danny! I doubt it's filled with crazy ideas." She thought about some of the people who'd made suggestions about Uncle Willie's health earlier. "Well, not entirely. And I didn't put it there. I guess Uncle Willie did."

"No, he didn't. I asked him. He said you did it."

"What? But if we didn't...that is so weird."

Danny laughed mischievously. "Let's bring it over to your place tonight after dinner and read what's in there. I'll bring the beer, you bring the dessert."

Cassie laughed with him. "Sounds fun. But just come over for dinner." What in the world might they find in that suggestion box?

And the bigger question — who put it in the store?

CHAPTER 15

*C*assie pulled out the ingredients to make a baked ziti for dinner, something Uncle Willie and Danny both loved. She put a pound of ground beef in a skillet, and heated a pot of water to boil the pasta.

Her mind whirled with a dozen thoughts of Danny. Could it really work out between them? Would he move back here and live in Loon Lake because he wanted to be with her? Could he be happy here?

He seemed happy enough. He seemed to want to start over with her. But that wasn't exactly right. Not start over — they weren't teenagers anymore. The man Danny had become was so much more striking. Despite his insecurities, he'd grown more confident. His gentleness had taken on a manly undertone that Cassie didn't understand, yet was incredibly attracted to.

And he sure had filled out nicely. She didn't mind admitting she liked how he looked.

Should she be worried about going too fast, pursuing him too hard? Tabitha had pushed her to declare herself, and when she had, she could hardly believe the results were so immediate.

She paused in breaking the ground beef chunks into smaller pieces in the skillet. He hadn't actually said "I love you" back.

Well...she'd surprised him. Shocked him. And he'd kissed her. That was the kind of reply one would expect from a man who felt the same, right? Plus, he'd called to ask her to say "I love you" again. So he must love her. Right?

She poured the box of ziti into the boiling water. Of course he loved her. Or something close to it. He wouldn't be acting this way if he didn't.

She shoved her doubts away as she continued to prepare dinner. It was far too early to worry about the minute details of Danny's feelings for her. No, she needed to chalk up her doubts to the effects of being dumped a few months ago. Conrad had chosen a job over his feelings for her. That had hurt.

Another thought sliced through her mind. When it came down to it, she'd chosen a town over Conrad. That couldn't have felt good to him, either.

Cassie sighed. Why was love so difficult? She needed to think about something else. When the casserole went into the oven, she started a batch of peanut butter cookies. When she rolled the balls of dough and placed them on the cookie sheet, one looked lumpy, kind of heart-shaped.

Cassie smiled and formed the cookie into an obvious heart. Should she bake it that way? Was it completely junior high to give it to Danny on the first day she'd told him she loved him?

The door opened and Uncle Willie called out a greeting. Cassie gasped and giggled and tossed the heart in her mouth.

"Hi," she called out, the word muffled around the cookie dough.

Uncle Willie came into the kitchen, saw the cookies, and glanced up in time to catch her chewing. "Ah-ha!" he said. "If you get one, I get one, right?" He plucked a ball of dough from the tray.

Cassie laughed and swallowed. At least he hadn't caught her with the embarrassing heart shape.

"Danny's coming over for dinner," she said. "He's going to bring the suggestion box from the store so we can see what's inside. You didn't put it there?"

"Not me, I thought you did. It's a pretty box. I thought you made it."

"I don't understand. Why would someone secretly put a suggestion box in our store?" Cassie chuckled, her brow wrinkling as she tried to think of who would do it and why.

Uncle Willie shrugged and walked into the living room, turning on the TV. "Someone with a sense of humor, I guess."

Danny arrived just as Cassie pulled the ziti from the oven. He said hello to Uncle Willie, then joined Cassie in the kitchen. She put the tray of garlic bread in the oven and felt Danny's hand at her waist. She almost dropped the potholder.

As she straightened, he pulled her close and kissed her. She let out a soft "oomf" of surprise, then kissed him back. Then she remembered that Uncle Willie would only have to turn his head to see them.

"Danny," she whispered. She pushed against his chest but he didn't move. "Uncle Willie's right there."

Danny ran a hand up and down her back. "So?" he said, and leaned in to kiss her again. "He's not paying any attention to us."

Cassie, spineless jellyfish that she was, returned his kisses. They were brief and chaste, but they made her feel like she was touching an electrical wire. Her breathing seemed to come in little bursts and gasps.

She pushed at him again. "Set the table." She giggled as he tried to hang onto her when she turned to get plates from the cupboard. "Go," she said as she handed him the dishes.

Dinner was a light-hearted affair despite the uncomfortable start to the day with Uncle Willie's will. Danny and Uncle Willie toasted Cassie's successful end to her studies and the three of them clinked their beer bottles. After leftovers were stored in the fridge, and dirty dishes were stacked in the dishwasher, the three of them sat down with the suggestion box.

Cassie put a plate heaped with cookies on the table as Danny tried to figure out how the box opened. He found the latch at the back and set the box on the table in front of them.

He pulled out a folded piece of yellow legal paper. "It looks like a recipe," he said. He scanned the paper as Cassie and Uncle Willie tried to read over his shoulder. "'Drink three times a day to kill off any bad juju in the body.'" Danny laughed and flipped the paper over. "It's unsigned."

"Well..." Uncle Willie leaned back in his chair. "Someone knows."

Cassie pushed the plate of cookies toward him. "Uncle Willie, I'm afraid a lot of people know. I'm not sure how." She told him about the people she'd run into today. "Somehow your secret is out of the bag."

Her uncle rubbed his chin. "I didn't think it would get out." He was quiet for a moment. Then he shrugged and nabbed two cookies off the pile. "Oh well. I'll just have to deal with it."

Danny slapped his shoulder lightly. "'Fraid so, old man. That's what happens when you're beloved. Everyone wants to be a part of your life and try to help."

Uncle Willie grunted. "Don't know about that."

"Are all the suggestions about your health?" Cassie grabbed a paper and unfolded it. "'When is Danny going to marry Cassie? It's long past time,'" she read. She felt the heat in her cheeks. She couldn't look at either of the men, so she put the paper down and grabbed a cookie. "Well..." she said, imitating her uncle.

"Now there's someone with a good idea," Uncle Willie said. He winked at Cassie and nudged Danny's shoulder.

"Uncle Willie," Cassie tried to chastise him but couldn't think of anything to say. She cast a quick glance at Danny. He didn't look at either of them, just pulled another paper from the box.

"'When are you going to get more trout lures? You've been out for two months.'" Danny laughed. "Do you know who wrote that one?"

"I'm sure it was Johnny Jenks," Uncle Willie said. "He's been bugging me about it."

Cassie pulled out a paper. "This one has the name, address, and phone number of a doctor in Traverse City. Maybe we should give him a call."

Uncle Willie snatched the paper and crumpled it in his fist. "I have a doctor. What else is in here? Anything worthwhile?" He dug another suggestion from the box.

Cassie met Danny's gaze. He shrugged a little. Cassie tried to keep her sigh on the inside. "Uncle Willie, we—"

"Oh, I like this one. 'Since Danny's back, is there a wedding in the near future?'"

Danny grabbed a handful of the papers that were left.

"Why don't we just separate them into piles by category. Then we can decide which ones have merit."

Cassie scooped up most of the rest and followed Danny's lead. All three of them read the notes as they sorted them. There were three more about her and Danny, five making suggestions for Uncle Willie's health or praying for him or wishing him well, and two about items people wanted to buy in the store.

"'If you bring in dark chocolate Reese's Peanut Butter Cups, I promise to buy one every day,'" she read. She laughed. "That sounds good."

Uncle Willie shrugged. "I could do that. Add it to next week's order."

"'If you die,'" Danny read, "'can I have Bessie?'" He started laughing. "Someone wants your boat?"

Uncle Willie gaped at Danny, then ripped the paper from his hand. He muttered some uncomplimentary things about his best friend, Dill, and shoved the paper in his pocket. "So what should we do with all of this?" He waved his hand at the piles as he and Danny reached for another cookie.

The three of them looked around at each other. "We still don't know who put the box on the counter in the first place," Cassie said. "Most of it is personal rather than store-related. I don't think we need to leave it out." Much as she loved her new relationship with Danny, it was half a day old. She didn't want to get teased about it quite yet.

"If you think so," Uncle Willie said, getting up from the table. "I'm going out. I'll see you later."

After the door closed, Danny looked at Cassie and grinned. "I bet he's going to Dill's. He looked pretty ticked about the note about his boat."

Cassie laughed. "Even I wouldn't tease him about asking

for Bessie when he dies." A moment after she heard her words out loud, she sobered.

Danny took her hand. "Look at him. He doesn't look sick. He doesn't act sick. I think Dill may be wrong. I know he's a good doctor, but he's old school. He doesn't know everything."

Cassie nodded, but didn't reply.

"Hey." Danny stood and pulled her up out of her chair, bringing her into a warm embrace. "Come on. Focus on today. Today he's having a good day. Tomorrow and Saturday will be good days because"—he tipped her chin up so she would look at him—"*you* are graduating with honors."

Cassie smiled a little. He was a good guy, trying to cheer her up even when he was as concerned about Uncle Willie as she was.

"Besides, you're always prodding me about taking my faith more seriously. Are we going to trust God with Willie's health or not?"

"But he hasn't pushed to get those other tests done or anything," Cassie complained. "Why won't he be more proactive?"

"He promised he would after your graduation," Danny reminded her. "So let's all enjoy the next couple days, and on Monday we'll press him to follow through on his promise. All right?"

Cassie felt another sigh building, but she held it in. Finally she nodded. "Okay. I'm so glad you're here, Danny. I don't think I could go through this without you."

He pulled her close and they wrapped their arms around each other. He kissed the top of her head and rested his cheek on her hair. "I'm glad I'm here, too."

After a moment, he whispered in her ear, "So now that we're alone, whatcha wanna do?"

Cassie giggled against his chest, feeling her heart race. "What did you have in mind?"

"IT'S WORKING," WILLIE SAID EXCITEDLY WHEN DILL answered his door. "I saw them kissing in the kitchen."

Dill glanced over his shoulder and made a shushing motion to Willie. "Shh, Barbara's here, she'll hear." He came out on the porch, and he and Willie took a seat. "What's going on?"

Willie could hardly stay seated. "I brought out my will after breakfast and explained what I wanted them to do. I wasn't sure Danny was going to agree, you know how that boy thinks everything through three times. He left and I thought maybe I'd pushed him too far, but Cassie went after him and tonight I saw them kissing in the kitchen!" He slapped his hand on his leg, then bounced out of his chair and paced the small porch.

"Well, I'll be. I didn't really think it would work." Dill leaned back in his chair. "You're sure?"

Willie turned and faced him, hands on his hips. "Whispering, silence, more whispering, you tell me. Isn't that how you and Barbara were?"

Dill grinned. "Still are. Makes the kids half sick."

"Well, then"—Willie threw his hands up in the air—"that's it then. We did it!"

"So you gonna tell them?"

Willie paced again. He couldn't let this charade go on too

long. He felt bad enough about how they'd been hurting. "If I tell them too soon, I don't want the whole thing to backfire on me and somehow pull them apart. I think we should give it a little more time, let their relationship set so it doesn't break later."

Dill shook his head. "The kids aren't a couple pieces of broken pottery."

"I disagree," Willie said vehemently. "They're both fragile — strong, but fragile. I just want to protect what they've finally found a little longer. Then I'll tell them you made a mistake."

"What?" Dill shot up out of his chair. "That wasn't the plan! You're supposed to tell them you're a big fat liar not that I'm an incompetent physician."

"Hey!" Willie stood toe-to-toe with his friend and was annoyed for the thousandth time at how far back he had to tip his head to meet Dill's eyes. He'd often called Dill "the stick figure giant" when he wanted to tease him. Dill hated it. He thought about saying it now, but then Dill said—

"I'll tell them the truth if you lie about my involvement." Dill folded his arms and planted his feet.

Willie knew that look. He held his ground another moment or two, then backed off. "Fine, have it your way," he grumbled. "But mistakes happen in medicine all the time. It's not that big a deal." He felt Dill's anger building like a volcano. "I wasn't going to blame it on you, you old hound dog. Just that you ran more tests and they came back negative." He threw his friend a hopeful look.

"The original plan, Willie," Dill said sternly. "We're all dying, that's what I said, and you took it from there."

Willie grumbled under his breath for a moment. The kids

were going to be mad as can be when he told them. He needed to defuse that anger beforehand. But how?

CHAPTER 16

*C*assie hugged her uncle hard. He hugged her harder.

"We did it!" she said, smiling so wide she thought she might pull a muscle.

"*You* did it. I couldn't be prouder," he said gruffly. He finally pulled away, and he and Cassie both wiped at their eyes.

She opened the leatherette folder to show him the diploma with her name, Cassiopeia Michelle Lane, in fancy, bold script.

Danny stood nearby and Cassie launched herself into his arms as well. He pulled her off her feet and squeezed until she giggled. "Congratulations, Sunshine," he said near her ear. "I'm so proud of you."

"Thanks," she said, beaming up at him. "I'm so, so happy."

Something shifted in Danny's face, softened, made him look younger. "Me, too." He leaned in and kissed her on the mouth, sweet, soft, quick.

"Danny," Cassie whispered. She turned her head just enough to see Uncle Willie smiling at them in approval.

"I don't care," Danny whispered back. "I've thought about it and I don't care who knows." He looked at Uncle Willie. "You mind if I kiss your niece?"

Uncle Willie grinned like the Cheshire Cat. "Please do, often as you like."

Cassie felt herself blushing and hid her face in Danny's chest for a moment. Graduation day had just taken on a new level of joy.

The three of them spent the next hour taking pictures of Cassie and her friends, getting dozens of pictures of the three of them along the way. Uncle Willie offered to take pictures of other people on their camera phones, telling each and every one of them that he'd been practicing and had become an expert just in time for his niece's big day.

The fourth time he told the parents of someone she didn't know that she'd graduated with honors, she finally made him stop.

"At least wait and tell people you know," she begged.

When everything began to wind down, when the pictures were taken and her cap and gown turned in, they headed for home.

Sitting in the front seat next to her uncle, she thought about what was next. "I'm not sure what I'll do with myself now. I've been in school for the last twenty years. What is life like without homework?" They all laughed.

"Enjoy your free time while it lasts," Uncle Willie advised. "It'll fill up before you know it."

"It's true," Danny said from the back seat. "Seems like I'm always busy with something."

"Well, I'm going to relax all weekend. No, *revel* in my

freedom all weekend." She laughed. "I'll start thinking serious thoughts about the next step on Monday."

"You don't have to move out," Uncle Willie said. "You're not taking up any space I need."

Cassie heard the wistfulness in his voice. "If you had it your way, I'd live at home forever."

"That's right." He laughed and patted her knee. "I like having you around."

"Someday I'll probably get married and have kids, Uncle Willie," Cassie said, trying not to think about what the man in the back seat thought of that.

"We'll build an addition," her uncle said promptly.

The three of them laughed and talked all the way home. When they would've swung past Sonny's, Uncle Willie pulled in. Before the car fully stopped, Cassie saw people pointing and waving through the windows. And was that crepe paper?

Uncle Willie opened the door to the restaurant for her and, one step inside, Cassie heard a loud "Surprise!"

Dozens of hands pulled her forward, hugging her, wishing her congratulations. A long line of tables had been pushed together, covered with bright paper tablecloths and swags of crepe paper, balloons bouncing softly against the ceiling.

Tabitha stood at the front of the table. She raised a hand and started everyone on a chorus of "For He's a Jolly Good Fellow" using the words, "For she's a jolly good graduate."

Cassie laughed and clapped her hands. The moment the singing stopped, Tabitha hugged her tight.

"Congratulations, my friend," she said, "you deserve every good thing coming your way. Love you."

"Love you back," Cassie said as she pulled away.

Jax swooped in for a big hug, almost squishing her to death. "Happy for you, Cass."

"Me! Me!" Tabitha's children couldn't wait any longer to give her hugs. Cassie bent down and hugged them both tight.

Summer pulled a gold paper crown from behind her back and put it on Cassie's head. "Now you're queen for the day," she announced.

"We got you a present," shouted Chas. "Want to know what it is?"

Tabitha put her hand on his head. "It's a surprise, remember? Wait until she opens it." She rolled her eyes at Cassie and moved her kids over to two seats with coloring mats and crayons.

The surprise party was more than Cassie could've hoped for. More people than she would've thought cared gave her cards and hugs and wished her well. Most people stayed to eat, though a few gave their apologies and rushed off to other Saturday obligations.

By the time Cassie was finished eating, she really did feel like queen for a day. She couldn't remember feeling so loved.

Danny leaned over from his seat next to her. "I'll meet you at your apartment, okay? I just have to run an errand." He gave her a quick kiss and someone whistled, which led to several more people hooting and clapping.

Cassie covered her face with one hand and tried to drink some water, but it was hard to swallow when she was blushing and grinning and laughing.

Finally, she and Uncle Willie headed home, arms full of cards, flowers, and a few gifts. She leaned her head back on the headrest. "Wow." That's all she could think of to say. "That was amazing. Thank you for the party."

Uncle Willie reached over and squeezed her hand. "I had

a lot of help. Everyone wanted to be involved. They love you, you know."

"If I didn't before, I do now."

At home, Cassie arranged her flowers into two big bouquets and put them on the table. As she set her cards up along the short bookcase under the front window, her phone dinged. A text from Danny.

Change into jeans. I'll be right there.

Cassie wondered what his plans were for the rest of the afternoon. She changed, and got another text as she was slipping on her most comfortable sneakers.

Open the front door, then sit on the couch and close your eyes.

Cassie giggled, did as he asked, and texted back a bunch of smiley faces and a check mark.

She sat on the couch, listening to him walking up the stairs, talking to himself. Then she could hear him walking toward her, and the sound of tearing paper.

"Okay, open your eyes quick," Danny said.

Cassie looked up to see Danny carrying a wrapped box. But the paper was being torn off through a hole from the inside. "What in the world?" She laughed.

Danny placed the package on the coffee table. "Go ahead, unwrap it." He stood next to her, one hand on his hip, the other pointing his phone at her.

Cassie leaned closer to see the paper that was ripping before her eyes. Was that...a paw? She gasped and started ripping the paper.

A little black and white head thrust itself through the hole, pushing against the *Congratulations* paper.

"Awww!" Cassie pulled the rest of the paper away. The

most adorable little puppy scrambled into her lap. "Oh my *gosh!*"

The little black and white ball of fur started climbing up her shirt, trying to get close to her face. Cassie scooped him up and held him against her chest. The pup licked her cheek and ear and neck, wherever he could reach, making her laugh even more.

"Oh, Danny, thank you!" She reached out with one arm and grabbed Danny's hand, pulling him closer until he sat on the couch next to her. If she thought her heart was full an hour ago, it was absolutely bursting now. "This is the best gift *ever*."

DANNY HURRIED TO THE FEED AND SEED AFTER CASSIE'S surprise party. Ted was waiting for him. They hauled all the things Danny had bought out to his truck — the pet bed, grooming tools, bowls, food. Back inside, Ted petted his dog for a few moments before reaching inside the fencing for the pup.

Danny took the squirming bundle, chuckling as it tried to climb up on his shoulder again. He knelt down by Ginger, scratching her head. "Thanks, Ginger, I promise we'll take good care of him." The dog licked her son, then nosed Ted for a treat, which he pulled from his pocket.

Danny took the tiny little collar he'd purchased and Ted helped him get it around the pup's neck. Then he attached the leash, just in case.

"Thanks, Ted, I'll talk to you later."

"Good luck! Have fun with him."

Danny got in his truck, placing the puppy in the box next to him. By the time he'd made three aborted attempts to back out of the Feed and Seed's parking lot, he gave up and pulled the pup onto his lap. He texted Cassie to leave the door open for him, and turned onto the main road.

The animal seemed happy to be on Danny's lap, looking out one window, then another, but otherwise not squirming around. Once Danny parked in the Fluff and Fold parking lot and put the puppy in the half wrapped box, it was another story. He finally cut a hole in two sides, putting wrapping paper over one opening but leaving the other clear. He kept the open part facing his body as he walked up the stairs to Cassie's apartment.

"Hold still, you little rascal," he chided softly. He held up the box and looked inside the opening. "And be quiet, so it can be a surprise."

The pup stared at him over his shoulder in the box, then promptly sat and waited quietly.

"Good boy," Danny said. "Don't worry, you're going to love her."

He walked in and saw Cassie sitting on the edge of the couch. He called a greeting to her, which got the puppy riled up. He started scratching at the wrapping paper that covered the hole facing Cassie. Danny heard the paper rip.

"Okay, open your eyes quick," he said. His excitement was burning a hole in his chest. He could hardly wait to see her expression. He set the box on the coffee table and pulled out his cell phone as Cassie gasped and started ripping at the paper.

He kept recording even when she pulled him down on the couch beside her. He hit the button to turn the camera to face them. He leaned in and said, "Happy Graduation, Sunshine!"

She giggled and faced him, the puppy tucked under her chin, her whole face shining with happiness. "I can't believe it — I love him! I love *you*!"

Danny's grin threatened to crack his face in half. The puppy was only part of what made this moment so special. "I love you, Cassiopeia Michelle Lane."

Cassie's face reflected her surprise, eyes wide, mouth open. The puppy slipped down onto her chest. He fought to get closer to her face, but Cassie ignored him.

"Say it again," she said softly. It was just what Danny had said to her two days ago. *Say it again*.

"I love you."

She let out a long breath as if she'd been holding it for a long time. "*That's* the best present ever," she said quietly. She leaned in and Danny kissed her.

Not just a little kiss this time. No, this was the *I love you* kiss, the *be mine* kiss, the *there's no one else for me but you* kiss. Danny poured all of those thoughts and emotions into it, hoping she would feel and hear and understand all the things that were hard for him to say.

The kiss felt to him like everything he'd hoped...until he started to feel something raspy and damp hitting his cheek. He pulled back enough to see the puppy licking Cassie's cheek, then reaching for Danny's again.

He joined Cassie in laughing at the dog. That seemed to be attention he liked because he sat back in Cassie's grip, grinning his little panting puppy grin, looking from one to the other and back.

Danny scratched his head, the pup leaning into his hand at such an angle that he would've fallen to the ground if Cassie hadn't had a good grip. Trusting little thing. He could probably learn a lesson or two from this little guy.

"So what are you going to name him?"

"Hmm, well," Cassie pulled the pup closer and giggled when he licked her face. She rubbed her nose in his soft fur. "Mmm, so soft."

"By the way," Danny said, "he's a he so don't give him an embarrassing name like Fluffy."

Cassie giggled. "I wouldn't do that to you, would I?" she crooned to the dog. "No, I wouldn't. No, I wouldn't, would I?"

Her hands never stopped petting him, scratching him, holding him up to her face, pulling him close against her chest. And the puppy didn't move away. He didn't try to climb all over her like he had with Danny. He didn't try to climb down to the couch or the floor to explore. He just stared at Cassie with his little tongue hanging out, taking in her every word, soaking up all the attention.

While Danny was pondering the change in the animal, the dog looked over at him and almost seemed to wink. His expression clearly said, *ain't this the bee's knees, dude?*

Danny laughed and rubbed the dog's head. The puppy closed his eyes for a second, then licked Danny's hand. "I know what you mean," he said softly.

"What?" Cassie asked.

"You've heard of that border collie, Chip, that's been living in Loon Lake recently?"

"Of course, everyone knows Chip. He's a great dog, gorgeous, well-mannered. Everyone likes him. Unless you have a female dog in heat. Then not so much." She paused, looking to Danny to confirm. "Oh!" She laughed.

"Well, apparently Chip is acquainted with Ted Grainger's dog. This is one of their progeny."

Cassie laughed again. "Oh dear, you little rascal. Maybe I

should call you Junior. But that's not a real name, is it? Chip Junior?"

The puppy just sat in her arms and stared at her.

"Maybe Rascal," Danny suggested. "That fits."

"That's a good one," Cassie agreed. "Or Patches. He's all patches of black and white."

"Or just Patch," Danny suggested, "since he has a black patch over his right eye."

"Oh, I know!" Cassie laughed and looked at Danny with mischief in her eyes. "I'll call him Pirate. I love pirates."

"Seriously?" Danny rolled his eyes. "You still read those pirate romance novels?"

"They're good, you should try one." She looked back at the puppy. "Do you want to be a pirate? Do you like that name? Pirate?"

The puppy yipped and tried to jump closer to her.

Danny and Cassie laughed together. "Are you sure you want to be called Pirate when you're old and gray?" he asked the dog.

The pup yipped again.

"Pirate it is," Cassie said, cuddling and petting the dog as she leaned into Danny. He put his arm around her and held her close as he petted the pup as well. "I love you, Danny. Thank you so much."

Danny kissed her temple and didn't say anything. He had something caught in his throat.

CHAPTER 17

Sunday dawned bright and clear with a forecasted high of seventy-three degrees. Perfect weather to be outside.

Cassie was going to need all the sunshine and fresh air she could get to stay awake today. Having a puppy in the house was exhausting. She and Danny had put a dog crate in her bedroom, but of course Pirate didn't want to be in it if he could be with his people.

Even if it was the middle of the night.

In an attempt not to wake Uncle Willie, Cassie had gotten up every time the pup had yipped last night. He'd probably nap in his crate while she was at church this morning. She hoped he'd be the only one napping.

With such perfect weather, she and Uncle Willie decided to walk to church. "I hope Pirate didn't keep you up last night," she said.

"I heard him once or twice, but I rolled over and went back to sleep." He laughed. "If Velma were here, she'd tell you I did that when Peter was a baby, too. Made her furious."

Cassie smiled. She liked to hear Uncle Willie talk about her aunt and cousin. Peter had died of leukemia when he was six, before Cassie was born.

"So," Uncle Willie said, "you and Danny are spending the day together?"

"Yup." Cassie felt her heart beat faster. "We're going to start training Pirate and, I don't know, hang out. You need anything? Want us to run any errands for you?"

"No, no, you have a good time." He paused. "I like seeing you together. Seems like things have changed between you."

Cassie looked away so her uncle couldn't see her blush. "Uh-huh," was all she could force out.

Uncle Willie chuckled. "No need to be embarrassed. Falling in love is one of the most exciting times in a person's life. Enjoy it."

"Well, it is a little embarrassing, under the circumstances," Cassie said. "I told Danny I don't care what people think, and that's mostly true, but the fact is the whole town is going to be watching us. Or at least everyone who knows us. It'd be nice to have some privacy while we figure out if..." She didn't know how to finish that thought.

"While you figure out if you're going to commit for the long haul?"

Cassie chuckled. "Yeah, I guess so. I mean..." She stopped walking. "This isn't like any relationship I've ever had. With Conrad...I don't know, I guess I thought that's what it would feel like to be mature and be in love in a mature way. I was crushed when he left, but not heartbroken, if you know what I mean."

Uncle Willie stood patiently at the side of the road and nodded. He was her rock, Cassie thought for the hundredth time. If she might lose him sooner than later, she needed to get his advice now, while she still had time.

"How do you know the difference between a teenage infatuation with hearts and rainbows, and a love that will last forever like with you and Aunt Velma?"

Her uncle grinned and stared into the distance. "Oh, there were hearts and rainbows there, too. I think every note she wrote me the first five or ten years, she drew a little heart next to 'Love, Velma.' And who would want to be in love without hearts and rainbows? It's fun to chase each other around the house and be silly."

Cassie smiled. She knew they'd been very happy. She didn't remember any chasing when she was around, but she could imagine it.

His expression sobered. "What you need to ask yourself is, could me and him get through the worst times together? When we lost Peter, it felt like our world had ended. But we'd already had a lot of practice in *deciding* to hang on. That's what you need to do. You need to both *decide* that you're together until 'death do us part.' Marriage is the best thing in the world, but it's also just about the hardest thing in the world. If you think you can go through the worst life has to offer and stay together — and have fun in the meantime, of course — well, then..." Uncle Willie looked directly at her now. "I think you should get married."

Cassie nodded slowly, processing what he'd said. She started walking again. "Danny and I have already been through a lot, and...here we are. What do you think that means? But we've also made a lot of mistakes," she added. "I don't know how to weigh the two sides."

Uncle Willie chuckled again. "I can promise you that if you have any kind of relationship with anyone, you're going to make mistakes. Even you and Tabitha have fought over the years. Remember that baby doll you two fought over in grade school? You thought the world was ending."

Cassie smiled and nodded. "Yeah, I see what you mean. It just seems a little scarier when…well, if you're married and you fight, the other person could…" She didn't want to say it. It had already happened once. What if it happened again?

"Leave? Get divorced?" Uncle Willie knew what she was afraid of. She'd moped around his house and cried on his shoulder many a time as a broken-hearted teenager. He stopped in the road and took her arm. "Listen to me, darlin', this is important."

Cassie stared hard at him, willing herself to ingest his wisdom. She needed it.

"This isn't the best advice for everyone, but I know you both like you're my own kids. Danny would only leave if he was scared. You've been his strength more than you know, the way you believe in him and defend him. You'd have to find that strength even if you were angry or hurt, and go after him. If you're thinking about marrying him, you need to *decide* that you're always going to be there for him, even if it means chasing after him when he gets wrong-headed ideas."

Uncle Willie paused and looked into the trees again. Cassie figured he was thinking about Aunt Velma again. He smiled wryly at her. "I have it on good authority that men specialize in getting wrong-headed ideas."

Cassie chuckled. She could see Aunt Velma saying something like that to him. She leaned over and hugged him tight. "Thanks, Uncle Willie."

He hugged her back, then started walking faster. "Come on, now, or we'll be late for church."

When they walked up, Cassie saw Danny waiting in a

sunny spot near the front door. "Good morning," he said to Uncle Willie. He leaned over and kissed Cassie on the lips, chaste but promising. "Hello, Sunshine," he whispered.

Cassie grinned up at him, lost again for a moment in the wonder of their new relationship. Then she remembered where she was and stepped back. "Good morning."

Danny grinned and took her hand, following a smiling Uncle Willie into church. After the service, Cassie said hi to a few people but let Danny know she was eager to go.

"Can't wait to spend the day alone with me, huh?" Danny said a little too loudly for Cassie's taste.

"Danny! Shh!" She giggled and pulled him toward the door. "Let's go. I want to get back to Pirate before he pees all over his crate."

The puppy started yipping as soon as he heard the front door. Cassie opened the crate door and Pirate jumped out. Danny caught him and ran for the stairs, Cassie laughing and following behind him. She watched as the minute the puppy hit the grass, he started peeing. "Whew," she called down to Danny.

"Good boy," Danny praised, "that's a good boy." He brought the dog upstairs a couple minutes later. "Okay," he said with an exaggerated sigh of relief, "now that that's done, we can relax and get on with the day."

They packed the picnic cooler and an armload of puppy paraphernalia into Danny's truck and headed out. Danny stayed on Lakeshore Drive, winding around to the northernmost part of the lake. It was a beautiful day to be out, and Cassie didn't care where they were going so she didn't ask.

Danny pulled into the driveway of the Hyatt's summer home. Nice people from down in the Detroit area. "Jax is caretaker for their house, and he asked if we could hang out here for the day. They said yes." Danny rattled a set of keys in his hand and Pirate jumped for them.

"Wow," Cassie said, surprised, "that was nice of them." She watched Danny pulling the picnic basket and Pirate's water bowl from the backseat of the truck.

"What?" he said, pausing.

"Nothing. I...this seems kind of romantic. I just..."

"You didn't think I was romantic?" Danny clutched his chest. "I am hurt."

Cassie giggled and followed him to the door. "I didn't mean that. I just meant—"

"Don't lie, we just left church."

She giggled again. "Okay, I meant that I'm surprised that you're romantic."

Danny groaned. "A knife through the heart, that's what it is."

"Well, it's not like I've seen you be romantic, remember?"

Danny put the picnic cooler on the kitchen counter and the dog bowl on the floor. He pulled Pirate from Cassie's arms and set him on the floor, putting the leash under his boot so the puppy couldn't wander far.

Then he pulled Cassie close.

Cassie felt her insides turning to mush under his gaze. It was so...tender, warm, loving. Danny Kessler really loved her? It was still hard to believe.

He ran his fingers lightly over her hair, then cupped her cheek. Cassie couldn't help but close her eyes and lean into his hand. Her body and mind were filled with two seemingly opposite emotions. On the one hand, every part of her from her hair to her toes seemed to tingle with joy in his presence.

On the other hand, she'd never felt so calm, so peaceful, so all's-right-with-the-world as she did now. She could stand here like this forever, just soaking up this peace and love without needing anything else, ever.

While she quietly reveled in the touch of his hand on her face, the feel of his chest pressed against hers, Danny kissed her. His lips were warm and soft and firm, all at the same time. Cassie leaned into the kiss and returned it with her whole heart.

One hand reached around his neck, pulling him closer, her fingers threading through the hair at the nape of his neck. All of the sensations — the warmth of his body, the softness of his hair, the tingling of her lips on his — combined to make her feel like there was a volcano building inside. It was a heady sensation. She felt dizzy and lighter than air.

She'd never been kissed like this.

And she wanted Danny to feel the same way she did. She pressed closer, opening her lips to a deeper kiss. All she could think was, *I love him so much.*

A few moments later, Danny pulled back, ending the long kiss with a series of shorter, softer ones. Their breath mingled as they both tried to steady their breathing.

"So," Danny sounded a little out of breath, "you still think I'm not romantic?"

Cassie's smile grew, encompassing everything she felt for him in this moment. "You sure proved me wrong."

His smile took on a satisfied air.

"But the day is still young," Cassie continued, "so we'll see."

Danny slapped her bottom and Cassie squealed, which set Pirate to yipping and jumping at her legs. Laughing, Cassie pulled away and reached for the picnic cooler.

"All right, Mr. Romance, what's your plan for lunch?"

Danny picked up Pirate, who settled down immediately. "She's mocking me, isn't she?"

"I'm not mocking you, I'm giving you an opportunity to show me what you've got."

"All right, you saucy wench, follow me." Danny marched over to the patio door that faced the lake and unfastened the security latches. He opened the door and reached for the food. "Please, allow me," he said with exaggerated courtliness. He bowed his head at Cassie and indicated that she precede him through the door.

After setting out the food Cassie had prepared, Danny opened another bag she hadn't seen. "And for dessert, my lady, fancy mini doughnuts from Lange, The Donut Baron."

Cassie clapped her hands. "Ooo, I love Lange's doughnuts!"

Danny pointed to a doughnut topped with red and white frosting and little red bits. He raised his eyebrows triumphantly.

It was the strawberry shortcake flavor, Cassie's favorite. "Okay, you're right, you're romantic." She gave him a big kiss.

Cassie couldn't remember laughing as much as she did over the next hour or so. Danny was like Prince Charming come to life. He sat next to her at the picnic table, served her first, kissed her hand or her lips or her temple a dozen times, laughed at everything she said, complimented her on the food. It was amazing.

The sort of thing you figure will end soon so enjoy it while you can.

But that thought seemed unkind. And it pointed out

Cassie's insecurities to herself just by sitting there in the back of her mind.

Her world had tilted when she'd told Danny she loved him, and it hadn't righted itself yet. But really, why would she want it to?

"You're looking a bit serious, Sunshine. What're you thinking?" Danny ran his fingers through her hair. It felt so good and made it hard to think.

She shrugged.

Danny's expression turned from teasing to understanding. While they'd always been good at knowing what the other was thinking when they were kids, life was more complicated as adults. Could they understand each other now the way they used to, sometimes with few words needing to be said?

"Jax put the dock out," he said. "The ducks haven't arrived to crap all over it yet. Want to—"

"Danny!" Cassie laughed.

"What? All right, then, poop."

Cassie squished her face up. So gross. She loved ducks, but wished there was a way to keep them off the docks.

"What? That's what it is. You have a problem saying poop? What do you call it?"

Just to tease him, Cassie said, "I don't know. Duck doo-doo?"

Danny rolled his eyes and laughed at her.

She loved his laugh. It had been far too long since they'd laughed like this. Years. And that was a really weird thought when she kept in mind they were only twenty-five and twenty-six.

"Well, there isn't any 'duck doo-doo'"—Danny made his voice sound funny, like a cartoon voice—"on the dock, so you want to go out?"

She wanted to say, *I'll go anywhere with you*, but instead she said, "Sure."

They put the food away, then decided to run around the yard a little with Pirate to get some of his energy out so he wouldn't want to jump in the water. The far end of the dock was double-wide so there was plenty of room to sit or lie down. Cassie relaxed onto her back, and Danny soon joined her. Pirate used the two of them as a jungle gym, climbing all over them both.

Cassie sighed. "This is nice," she said after a few minutes of silence. "It's been awhile since I relaxed like this."

Danny didn't say anything.

Cassie looked over to see if he'd fallen asleep.

"I'm awake," he said. His voice was quiet, almost gruff. It was a tone that said he was thinking big thoughts.

She waited. Pirate flopped down on her chest and settled in for some petting and probably a nap. She rubbed his head and back and belly, fingering the incredible softness of his ears. She thought she could see some of the characteristics of his golden retriever mother, but he really looked like his border collie father, Chip. Pirate was going to be gorgeous when he grew up.

Just like Danny. He'd been a good-looking kid, and more good-looking than gawky as a teenager, but he'd grown into a handsome man. She wondered if he noticed women looking at him down in Lansing. If they weren't staring and wishing they could get to know him better, they were idiots.

"I think I gotta tell you something," Danny interrupted her thoughts. "I don't want to, but it seems like I should."

DANNY SHIFTED UNCOMFORTABLY ON THE WOODEN PLANKS.
Everything he'd been taught about how men were supposed
to act shouted at him to keep his mouth shut. On the other
hand, he'd been doing all the "right" things and getting
terrible results. So maybe he should do something different.

Cassie's hand stilled on Pirate's head. Danny felt her
tense beside him. He wanted to tell her not to worry, it was
no big deal. But it was a big deal. He had no intention of
making the same mistakes twice.

She waited for him to speak like she always did. Lily was
never patient with him. She was always pushing him to say
what he was thinking, to stop making her guess. He hadn't
been trying to make her guess, he just hadn't had anything on
his mind that he felt like sharing.

How should he begin? He should probably just come out
and say, *I'm scared*. But he wanted to try to spin this
conversation in a positive way, looking for answers rather
than focusing on the problems.

"I've been thinking about Lily," he began.

Did Cassie lean away from him? Uh-oh.

"Not like I miss her or anything," he hurried to add. Good
job, Kessler. He tried again. "I've been thinking about the
things we did wrong, the reasons we got divorced."

Still quiet, Cassie hadn't moved. Good sign? He kept
going.

"I made a promise to myself to never go through that
again, never get married again."

Cassie turned her head to watch him while she listened.

Danny stared at the bright blue sky dotted with a few
puffy white clouds. That sky was his life with Cassie, mostly
awesome with a few clouds that didn't get in the way. His
life with Lily was one summer thunderstorm after another

with a few sunny days in between. What he didn't know, couldn't decide, was whether the thunderstorms were because he was bad at marriage, or because he'd picked the wrong partner.

"I don't want to hurt you," he said.

After a moment, Cassie spoke. "I'm trying to figure out what you're saying. You love me but you don't want to marry me because you're never getting married again?"

Her voice wavered a little at the end. Danny forced himself not to take her hand or kiss her or do anything to try to distract her from his words. They needed to be said. They needed to be dealt with.

"I'm saying I...I don't know. How do you fix something that's broken? How do you know when it's fixed?"

"Danny, you aren't broken." Cassie's voice had some heat to it, but she didn't punch him in the arm like she had before when he'd been critical of himself. Did that mean she was less sure?

"I'm not explaining this right," he muttered.

Cassie was quiet again for a moment and he wondered if she was praying. She said she often prayed in the middle of conversations that she didn't know how to proceed with. Heaven knew, he needed as much prayer as he could get.

She moved Pirate from her chest to her lap and sat up. She twisted to face him. "I still don't know what you're trying to say, so no, I guess you're not explaining it well. It sounds like you're trying to talk around what's really bothering you. Just come out and say it. I won't run away, I promise."

Danny covered his face with one arm. The sun was getting in his eyes. She was probably right, but he didn't want to put his feelings into words. It made them too real, made him feel even less capable of handling things maturely. It made him vulnerable.

But if he wanted Cassie in his life, maybe he was going to have to be vulnerable. He sat up slowly. Looking out over the lake he tried to spit out the words. "I…I'm…I might be a little…scared."

Cassie sighed heavily beside him. She must think he was a real loser.

She chuckled. "Oh my gosh." She sounded relieved.

Danny glanced over at her. She looked relieved.

"Is that all?" she said. "That is so normal!"

"No, I'm not talking about the normal kind," Danny said, frowning. He had to make her understand. "I'm talking about me being scared of ruining your life. I've already ruined one person's life, and I refuse to mess up yours."

Cassie took his hand and held it tight. "She really did a number on you. What will it take for me to undo the damage, for you to believe the truth and forget her lies?"

"Lily didn't lie. Everything got screwed up. That's the truth."

"People don't call her Bright Shiny just because she caught your eye and turned your head. You're not the crow in the analogy. She is. She picks up pretty things and drops them for other pretty things. I'm not going to gossip, but I've heard things from people I trust, and it seems to be true — she doesn't stick to things. She starts something, and then starts something else, and something else. Same with her relationships."

Danny would normally say he completely trusted Cassie. He trusted that she wouldn't lie to him, that she wouldn't gossip about someone even if she didn't like them, that she wouldn't try to make him believe her just to be on her side.

So if that was true, why couldn't he believe her now?

Cassie sighed. "Okay, if you don't believe me, then let's look at it a different way. You were eighteen when you got married. You're twenty-six now. How have you changed?"

Danny frowned.

"I mean, say, have you gotten healthier or less healthy?"

He shrugged. "About the same."

Cassie rolled her eyes. "Have you looked in the mirror? You are *not* the same. You're bigger and you have more muscles and you look like a man instead of a boy."

Danny felt his lips twitch. Cassie liked how he looked.

"Okay, what about work? Are you at the same level now or higher?"

"Higher."

"Right, because you've worked and learned and been successful and been reliable and so you've gotten promoted, right?"

He nodded. That was pretty true. And now he was seeing where she was going with this.

"What about emotionally or spiritually? Do you think you've grown or are you about the same?"

He felt his brow furrow as he thought about it. "Is this a trick question? If I say I think I've grown, does that mean you're saying my arguments aren't valid?"

"I'm not trying to invalidate your arguments. I'm trying to show you that over time we generally grow, learn, change, and we have to at some point leave our mistakes in the past. At some point, to keep on growing, you're going to have to move forward instead of slogging around in the same mud that's been thrown at you for years by women who don't—" She stopped abruptly.

Danny knew what she was going to say. "Who don't love me."

"Of course she loves you, just not…she does her best."

Cassie wasn't talking about Lily anymore. She was talking about his mom. He wasn't so sure she did love him, but he grudgingly agreed that she probably was doing the best she could.

He stared at their joined hands. It seemed like a dream that Cassie would still want him. But she probably wanted other things that went along with marriage. Like children.

"I don't think it's a good idea for me to procreate," he said, his voice feeling as hollow as the thought left his heart. "Look at how I was raised."

His father had left early in Danny's life, leaving his mother to try to get by on her own with two little boys to feed and clothe. Then his older brother, Paul, started getting in trouble with the law.

One drink led to another until his mother couldn't get through the day, let alone the night, without a few hits on the bottle. Even with Paul in prison in Ohio, his mom still told Danny he'd turned out the worst. He had a shot at getting them all out of the hole, that was how she'd said it. She'd always thought that Lily's family could lift them up, give the Kessler's a seat at the table of respectability.

"Uncle Willie and Aunt Velma were great role models for you. You know how to act."

"They're wonderful," Danny said, "and still look how things turned out." This conversation was making him feel worse, not better. He finally had something good in his life and he was going to have to let her go.

"I don't agree, but let's look at that children thing. You're afraid to be a dad, well…maybe we won't have kids."

Danny's head shot up and he said fiercely, "No! I'm not asking you to give that up for me."

Cassie closed her eyes and took a deep breath. He recognized that he was getting on her nerves, annoying her with his answers, but this was the best time to be honest and lay everything on the table. Not *after* they got married and realized they had completely different ideas about life.

"Okay, let's say you had a son and he got in a fight at school and you were called into the principal's office. What would you do?"

Danny gave it some thought. "I'd want to talk to my son first, not the principal, so I could take all the circumstances into account before I decided what to do."

"And what if you lost your job, something happened that wasn't your fault, but suddenly you're out of money and have mouths to feed?"

"I'd get another job, whatever it took. I'd move the family if I had to. I wouldn't leave my family."

He didn't realize the emphasis he'd put on the last sentence until he saw Cassie's reaction. Her smile turned soft and she squeezed his hand.

"Good. So what if you and your wife had three kids, two in diapers, one sick and crying, and you came home to find your wife crying in the kitchen?"

That sounded pretty awful. What would he do? He thought about it for a minute, still playing Cassie's game.

"Well, if that was my life, then I'd already know how to change diapers, so I'd start there. Then I'd put the kids in the playpen, or whatever safe place you put kids, and hold my wife until she stopped crying." He thought about it some more. "And then I guess I'd do whatever she told me to."

Cassie laughed. "Don't make me propose to you! That sounded pretty perfect to me."

Danny laughed with her for a moment. "But life isn't a game, Cass. It's made up of real people who get hurt, sometimes without you ever intending it." He moved closer to her, pulling her close. "I hurt you without meaning to. It happens."

She curled up against his chest. "You're right, it happens. And you get through it, and you get over it, and life goes on."

If only that were true. If only he could believe that you could get over and past your mistakes, no matter how big, that people could forgive you and not leave you.

If he could believe that, he had a shot at being happy.

CHAPTER 18

$\mathcal{M}$onday morning, Cassie awoke at 6:30 to music from her alarm clock. Normally, she didn't need an alarm, but when it was her turn to open up the Fluff and Fold, she set it just in case. Since it was on her favorite radio station, she usually didn't mind.

Today, however, she wanted to throw the clock against the wall.

She'd been having the most delicious dream about Danny, and now she couldn't remember it all. Part of it involved him feeding her strawberries and kissing her. That was enough to stay asleep even without the parts she couldn't remember.

She groaned and rubbed her eyes. She had to get out of bed and get to work, despite fantastic dreams. She let Pirate out of his crate, and threw on jeans and a T-shirt. She poured herself a glass of orange juice, tied her hair in a ponytail, and pounded down the stairs, setting Pirate on the grass just in time.

Ack! She shivered. The sun made it look warmer than it

was this morning. She unlocked the front door, turned on the lights, and dashed back upstairs for a hoodie. Ahh, better. Pirate crawled around inside the sweatshirt until his head poked out near hers. Cassie laughed as he stuck his tongue out at her. She grabbed her phone and a protein bar and headed back to the laundromat.

She tied a long clothesline rope to the leash loop of Pirate's collar and tied the other end to a sturdy cement column in the center of the room. Pirate immediately started sniffing everything in sight.

In the cleaning closet, Cassie pulled out the mop bucket and wrangled it into the sink where the faucet was. She filled it halfway with soapy water and got it back onto the floor without splashing herself. Victory.

She was rolling the bucket out into the main room when the bell over the front door jingled. This early on a Monday morning, it must be someone who forgot to get their laundry done over the weekend. She looked up to see the man of her dreams walk in.

Cassie didn't realize she'd stopped suddenly until water sloshed over the edge of the bucket onto the floor. A quick step and she just managed to keep her sneakers dry.

Danny smiled at her, and Cassie was embarrassed to feel her knees go weak. His wrinkled T-shirt barely contained his muscular pecs and biceps, all naturally obtained, no gym-muscles on this guy. His strong legs were half-covered by worn cargo shorts even though the morning air was brisk. Everything about him exuded a masculine strength and confidence that Cassie found intoxicating.

He walked straight toward her, bypassing the washing machines and stepping around the puddle. She could smell his aftershave before he even reached her. Whatever it was, he smelled marvelous. She felt her body tingle right down to her toes. She inhaled deeply.

He chuckled. "Good morning, sleepyhead. Making a mess here, huh? I keep you out too late?" He leaned in and kissed her, one hand cupping the back of her head, making her feel safe and protected. She closed her eyes and kissed him with her heart as well as her lips.

The kiss ended too soon. Danny stepped back and Cassie fell forward. He laughed and grabbed her around the waist before she tripped. Her hands fell against his hard chest and she remembered part of her dream from this morning. She felt her face heat up.

Unbidden, a picture of him standing shirtless on the roof crowded out her other thoughts. Thoughts like *be calm*, *breathe*, and *he's just a man*.

"Cassie?"

"Huh? Yes, right, I'm mopping."

He chuckled again. "You okay?"

She pulled her thoughts together. "Of course, just trying to wake up." She couldn't think about how wonderful he was, what a magnificent kisser he was, how fabulous he smelled. She had to work. But how could she focus on something as mundane as cleaning when Danny stood a foot away?

He walked over and swung a full duffle bag onto one of the washers. Pirate came racing to the end of his lead, just barely able to stand on his hind legs with his front paws on Danny's leg.

"Hey, buddy, how you doing?" He reached down to pet the puppy, playing with him for a few moments before standing. "Sorry, I gotta get these clothes washed and get to work. I'll play with you later."

He unzipped his duffle bag and sorted his clothes into two machines for lights and darks. Shocking. That's something she'd never seen him do before. Cassie had the presence of mind to take one of the keys from the ring and open the coin compartment on both machines.

"You don't need to do that," Danny protested. "I've got quarters."

"Well, you're family, you don't need them. You know that." Cassie arched her eyebrows at him, daring him to argue.

"All right, well, I'll help you clean while I wait."

So sweet. Such a hard worker. But how was she going to get anything done when he was so temptingly close? Now that she'd found that being his girl was even better than she'd imagined, she wasn't ready to get back to real life. Determined to focus on what needed to be done, she sloshed her mop through the puddle she'd accidentally created and got to work. The familiar routine was soothing.

Until Danny got some cleaning cloths out of the closet and began emptying lint traps and wiping down the dryers. No matter whether he stood up straight to get to the back of the upper level of dryers, or bent over to reach inside the lower dryers, the view was fabulous.

God, you sure did a good job when You made him. Inside and out.

She figured the Almighty didn't mind a few compliments to start the day, just like anyone else.

The two of them found their groove as his clothes washed and dried, working in harmony, both of them noticing and enjoying the long glances from the other. Pirate was oblivious to the tension in the air, running back and forth from one to the other, chasing the mop around the floor, and making them both laugh.

When Cassie was done with the floor, Danny dumped the dirty water for her and rinsed out the bucket and the mop. Cassie opened the wall machines with the single use boxes of detergent and fabric softener and refilled them both.

"You know," Danny said from a few steps away, making her jump. "Sorry," he said as he rubbed her back. He picked up Pirate and scratched his belly. "I'd rather have Uncle Willie alive and well, but if we were to inherit this together, we make a great team."

Cassie turned and smiled. "I agree. We always have." Her smile faded. "You know, it's after graduation. We promised we'd wait until today, but I don't want to wait any longer."

Danny knew what she was talking about. His expression turned solemn and he stopped tickling Pirate. He sighed. "Yeah."

"Maybe one of us should go talk to Dr. Dillon, try to get him to tell us something."

"I'm technically not family," Danny said, "so it'll have to be you. I'll go with you if you want."

Cassie nodded. "Lunchtime?"

"Find out when they're open. Doctor's offices are closed for lunch, aren't they?"

"I'll find out and text you."

Pirate looked from Danny to Cassie and yipped. He wiggled and squirmed in Danny's arms trying to get to her. Cassie laughed, and Danny handed the dog over.

"He knows who he belongs to, that's for sure," Danny said. "I'm glad you like him."

"I love him," Cassie crooned to Pirate. "Don't I? I love you so much, and you love me, don't you?"

Pirate responded by licking her chin. Over and over until Cassie made him stop. "I'm going to have to teach you not to do that, but it's so cute."

"Don't worry, buddy," Danny said, petting the pup. "I'll kiss her for you." He bent his head and followed up.

One of the dryers beeped. Stupid machine.

Danny opened the dryer, grabbed his duffle bag, and started stuffing clothes into it. Directly into the bag, bypassing the folding stage altogether.

Cassie gaped. "What are you *doing*?" she asked, setting Pirate down and hurrying over. "You're going to ruin your clothes that way."

Danny snorted. "It won't ruin them."

"I mean, you can't wear them when they are the wrinkled mess they *will* be when you take them out of the bag." She plucked a shirt out of the duffle and folded it neatly. "If you fold them while they're still warm, they won't wrinkle."

Danny shoved another handful in the bag. "I don't mind if they're wrinkled. They won't be after I've spent all day in them."

Cassie groaned and pulled another shirt out and folded it. When he did it again, she finally glanced up and caught his mischievous grin. She swatted his arm with the shirt she'd just folded and turned on her heel to walk away.

"Fine, have it your way. You're going to look like a country bumpkin in those wrinkly clothes." An excusable weakness, perhaps, in light of the multitude of his admirable qualities.

His arm snaked out around her waist and pulled her back before she got very far. "You're so easy to tease," he said in her ear.

The vibrations from his voice traveled through her ear

and down every nerve ending in her body. She couldn't help but turn in his arms and kiss him, swatting his arm for teasing her. She could live with being teased like this for the next fifty or sixty years.

An image crossed her mind of how Paul Brighton from Ann Arbor seemed to be the epitome of the well-dressed, professional, going-places kind of man her sisters wanted her to marry. He was a magazine-model kind of guy, the kind that advertisers assumed she wanted.

But they were wrong. She wanted someone who was as happy eating her egg salad sandwiches sitting on a fence as he was watching a movie with her knowing she'd be asleep before the end. Advertisers might always use the Paul Brightons of the world to get inside her head, but she was sure she'd never get this salt-of-the-earth country boy out of her heart.

DANNY DROVE CASSIE OVER TO DR. DILLON'S OFFICE AT eleven o'clock. The receptionist said there should be a lull for a few minutes then. During the short drive, she squeezed her hands into fists, then spread out her fingers on her legs trying to relax them.

After a few minutes, Danny grabbed her left hand. "It's going to be fine."

Cassie could tell by his voice that he wasn't sure he believed his own words. But it was kind of him to try to reassure her. She held onto his hand, praying for Uncle Willie and for strength to get through whatever was to come.

In the doctor's office, she introduced them and asked to

see Dr. Dillon. A few minutes later, the doctor appeared at the window.

"Cassie Lane is here to see you, doctor," the receptionist told him.

Dr. Dillon's head bounced up, eyes wide. "I, uh…"

He looked ready to flee, so Cassie hurried up to the window. "I just have a few questions. I won't take much of your time."

His professional mask slid into place. "I can't talk to you about another patient, I'm sorry." He turned as if to leave.

"Please," Cassie cried. She heard her voice break and felt embarrassed.

But the doctor must've heard it, too, because he stopped. He looked from Cassie, behind her to Danny, and back. He sighed heavily. "Come on back to my office, both of you. But I only have a minute."

Cassie felt Danny's hand at the small of her back as they walked through the door separating the reception area from the exam rooms. She hurried to follow the long-legged older man. He turned into an oak paneled office with a massive wooden desk and leather chairs. He motioned to two chairs as he walked in.

"I'm sorry that you're so distressed," Dr. Dillon said, sitting down and folding his hands on the neat desktop. "But I don't know what I can do to help you."

"We understand you can't talk about specifics," Danny said, "but Uncle Willie said there were other tests that had to be run before you could confirm a diagnosis. He doesn't seem to know when those tests are supposed to happen or where. Are they going to be done here? Does he have to go to Munson in Traverse City? What can we do to help?"

Cassie heard the same helpless fear in Danny's voice that

she felt herself. In a way, it was comforting, knowing she wasn't alone in this.

The doctor stared at his hands for a moment, seeming to almost make a fist of them. Was that a flash of anger? No, the doctor started to smile.

"We don't know anything for sure," he said, "so for now you can make sure your uncle eats very healthy food, lots of vegetables, less meat, and no desserts. Cut back on his sugar and junk food intake immediately."

Cassie pulled out her phone and started taking notes. Finally, something she could do to help.

"Be sure he doesn't overwork himself," Dr. Dillon continued. "He needs to get plenty of rest, no more night fishing, he needs sleep and a lot of it. And don't let him do a lot of lifting. These tests will involve a lot of needle sticks, so his skin will need to be free of scratches or bruises." He looked at Danny. "Whenever you see him lifting something, take it. He'll complain, but ignore him. He needs you two to take good care of him. You know he's too stubborn to listen to me."

Danny and Cassie both nodded, sharing a look of relief. They could help. Finally, actual things to do.

Dr. Dillon stood, and they followed suit.

"Dr. Dillon, thank you so much for your help." Cassie reached to shake his hand. When he clasped it in both of his and looked at her with such a compassionate expression, she had to pull away and wipe her eyes.

"Thank you, sir, we appreciate your time," Danny said, shaking the doctor's hand. "If there's anything else we can do, please let us know. Anything."

Cassie and Danny started out the door, but Dr. Dillon called out to them.

"Kids," he said. He paused and rubbed the bridge of his nose. "Medicine isn't perfect. We're all going to die, we just don't know when. Just...keep that in mind."

"Are you saying it may not be...maybe he's not dying?" Danny asked, hope infusing his voice.

"I can't say any more. But I promise you, I'll call Willie today and try to get him to open up to you both. Okay?"

Cassie and Danny thanked him again and left. Outside the office, Danny pulled her into his arms. They held each other tight. "Maybe it's not as bad as we think," Danny said against the top of her head.

"We've got to pray harder," Cassie said, feeling more hopeful than she had in a long time.

Danny nodded. They got into the truck and he turned the opposite direction from the Laughing Loon. "Let's go shopping," he said. "Apparently, we've all just become vegetarians."

Cassie chuckled. "I'll have to figure out what to do with that venison in the freezer."

Danny patted her knee. "No need for Uncle Willie to know what we're eating at Tabitha's or Jax's."

The sound of relief echoed in the laughter of the truck. Maybe things were going to be okay.

CHAPTER 19

*D*anny waited for Uncle Willie from the porch of the Fluff and Fold. He wanted to talk to him before they went upstairs to dinner. When he saw him crossing the street, Danny took the two cold beers from his lunch cooler and intercepted the older man.

"Hey, there, Danny boy, how's your day so far?" Uncle Willie slapped him on the back. "I'm sure it's only going to get better having dinner with a pretty girl."

Danny smiled. "It's been a good day. Do you have a minute?"

They walked to the back yard and settled into the wooden Adirondack chairs Danny had wiped down earlier. He twisted the cap off one of the beers and handed it Uncle Willie. When he hesitated, Danny said, "Enjoy it, it might be the last one you get."

Uncle Willie raised his eyebrows and they clinked bottles. They each took a drink and sat back quietly, staring at the bare woods just coming alive with green buds and unfurling leaves.

"Haven't seen that downstate fellow around for a while," Willie said out of the blue. "He go back home?"

Danny gritted his teeth thinking about Mr. Beamer. He took a drink of beer to cool down. "It might've been suggested to him that the dry cleaner could better serve his laundry needs."

Uncle Willie laughed. "Is that so?"

He didn't sound upset. Thank goodness.

Danny tried to focus on the topic at hand. He had run this conversation through his mind a dozen times. He could hardly start out with, *If you die soon, I wanted one more opportunity to ask your advice*. But where to begin?

He cleared his throat, took another swallow of beer, and cleared his throat again.

"Just spit it out, son, it'll hurt less."

Danny sighed. Without thinking, he said, "I don't know how to tell when I should believe what a woman says and when I should assume she's not telling the truth."

Uncle Willie burst out laughing. He slapped his knee and laughed some more.

Danny peeled at the label on the bottle. He smiled a little. "That didn't come out quite right."

"Oh no," Uncle Willie said, trying to stop laughing, "I think you said it exactly right." He wiped at one eye and sipped his beer. "I don't know why you think I know the answer, though."

"You were married for forty years, right?"

"Forty-two," Uncle Willie said, a touch of both pride and sadness in those two words.

After a moment, Danny prodded him. "So...?"

Uncle Willie grinned at him. "Women are a mystery. That's the truth."

Danny rubbed his head and sighed.

"All right, I see you're looking for a real answer." Uncle Willie took a deep breath and leaned his head back on the tall chair. "Let's see...I'd say first you start with a woman you can trust. It's takes time to learn to trust each other, but let's say you already found someone like that."

Danny glanced at him out of the corner of his eye. What did Uncle Willie think of him and Cassie? Sure, he loved them both, but when the rubber hit the road, would he really want a divorced man for his precious niece?

"Then — and this is something it took me a few years to learn, but let me save you the hard knocks — you gotta assume she's being honest with you. Tell her you trust her. Tell her you expect her to be honest and that she should expect honesty and integrity from you. Set those expectations early and then work every day to make it a habit."

He and Cassie used to trust each other implicitly. But he was pretty sure his actions had broken that trust. "You make it sound easy."

Uncle Willie grunted and shook his head. "Far from it. It's in our nature to lie and cheat and steal — even little things like lying about where you've been to keep her from worrying, or stealing her joy with something you said or didn't say. Remember, as much as we think we're uncomplicated, for reasons you and I will never understand, women say they don't understand us either."

Lily had always complimented him when they were dating. She seemed to agree with him on important matters, and she didn't seem to want things he didn't want. She wanted a nice house — sure, so did he. He just couldn't afford one. She wanted new furniture — so did he, but that credit card bill about killed their budget.

She said she loved him. He loved her. But it finally sank in — for both of them — that love wasn't enough. Not for Lily.

Cassie said she loved him. It was definitely different from the way Lily loved him. And he loved Cassie. More than he let himself dwell on. It seemed enough to see her as one of his best friends — he certainly couldn't see her as a sister. But of course, when he was dating and then married to Lily, he couldn't let himself think about Cassie.

Now there was nothing standing between them. But was love enough?

"Did you have a house when you and Aunt Velma got married?"

"It took us about five years to save up. We both worked two jobs and saved every penny we didn't need to eat. We argued when one of us wanted to buy something and the other didn't, but we got through it."

That's exactly what he'd been wondering. "How?"

Uncle Willie shrugged. "We talked. Sometimes loudly." He grinned. "And when we fought, we made up. And that's usually about the time we both came to our senses and made a decision together. Sometimes we bought the gizmo or dress or whatever, sometimes we didn't." He looked over at Danny. "Disagreeing is never easy, but it's part of the package. You're two separate people after all."

It seemed that Uncle Willie was done talking, but Danny still had questions. He drank his beer and stared into the woods.

Uncle Willie looked over at him, but Danny didn't meet his gaze.

"I don't know if I'm worthy of her," he said quietly. "Worthy of you. I don't want to make another mistake."

Uncle Willie sipped his beer. "Marriage is all about forgiving each other for all the mistakes. If you decide in advance that that's the way you're going to play it, then you're both going to win." He paused. "And don't let the devil get in your head. In many ways, none of us are worthy. But which is the bigger mistake — to sign on for a lifetime of joy like you've never known before, or walk away because it's the hardest thing you'll ever do?"

After a few moments, Danny said, "Thanks, Uncle Willie. I appreciate it. I don't know if I say it enough, but I appreciate everything you do for me."

Uncle Willie tipped his beer bottle and they clinked them again. "I feel the same. Now let's go inside, I'm getting cold."

Danny stood. "I'd finish that beer first. Enjoy it like it's your last one."

Uncle Willie raised his eyebrows.

"Trust me," Danny said. "You'll understand in a few minutes."

"WHAT DO YOU MEAN, NO MEAT?" UNCLE WILLIE GROUSED. He'd been a little surprised that Cassie had made a vegetable lasagne instead of one with ground beef, but it wasn't until Cassie started explaining why there was no dessert that he'd really started listening.

"Dr. Dillon said no meat, no dessert, no junk food. That's the way it is," Cassie said with steel in her voice.

"He's an idiot, making up stuff just to punish me. I'll do what I darn well please!"

Danny saw Cassie clamp her jaws together, and he knew she was trying not to cry.

"Don't you want a shot at getting better?" she asked quietly.

Uncle Willie must've seen it in her expression, too, because he backed down immediately. "I'm sorry, honey, of course I do. Here, let me have some more of the lasagne. I didn't know you could put vegetables in it. Since I don't have to save room for dessert, I need to fill the space."

Cassie paused as if trying to decide if he was serious. She cut another piece and put it on his plate. "I know you're probably thinking you can just eat what you want over at the store and no one will notice, but that's not true. Everyone cares about you and no one is going to allow you to eat junk food over there. I've sent out an email."

Uncle Willie paused in his chewing. Danny wanted to laugh, but it wasn't funny. Tonight would be the last time he slid him a beer on the side.

The older man muttered under his breath.

"I'm not going to be shaken from this. I'm serious about helping you. Dr. Dillon made it sound like his diagnosis isn't absolute. But until we know what's wrong and what can be done, we're following his directions. Period."

"All right, all right, I heard ya," he said.

Danny's phone rang. He pulled it out of his pocket and looked at the screen.

Mom.

He ran his hand down his face. She didn't call often, but it was rarely good when she did. "I'm sorry, I should take this," he said and pushed back from the table.

"Everything all right?" Uncle Willie asked.

"It's my mom." For Cassie and Uncle Willie, those three words explained everything.

He stepped into the living room and hit the Talk button. He picked up Pirate, hoping that petting the animal would help him remain calm. "Hello, Mom."

At first, all he heard was crying. His stomach tightened. Great. She was drunk-dialing him. He waited for her to speak.

"I always end up alone," she cried. "Everyone leaves me. Everyone. But you came back. You came back to me." She cried harder.

Danny closed his eyes and asked for patience. Experience had taught him that nothing he said or did would make her feel better for more than a minute. But it was hard to fight the urge to try. The very fact that she was his mother was a difficult obstacle to overcome in setting healthy boundaries.

He sat on the couch and listened to her cry, then rant, then cry again. Finally she said the words he'd been dreading.

"Come over. I need you. I don't want to be alone."

Every nerve in his body, every thought in his head screamed to say no, that he couldn't help her, that he'd never been able to help her. He wasn't enough to make her better.

"I'll be right there." Before she could say another word, he hung up.

It was tempting to stay here, his haven so many times throughout his childhood, petting the dog and talking with people he loved. Even arguing with Uncle Willie about dessert seemed like a great way to spend the evening. Now.

He stood and gently placed Pirate on the floor, petting him one more time. The sooner he got going, the sooner it would be over.

Cassie walked over with a section of the lasagne in a plastic container. "Want company?"

He shook his head. He did, but then the vitriol sure to come would spew onto her as well. He wanted to protect her from that.

She pressed the food into his hand. "I don't need the container back. Praying for you."

He hugged her tight, kissed her forehead, and let her go. He nodded to Uncle Willie and left for the hellhole he'd grown up in, his stomach already tying in knots.

The two-mile drive took forever and ended too quickly. Danny sat in the truck for a moment, trying to find the words to pray, and finally ending up with *Please*.

He knocked on the trailer door and walked in. The stench of stale cigarettes, alcohol, and body odor hit him hard. He propped the door open to get some fresh air inside. At least he didn't smell vomit. Yet.

It took him a moment to find her. She was curled up on the couch under a pile of blankets and pillows. No sound, so maybe she'd already passed out and he could go.

He walked closer. She moaned. Just as he stepped back, her hand shot out from under the blankets and grabbed his wrist. He pulled but she held on. For a moment he was ten, too small to get away if she grabbed him, too small to defend himself.

But he wasn't ten.

He twisted his wrist hard enough to get loose, trying not to hurt her. He moved some papers and clutter from a nearby chair and sat gingerly, leaning his elbows on his knees.

He waited, counting like he used to.

After a minute, instead of falling asleep, she started crying and mumbling. It took him awhile to figure out that she was crying about her latest boyfriend. What was his name, Ralph? Rod. Apparently, that's who had left her. Most recently.

Danny went to the bathroom and tried to find a clean washcloth. No luck, so he chose the least offensive one and rinsed it in cool water. He brought it back into the living room and laid it on his mother's forehead. Then he went to the kitchen and filled a plastic cup, not a glass, with water. He remembered all too well what happened when glasses were thrown around the trailer. He still had the scar on the bottom of his foot.

He set the cup on the table and sat again, waiting.

Her crying eased and she sat up, wiping her face. "I need a drink."

"Right there, Mom." Danny pointed, knowing she wouldn't take it even if it was what she really needed. "You're dehydrated. Drink a little water. You'll feel better."

"Tequila will make me feel better," she mumbled, her words slurring together. "Or vodka. Or even gin." She pointed at him. "Good gin. Not the cheap stuff." The rest of what she said was punctuated by heavy cursing.

Danny closed his eyes.

"What's wrong? You gotta problem with swearing? What kind of man doesn't swear, huh? You a goody-two-shoes? You're too good for your momma? You always were. Running off and leaving me. Everyone's leaving me. Your father left me. Your brother left me. You left me. Rod left me." She started crying again, digging around in the blankets.

It took Danny a few seconds to realize what she was doing. He jumped up and rushed to the couch, but it was too late. She'd found her bottle. He tried to grab it from her but she was surprisingly strong. Alcohol and a narcissistic disposition had aged her more than time had, and the results were worse. She was shrunken and skinny and gray, but she had the strength of two men when it came to the bottle.

Danny gave one last pull and she scratched his arm with her long fingernails, drawing blood. When she lunged to bite him, he jumped back, withdrawing to his chair. He ignored his arm, ignored his mother lifting the bottle to her lips once, twice. He waited. When she finally passed out, he could cover her with a blanket and leave, knowing she was as safe as he could make her.

She started shouting again, and Danny realized she was talking about Lily. "You finally had a chance, a way to get us out of this dump, and you ruined it. You ruined it! She was an angel, beautiful and kind and sweet. She loved me and you pushed her away!"

Danny had never understood the relationship between Lily and his mother. Perhaps Lily just needed someone to complain to about him who would agree that Danny was a screwup. Perhaps she took a sick pleasure in making his relationship with his mother worse. Perhaps they'd actually liked each other.

"Bring her over. Go get her," his mother insisted, leaning toward him. "I want Lily to come over and hold me. She makes me feel better."

"She doesn't live here," Danny said, his voice devoid of emotion. "She lives downstate."

His mom looked confused for a moment. Then she turned angry again. "You ruin everything. Everything! If you touch it, you break it. You've always been that way." She stopped for a second and her eyes widened. "You're with Cassie again," she whispered. "I heard it. Someone said it. That tramp who lives over the laundry mat. She's always been sniffing after you, that little—"

"Mom!" Danny took a deep breath. "Can I get you some coffee? I brought you some lasagne. It's in the fridge. Do you want it now?"

"Fine, fine," his mom said as she leaned back into the couch cushions and took a long drink. "Ruin her, too. Go ahead and ruin her life. She deserves it. You deserve each other. You ruin everything. Just go. I don't care, just go. Go!"

She screamed the last word, making Danny jump. He stood, unsure of what to do. He'd always been afraid she'd somehow set the place on fire, or drown in her own vomit. If she'd just fall asleep, he could worry about her a little less and go home.

Well, not home. He didn't have a home. He slept on someone's couch. What kind of a man does that? What kind of a man can't provide for his wife? What kind of a man—

The litany of his mother's abuse rushed through his mind, giving him a headache and making him feel nauseous. He was so caught up in the noise in his head that he almost didn't see the empty bottle. He ducked just in time. It crashed against the wall.

"Everything's ruined. Everything's ruined," she mumbled. It had been her favorite phrase as long as he could remember.

Danny went to the kitchen and pulled a dustpan and a whisk broom from under the sink. Trying not to shrink as she yelled at him, he swept up the worst of the broken glass and threw it in the trash.

As he neared the living room area again, she started cursing and screaming again. She picked up the cup of water and threw it at him.

She'd always had a remarkably good aim, Danny thought as the cup hit his upraised arm and splashed cold water over him.

Whether it was the cold water or the sense of helplessness, he decided he'd had enough for tonight.

"That's right! Leave!" she screamed. "You're good at that. Always leaving people. Just go!"

Danny walked to his truck, turned it on and blasted the heat. He couldn't stop shaking. He didn't know how long he sat there because he hadn't looked at the clock when he left. But he'd left Cassie over an hour ago.

He put the truck in gear and backed out. At the bottom of the driveway he stopped.

He wanted Cassie. He needed her. She'd always been able to soothe his wounds. Uncle Willie and Aunt Velma and Cassie. They healed him. He knew she waited for him.

But he sat there in his truck, not moving. How could he bring this wretchedness back into her life, into her arms?

He pulled out his phone and texted Jax.

> Feel like some Call of Duty and ginger ale?

It was a code they'd developed long ago. Danny needed a friend and something to settle his stomach. And not beer. The last time he'd been around his mother like this, he hadn't been able to drink for a month.

A minute later, his phone beeped.

> I will by the time you get here, brother.

CHAPTER 20

*C*assie slept surprisingly well considering she went to bed worrying about Danny. She understood his need to go shoot things in video games with Jax — Jax was good for him, and she was rarely jealous of their friend — but she wished she could've helped comfort Danny and cheer him up.

Maybe she should learn to play *Battlefront*. It was a *Star Wars* game, after all, how bad could it be? On the other hand, maybe she was glad Jax was Danny's Xbox buddy.

She spent the morning on the computer, finalizing reservations that had come in for Idle-Awhile Cabins, working on bookkeeping, and staring out the window thinking about Danny. Around the eighth time her mind wandered to him, she was rewarded with a text.

Hey Sunshine, wanna have lunch?

She giggled. Good thing no one was around but Pirate. "Wanna have lunch with Danny?" she asked.

He looked up from the chew toy he was working on and wagged his tail.

> Pirate thinks we should. How about Oahu?

It was a silly game they'd played since they were kids. If they could have lunch anywhere in the world, where would they go? Whichever place they chose, they'd pretend to eat food from that area. A peanut butter and jam sandwich could become a panini in Italy, or a taco in Mexico, or a gyro in Greece.

> Maybe Cancun?

> We haven't been to Turkey.

> I have a better idea. I'll pick up you and Pirate in an hour. I'll bring lunch, you bring a picnic blanket.

> Deal.

Cassie scooped up Pirate and petted his cute little head. "We have a date," she said with another giggle.

She really had to stop doing that. Someone was going to hear her sometime and she'd be horribly embarrassed. She wasn't a teenager.

Pirate licked her chin.

"You're right," and she giggled on purpose, "I shouldn't care what other people think. I'm happy. You're happy. And we'll cheer Danny up today so he's happy, too. Right?"

Pirate wagged his tail so hard, his whole body wiggled in her arms.

A new thought stilled Cassie's hands on the soft fur. Huh. She and Danny had never actually been on a date.

She absently stroked Pirate's back as she thought about it. Did it matter? They spent all their time together. They both said they loved each other. Due to their twenty-year — gosh, was it that long? — friendship, maybe they didn't need to date.

She would've liked it though. Getting dressed up and going someplace nice. Maybe dinner and a movie in Traverse City. Maybe a play. Did Danny go to plays?

Or maybe those were things that society said they needed to do.

"I don't care," she told Pirate. "I'll take him any way I can get him. Who knows? Maybe I'll ask him out on a date. I'm a modern woman. I could do that."

Pirate wiggled his little butt some more, and Cassie took that to mean, *good idea*. She laughed and put him back on the floor.

"Now don't distract me. I have to work before he gets here."

An hour later, Cassie and Pirate were downstairs waiting when Danny pulled up. He swung through the parking lot, waited for her to hop in, and off they went. Danny took her hand and kissed it as he pulled back onto the road. He didn't let go.

"For once, I hate these bucket seats," he said.

Cassie smiled at him. If there was any way to sit closer, she would have. "Remember that old pickup you had in high school? I remember you saying, 'I can't wait to get a new truck. It'll have bucket seats and a working air conditioner—"

"Yeah, yeah." Danny chuckled. "I don't think I was

dating when I said that. I hadn't thought things through, didn't realize how great those old bench seats were."

Cassie had the fleeting thought, *I wonder if he pulled Lily against his side in that truck?* But she kicked the thought away. She'd been practicing a new habit of taking every thought captive and checking to see if it was a helpful and healthy thought. If not, in the garbage it went.

She sighed contentedly and watched the lake go by as they drove. Danny didn't seem to feel like talking, and that was fine with her. He turned left onto Lakeshore Drive, passing dozens of houses owned by locals and out-of-towners alike. Jax was caretaker for several of these summer homes.

They circled around the S-curve where Mr. Billings got in an accident almost every winter. For reasons no one could understand, the man insisted on buying white cars. Then he'd back out of his driveway at the top of the S-curve and drivers wouldn't be able to tell his car from the snowbank until it was too late. Maybe he just liked the attention he got from complaining about it every year.

Another strip of lakeshore crowded with houses on both sides of the road nearly obscured the lake, then a left turn took them through the woods, then back around to the lakeshore again.

"Looks like the Harpers are building an addition," Danny noted as they drove.

"They just had their fourth kid. I guess they need the space."

When they hit another patch of woods between houses, Cassie gasped and pointed. "Trilliums! I haven't seen many this year." It was one of her favorite flowers, but you weren't supposed to pick them. They were so fragile that they often wouldn't grow back.

Cassie was still trying to figure out where Danny was going. There weren't any restaurants this direction — of course, he did say he'd brought their lunch. Looked like they were going to the Hyatt's house again.

A few more curves, and then...no slowing to turn down the road for the Hyatt's.

Cassie smiled. She'd figured it out. Just as the wheels of the truck left the pavement for the dirt road, they both said, "Where the sidewalk ends."

Danny looked over at her and kissed her hand.

It was one of their favorite places, a private place they'd found riding their bikes as kids. They'd read the Shel Silverstein poem and decided, at Loon Lake, it was the northernmost part of Lakeshore Drive where the pavement ended. At this time of year, it should be perfect since the mosquitos weren't out yet.

Cassie rubbed Pirate's ears. "Your first time in the woods. You're going to love it." He climbed up her shoulder and put one paw on the doorframe, staring out at the budding trees.

Danny turned off the dirt road onto what could only generously be called a two-track, more of a space between the trees large enough for a vehicle to pass. A hundred yards or so and it opened into a small clearing. At the far end, a creek bubbled along the edge of the woods.

Cassie sighed happily. She opened her window partway and breathed deeply. "I think I smell a peppermint wind," she said referring back to the poem again.

Danny grinned. "That will go perfectly with our lunch." He got out and opened the back door on his side, pulling out a box and a small cooler. He tapped the ground with his foot, then bent to press his hand against the dead grass and leaves.

He put the food back in the truck. "I think we're a little

early for sitting on the ground. It's still wet from the last rain. I guess we'll have a tailgate party instead."

Cassie finally got Pirate's leash tied to the long rope she'd been using when she wanted to give him more room. She opened her door to find Danny reaching for the puppy. She started to give him the animal, but he pressed closer.

"Hang on," he said. "You haven't gotten a proper hello yet. I should've done this earlier," he whispered, moving his lips closer to hers as he spoke, "but I really needed to get away."

On the breath of the last word, his lips touched hers. A light, feathery kiss made her catch her breath. Half a dozen little kisses, each one hungrier than the last, made her insides melt. Their mouths opened together and the last kiss burned like a waking volcano. It was perfect except for the scratching at her chest.

Yip, yip, yip!

Oh, right, there was a puppy squished between them.

Danny pulled a few inches away, laughing. "I'm sorry, buddy, did I crush you? Or do you just want some attention, too?"

His eyes caught hers and he sobered a little. He must've read her longing for more on her face because he leaned in close and kissed her passionately again.

She pulled him closer, trying to get more of him somehow. The hand on her face traveled down her neck, and her body burned with longing.

Then he started laughing.

Cassie opened her eyes and blinked at him, confused.

"I'm so sorry, but Pirate is licking my hand. It's hard to concentrate."

Cassie burst out laughing. "I guess he's keeping us honest, huh?"

Danny's laughter sounded strained. "Unfortunately." He pulled Pirate from her arms and set him on the grass. He tied the rope to the door handle and made sure it wasn't long enough to reach the creek. The puppy started exploring, ignoring the humans.

Danny turned back to Cassie, still in the truck. His eyes went to her lips and drifted lower. Cassie swallowed. She wanted him, too, but now was not the time or the place. She wanted their first time to be after they'd truly committed to each other, not as an escape from a bad day.

She quickly jumped out, grabbed the blanket from the backseat, and hurried to open the tailgate. She folded the blanket in quarters to make it big enough for the two of them to sit on, but thick enough to be moderately comfortable.

Danny sauntered over and leaned his hip against the side of the truck. He looked so sexy, looking at her like he wanted her more than lunch. She tried to clear her throat but it had gone dry. She really should stop staring at him. That would help, surely.

But she'd never seen him look at her this way. It was…intoxicating.

He walked closer, one measured step at a time.

Like stalking.

She felt her breath catch in her throat as he stood in front of her, one hand on each of her legs. A shiver raced up her spine as if electricity were shooting out of his fingertips.

He leaned in to kiss her. She raised her face, her eyes on his lips.

Yip!

Cassie heard the little claws on denim. Pirate stood on his back legs, his front legs pawing at Danny's jeans.

"For Pete's sake," Danny exclaimed loudly. "What are you, Heaven's guard dog?"

Pirate yipped again, making Danny and Cassie laugh, albeit laughter threaded with frustration.

"Fine," Danny shouted to the sky. "I get it! Hands off." He picked up the puppy and dropped him in Cassie's lap. Then he went around the truck to get the food. He dropped the box and cooler on the blanket. "Let's keep the food between us, okay?" he said as he hopped onto the tailgate.

He wouldn't look at her. Cassie tried to work through what had just happened. If it wasn't for Pirate...

She felt her face get hot as she thought about where they'd been headed. She wondered how long she would've followed his lead. Of course, she wanted to. But...not yet. She stared at his profile as he set out their lunch. For all the imagining she'd done, it was nothing like the reality.

In the past, the guys she'd dated were mostly gentlemanly. Several had obviously been willing, but had respected her wishes in the end. Even when she was with Conrad, it had gotten hot and heavy a few times — which was part of the reason she naively assumed he wanted to marry her — but she'd been able to control herself.

Now, well...she wanted to rip Danny's clothes off.

The thought was startling in its intensity.

She knew sex wasn't love. She'd been attracted to the men she'd dated, and understood that wanting to have sex was a natural human urge. But this was different.

What she felt for Danny right now wasn't just wanting to have sex. She wanted to entwine her entire life with his, in every imaginable way, starting right this second. Sex, yes, but also hopes and dreams, careers and finances, friends and family. Well, some family more than others.

It was almost painful not to reach out to him.

She'd never wanted anything as much as she wanted Danny Kessler.

"I'M BEGGING YOU TO STOP STARING AT ME," DANNY SAID, his voice tight with tension. "Your uncle is going to come after me with a shotgun if you don't."

It was all he could do to sit on his side of the truck and pretend to eat. He wanted her desperately. If it wasn't for the dog, who knows what they'd be doing now. There would certainly be more skin on skin. But he hadn't even gotten as far as sliding his hand around her waist and hips and —

He had to stop thinking about it.

An image of a bumper sticker he'd seen once flashed into his head: *Dog is God spelled backwards*.

Danny looked up at the sky and shook his head. *I don't remember you being this interested in my actions in the past.*

Before the thought was fully formed, Danny knew he was wrong. God hadn't been the one who walked away. Coming back to Loon Lake seemed to have been a homecoming in more ways than one.

It felt better than he would've thought. Except for right this second. He was pretty darned uncomfortable right now.

"Please talk about something," he said, risking a glance at Cassie. She was red-faced and quickly looked away. What was she thinking? Well, duh, he could guess. They both needed to think about something else.

"So how about those Tigers?"

Danny paused, his sandwich halfway to his mouth. He chuckled. "Spring training went well. Looks like the pitcher's arm healed over the winter. I think they've got a shot."

She stared at him blankly.

"You have no idea what I'm talking about, do you?"

"You wanted a change of topic, you didn't say it had to be something I knew anything about." She bit into the crusty sandwich he'd bought her. Piles of smoked ham, sliced so thin you could almost see through it, layered with melted mozzarella cheese and tomatoes and pesto. Her eyes closed in pleasure and she groaned. "Oh, wow, this is amazing."

Danny clenched his teeth. "Could you eat without the sound effects?"

Her face turned bright red.

"Please," he said, trying to keep his voice even.

"Sorry," she whispered. If anything, she got redder. "Um, how was last night?"

This time, Danny was the one who groaned. "Bad. Really bad. I don't want to talk about that either." He had no idea what to do about his mother, but he definitely didn't want to think about it right now.

"Sorry," she said again. "It was the first thing I thought of. Um..."

"I've been thinking about Dr. Dillon," Danny said after a moment of silence. "I like him and all, but remember the message in the suggestion box with that other doctor's name? I looked him up on the Internet. Seems everybody loves him. I think we should give him a call."

Cassie raised her eyebrows and stopped chewing. Then she swallowed. "Um, okay. I guess it couldn't hurt to get some more information."

"I hate to say it, but—"

"I know. I'll call him."

If he married Cassie, he would truly be Uncle Willie's nephew. Then he could help more with the medical and legal issues that Cassie got saddled with now. The idea was tempting for more than one reason. Not only would he be with Cassie, he'd have a whole new family.

He'd actually be related to the man who'd been a substitute father to him since he was a kid. Cassie's annoying sisters would become his annoying sisters. He'd have nieces and nephews and obligations to remember birthdays and buy Legos and action figures.

Lily's family had been kind to him at first, but even at the best of times he'd felt like an outsider. If he married Cassie, he'd never be an outsider again.

But then he remembered his mother's words, how he ruined every relationship he was in. That was true. No way around it. Even drunks can be right sometimes.

He took a swallow of Faygo Black Cherry pop — last one in the refrigerated case at the Laughing Loon today — and eyed Cassie. She was trying to keep Pirate off her lap and away from the people food.

He loved her. He was absolutely sure of it. He just didn't know what to do about it. Follow Uncle Willie's advice and chase her around their home until they died of old age? Or follow his mother's advice and leave her alone before he ruined her life again?

Even praying hadn't helped. Great.

The thing was, no matter what Cassie or Uncle Willie said about forgiving the past, marrying Cassie would put her in the bull's eye of his mother's wrath. If he lived here again, last night would only be a taste of what was to come. How could he ask that of someone he loved?

He finished the last bite of his sandwich and wiped his hands on his jeans.

Cassie gave him an arch look, glancing down at the pile of napkins between them, and back at Danny.

"What? They're already dirty. Come here, Pirate. Cassie needs to finish her lunch."

"I'll save the rest for tomorrow. You brought enough food to feed Jax, not me," she said. "And no, you can't have my other half. It's too good. Where'd you get it?"

Danny moved the food box to the other side of the truck bed. "Let me lie on your lap and I'll tell you."

She gave him her best stern look. He gave her his best sweet and innocent look. She giggled. He loved that sound.

She rearranged the blanket and leaned against the side of the truck. Danny lay down with his head on her thigh. When she started running her fingers through his hair, he closed his eyes and sighed. Other than the firm grip he kept on Pirate's leash, he felt more relaxed than he had in weeks.

Years.

If only he could stop time and lie here with her until he made a decision.

CHAPTER 21

Cassie couldn't remember a better day — the most delicious lunch she'd had in ages plus a sexy, romantic interlude equaled one of the best memories she and Danny had ever created.

And then there was the other part.

She wasn't used to wanting to rip off a man's clothes, or wanting to help him rip off hers. If Danny hadn't stopped them, there definitely would've been some skin-on-skin. She figured she would at least feel guilty about it, her whole "good girl" way of life and all. But yesterday, honestly, all she felt was a longing for more.

Not only more physical contact, but more of everything. She wanted more days lazing in the woods with Danny napping on her lap. She wanted more nights hanging out with their friends. She wanted more laughter and talking and playing with Pirate. They kept saying they were training him, but so far they'd only laughed at his antics. She didn't care though. Any reason to hang out together was a good one.

She stared out the window and sighed. She couldn't read

what was going on in Danny's head. Not the big stuff. They could finish each other's sentences, order take-out the other would like, and think of where to find the other person without sending a text.

But what did Danny think about *them*? She felt giggly and foolish and wonderfully sexy when she thought about yesterday and his first obvious sign of intense attraction to her. But she knew him well enough to know he had a lot of things on his mind. Past experience had taught her that when he was trying to decide what to do about something, he took his own sweet time. He didn't rush into things.

That was normally a great attribute in a person. But sometimes Danny went off and did something half-cocked for no reason she could discern or understand.

So while Cassie might normally assume this relationship of theirs was headed full-speed ahead, with Danny she had her doubts. Not doubts about how he felt about her, but about what he would think was the best way to deal with it.

She sighed heavily and looked at her watch — 8:32 a.m. She'd called that doctor in Traverse City yesterday, Dr. Bonner, but his office had been closed. Since Uncle Willie was over at The Laughing Loon, it was safe to make the call from home today.

"Dr. Bonner's office."

"Hi, my name is Cassie Lane, and I was referred to Dr. Bonner by a friend." She hoped they didn't ask who. No one signed those suggestion box cards. "My uncle, who I live with, was recently told by our local doctor that he's" —she couldn't form the words *going to die*— "got a terminal disease. I don't want to discredit this doctor or anything but..."

"You'd like a second opinion. What is your uncle's doctor's name?"

"Dr. Bob Dillon in Loon Lake."

"Please hold."

Cassie gripped her cell phone hard enough that her hand hurt.

"Thank you for holding, Miss Lane, Dr. Bonner knows Dr. Dillon. He suggested you come in today at two o'clock. Can you make it?"

Cassie almost choked. Today? Holy cow. That was faster than anything Dr. Dillon had been doing.

"Um, yes, sure, but…he can talk to me even though—"

"Of course, the appointment is for your uncle, but you can come with him. Assuming your uncle doesn't mind. Will today work for you?"

Cassie thought about how Uncle Willie would react. Not well. He was happy to tell her to stay home if she had a cold, but he refused to ask questions when he'd been told he was going to die. She wished she could ask Danny what he thought before she had to decide.

"The next available appointment looks to be in…three weeks."

"We'll be there," Cassie said. "Today. Two o'clock." A part of her brain was reeling with what she'd have to do to make this happen. "Can you give me the address, please?"

After she hung up, Cassie leaned against the wall. She didn't even know who this doctor was. Danny had researched him and been impressed. That was the only reason she'd agreed to take today's appointment. Well, that and the fact that the doctor knew Dr. Dillon. That was probably good, right?

She called Danny.

"Hey, what's up?"

"I just got off the phone with Dr. Bonner's office. We have an appointment for two o'clock. *Today.* How are we going to get him there?"

"What? Today? Wait, how…"

"Yeah, that's how I feel," Cassie muttered. "I think he made an opening for us because he knows Dr. Dillon. The next appointment is in three weeks. How do we…"

There was a short silence. "Then we get him in. We'll carry him to the car if we have to. Let me think. Okay, if we leave by one o'clock, we should get there in plenty of time since the weather's clear. Get him home for lunch. I'll join you. Then we'll just…not back down."

"Yeah." Cassie stared out the window at The Laughing Loon. Her uncle had a backbone of steel and a will of iron. He didn't do anything he didn't want to do. "I don't know how we're going to convince him either."

After a moment, she squared her shoulders. If it was possible to save her uncle's life, she would do whatever it took, even if Uncle Willie was mad at her forever. "Okay, I'll see you at lunch."

WILLIE FELT HIS PHONE BUZZ IN HIS POCKET. HE FINISHED stacking the soup cans on the shelf, arranging them so the labels all faced forward, then checked his phone.

> Trying to arrange lunch around everyone's schedule. Can you come home at noon?

He smiled. Cassie and Danny were doing everything he'd

hoped for. Now he just wanted a proposal and a wedding, and he could die a happy man.

In ten or twenty years.

> Sure thing.

He wasn't much of a fan of the food she'd been making the last few days, and the "no desserts" bit was making him cross. He had a loud conversation with Dill Monday night, which ended with being invited in for a piece of Barbara's Boston cream pie.

Barbara, of course, was the one who offered him the pie. Dill just said, "It wouldn't hurt you to eat healthier."

"Apparently, I'm going to *have* to eat healthier for a little while. So you can bet I expect to be invited over for the good stuff."

Dill laughed and said it was his own fault.

But Danny was coming around, Willie was sure of it. When the two of them were a done deal, he'd share the good news.

Customers came and went, and Willie managed to get home by twelve-ten. Cassie usually made sandwiches for lunch, and today it smelled like she'd made homemade bread in the bread machine. Wonderful. Only problem with getting her married off was thinking up what he'd eat every day. Small enough sacrifice.

"Smells wonderful," he said, walking into the kitchen to see what was on the menu. He squeezed her shoulders and washed his hands at the sink.

Someone pounded up the stairs, and a moment later Danny entered.

Willie looked around. "Where's Pirate?"

"Um, Tabitha's watching him," Cassie said brightly.

"The kids wanted to play with him," Danny added.

"In the middle of a school day? Is one of them home sick?"

"Yeah, unfortunately—"

"Nope, Tabitha just—"

Willie watched the kids look at each other, changing their stories. He'd seen them do this dozens of times over the years, but not since they'd become adults. Interesting. He'd pretend to buy it. "Well, I hope whoever it is feels better."

Danny helped Cassie as she slid hearty grilled cheese and tomato sandwiches off the grill onto plates. When everyone sat, Willie said grace and they ate.

"How's your day been?" he asked them both.

"Busy," they answered together.

"I found a short in the living room light fixture in cabin two," Danny said. "I'll call Barney's Electric tomorrow and get it fixed before the first guest arrives."

Willie nodded. "Sounds good. But you might as well call him today and get on his schedule."

Danny and Cassie exchanged another glance. "Sure, right, good idea," Danny said.

Yup, something was definitely up. Now he just had to put on the pressure until they hollered "uncle." He smiled to himself and took another bite of the sandwich.

"Cassie, this might be the best grilled cheese sandwich you've made yet."

"Thanks," she said, shooting him a bright smile. He watched her out of the corner of his eye while pretending to look out the window. Her fake smile turned into a frown.

"Everything all right?"

"Of course. Fine," she said. "Finish your lunch. I don't want you to be hungry today."

He felt his eyebrows come together. He tried to act natural, forcing a neutral expression. "Why would I go hungry? I own a store full of food."

"All I meant was..." She stopped, looking at Danny for help.

Danny sat up straight and looked him in the eye. "Uncle Willie, we made an appointment for you today with another doctor in Traverse City. A specialist."

A what? With another doctor? Oh, no, *not* good.

"He's got an excellent reputation, and apparently he knows Dr. Dillon, so he made room for you to come in at two o'clock. We're leaving in twenty minutes."

So that's what all the cloak and dagger was about. "We most certainly are not. I'm not seeing another doctor when I have a perfectly good one right here."

Willie tried to stay calm. They couldn't make him go.

"Dr. Dillon is good at the regular stuff," Cassie said, "but he can't seem to find what's wrong with you. We've waited three weeks. We can't wait any longer."

Willie saw the tears in his niece's eyes. Dill was right. He needed to bring this charade to a close. "All right, you two..."

But he wasn't sure how to say it. He sat back in his chair and looked from one to the other. He opened his mouth to try to explain, but he couldn't. He hadn't figured out yet how to come clean without tearing them apart.

Danny gave a short nod. "All right, then."

"No, no, no." Willie tossed his napkin on his plate. That's not what he meant.

He stood up. He couldn't remember the last time he'd

walked away from a perfectly good meal. "I'm not agreeing to go with you."

Danny stood and took a step closer. "We're not going to let you die just because you're afraid of the hospital."

Willie looked up at the younger man, several inches taller with a lot more — and younger — muscle. He narrowed his eyes. "What are you going to do about it?"

"Hog-tie you and toss you in the back of my truck, if I have to," he shot back, fire in his eyes.

"Danny—"

"Exactly what you'd do to me if you thought it was necessary."

Well, he had him there. If Willie thought Danny was dying and not going to the hospital to do something about it, neither youth nor strength would keep Willie from finding a way to get Danny the help he needed.

He grunted and turned away. Dagnabit! How had he gotten himself into this situation?

Willie heard Danny follow him. He shouted over his shoulder, "I'm going to the bathroom! Can't a man go to the toilet in peace anymore?"

"Fifteen minutes," Danny called back. There was a mile of steel in his voice.

Inside the bathroom, Willie locked the door and leaned against the sink. He needed to come up with the right words to clear up the situation without hurting the kids. Bad enough the whole town thought he was dying. He'd have to deal with that later.

If only he'd said Dill *had* done a few more of the tests. He could call him now, and together they could proclaim a miracle, that he wasn't dying. But Willie had made the wrong move there saying Dill was still deciding which tests to run.

Okay, then maybe he should go to the other doctor and let him proclaim Willie healthy. The kids would believe him.

But it might ruin Dill's excellent reputation. He couldn't do that to his best friend. And besides, Dill would certainly defend himself when push came to shove.

Willie sighed and shoved his hand through his hair. Think, think. He finally pulled out his phone. Dill had helped him get into this pickle, he could help him get out.

"I told you it was a bad idea," Dill sputtered when he got on the line.

"You did not," Willie whispered back fiercely. "You loved it. You wanted to help me, and it worked. They're together. Now help me put a stop to the dying part."

"The older you get, the worse your memory is—"

"Dill, they're waiting in the kitchen ready to take me by force to some doctor in T.C."

"Oh." The surprise came through in his voice. "Well... where are you?"

A knock sounded on the bathroom door. "You okay in there?" Danny asked.

"Privacy!" Willie shouted. He turned on the water tap. Into the phone, he said, "I'm hiding in my own bathroom trying to think of a way to convince them I'm not dying — without screwing up the good work we've done. I don't want to see any doctors, not even a friend of yours. I hate hospitals."

"A friend of mine? Who—"

"Focus, Dill. I'm hiding in the *bathroom*. What are we going to do?"

Dill was quiet for a moment. Finally, he said, "I don't see how you can tell them anything but the truth."

Willie rubbed his eyes. That's the only plan he could

come up with, too. Stupid plan. It was going to hurt the ones he loved most. "How?"

Dill must've heard the crack in his voice. Willie didn't know if it was the doctor part of him that wanted to help people, or the best friend part of him who had always been there for Willie. But he said, "I'll be right there. Hold them off."

CHAPTER 22

 $\mathcal{C}$ assie twisted her hands together and paced the living room. "I knew he wouldn't want to go. We both knew it. What are we going to do? Break down the door?"

Danny stood at the front window, arms crossed tightly in front of him, staring into space. "Give him time to adjust. He'll come with us."

His voice sounded strained. Cassie paced over to him and put a hand on his arm. "We'll find a way to help him. We won't let him die."

Danny stood stiff and still until she started to turn away. He pulled her into his arms and they held each other tightly. She felt him press his face into her hair and breathe heavily. He was dealing with this about as well as she was.

Which was to say, not well at all.

It was impossible not to wonder what was going to happen, how long until Uncle Willie started showing symptoms of his illness, how long until...

They had to get him to Traverse City. Munson had

amazing doctors and specialists there, some of the best in the country. Surely they could help.

"Maybe we should call Dr. Dillon," she said. "He can convince Uncle Willie that it's time for a second opinion. We'll tell him about his friend over there making time for us today."

Danny kissed her forehead. "Good idea. Do it."

A touch of relief mingled with a ray of hope. Of course Dr. Dillon would help. That's what doctors did.

Cassie pulled out her phone and checked her Contacts. Darn, she hadn't added him. She found her purse, pulled out her wallet, and found Dr. Dillon's card from when she and Danny had visited him. She dialed and waited.

"I'm sorry, but the doctor had to leave for an emergency," the receptionist said.

Cassie felt her stomach twist. "Do you know how long he'll be gone? Is there any way to contact him? Cell phone?"

"I'm sorry, I can't give out his cell phone number. I can take a message."

It would be too late. If they didn't leave soon, they'd miss the appointment in Traverse City.

"No, thank you, I'll try back later." Cassie hung up. "He had to leave for an emergency," she told Danny. "We've got to get him out ourselves. What can we say to make him want to go?"

Danny snorted. "No one wants to go to the hospital."

Cassie marched over to the bathroom. "Uncle Willie," she called through the door. He didn't answer. "It's not really the hospital, it's just a doctor's office. And he's not going to take your blood or anything, no needles, just talk to you, ask about your symptoms." She waited. Nothing. "It's really nothing to be afraid of. And Danny and I will be with you. Or not. Whatever you want."

She looked to Danny. He shook his head. Cassie leaned her head back against the wall. What else could she say?

A knock at the front door startled her.

She met Danny's questioning gaze, then hurried to open the door. "Dr. Dillon! We were just trying to reach you at your office. Please, come in."

The tall, kindly man ducked his head as he entered, his expression grim. He nodded at Cassie and Danny but didn't say a word. He stopped in the middle of the living room and cleared his throat. "Willie," he called toward the bathroom.

Cassie reached for Danny's hand. He wrapped his arm around her and held her close. She put her other hand on his chest, feeling his heartbeat under her hand. Normally, the strong, steady beat calmed her. But it pounded faster than usual. She held on tight. Whatever happened, they'd get through it together.

The click of the door lock, the soft squeak of the hinges, and Uncle Willie poked his head out of the bathroom. Cassie had the oddest sensation, just for a moment, of watching a child peek out to see if he was in trouble.

Her uncle nodded to his friend. "Thanks for coming."

"We're not giving up," Danny said suddenly. "We're not going to sit back and wait for you to die. You're going to the hospital. If not today, I'll kidnap you in your sleep."

Uncle Willie looked startled. "Ya see?" he said to Dr. Dillon.

The doctor shook his head. "It's time," he said. "Long past."

Cassie took a step forward. "Tell us." She brushed a tear

off her cheek. She was determined to be strong for whatever came next.

"Everybody sit," Uncle Willie said, motioning Cassie and Danny to the couch.

They complied, sitting on the edge, leaning forward, holding hands tightly. Uncle Willie and Dr. Dillon sat awkwardly on the loveseat.

Uncle Willie cleared his throat. He looked at his hands, at his friend, at the floor, but not at them.

Danny squeezed her hand painfully. She reached her other hand over and ran it soothingly up and down his forearm. He relaxed enough to let circulation return to her hand.

Uncle Willie cleared his throat again. "I, uh...I have to tell you two something, and you're not going to like it."

Cassie sucked in a breath. Danny let go of her hand and put his arm around her. She looked up at him and they shared a look. She took a calming breath. They could do this. She settled in closer to him and looked back at her uncle. "Go on. Just tell us."

Still staring at the floor, he said, "Let me start at the beginning. For as long as I can remember, Dill here has been my best friend. We've done half of everything together, including getting into trouble, and standing up for each other at our weddings, and pledging to be godfathers to each other's children. We've got a bond."

Cassie wondered where this was going.

"Back before we knew better, we took our pocket knives and we made a blood bond not to let anything come between us, especially girls. And we never did. If both of us liked a girl, neither of us dated her. Thank God, Velma and Barbara hooked us early enough that we never really had to put that promise to the test."

Uncle Willie finally looked at them. "You two have the same bond. I've seen it since you were tiny things. You did everything together. I watched you communicate without words. You were there for each other when your lives went to pieces. But then you let a girl come between you."

Cassie felt Danny stiffen. She put her hand on his knee, refusing to let him pull away.

"I understand. She was new and pretty and turned all the boys' heads. I don't blame you, Danny, for wanting to marry her. But when it didn't work out, you decided you were tainted somehow, no longer good enough for Cassie. Or maybe you were too proud to apologize and come home."

Danny opened his mouth and closed it, staying silent.

"Cassie, I wouldn't have blamed you for trying to move on with your life. But you didn't. Sure, you made a fine show of it. Except when Danny came home for this or that, your heart was on your sleeve for all the world to see."

Cassie wanted to argue, but she didn't know what to say. It was more true than she wanted to admit. Still, how did all this fit into his illness? Had worrying over them made him sick?

"Clearly, you didn't know how to get back to where you'd been, so I thought...I wanted to help. I..." Uncle Willie looked to his friend.

Dr. Dillon's expression slid into professional mode. He said softly, "Remember how I told you in my office, we're all dying, we just don't know when?"

Cassie nodded and felt Danny do the same.

"Knowing that, we need to live every day with purpose

and intention. Don't waste life wandering aimlessly. Decide what you want and go after it."

"What does this have to do with Uncle Willie?" Danny asked. "Are you saying you want to travel before you die? That's fine. Say the word and I'll max out every credit card I can find to help you do everything on your bucket list. We'll do anything we can to help you. But we don't want you to give up so fast. Just get a second opinion. That's all we're asking."

A thought grew in the back of Cassie's mind. She watched Uncle Willie and Dr. Dillon, their expressions, their body language. She thought back, trying to remember Uncle Willie acting at all unwell since he'd made his announcement three weeks ago. What struck her most was this: he'd seemed happier than he'd been in months since Danny had come back. Even more so since she and Danny had started dating.

"Oh my gosh," she whispered. Her hand slowly covered her mouth as the thought grew and formed. She sat up straighter. "Oh my gosh."

When Uncle Willie finally made eye contact, she knew. Without a doubt.

"What?" Danny asked. He looked from her to Uncle Willie and back. "What?"

Cassie felt tears run down her face, gathering speed as a myriad of emotions overwhelmed her. Shock and relief and anger and...fear. Fear that Uncle Willie's plan was going to backfire in about five seconds.

She speared the doctor with a look. "He's not sick, is he?"

"No," he said before turning to stare at his shoes.

Cassie could tell in Danny's posture, feel it in the pressure of his hands, when the full impact hit him.

"You-you lied to us," he stuttered, "about *dying*."

DANNY FELT THE BLOOD DRAIN FROM HIS HEAD. HE FELT dizzy, sick to his stomach. He'd felt this way a few times when he'd fallen or cut himself at a job site. Only this time, it wasn't his body that hurt.

"Why?" His voice came out as a croak. "The funeral plans and the will and leaving everything to..." He stopped as comprehension dawned.

He looked at Cassie and saw her tears, a pleading expression on her face.

He stood up suddenly, filled with rage. "Look what you've done to her." He pointed at Cassie as Uncle Willie shrank back. "*You* haven't held her while she cried for you. *You* haven't wiped hundreds of her tears—"

"Danny—" Cassie pulled at his hand but he ignored her.

"*You went fishing* while we begged God for answers, for a little more time with you. I've turned my life upside down for you, and now you're telling me it was all a lie? I might lose my job over this."

He heard Cassie's gasp and realized what he'd said. But he blamed that on Uncle Willie, too. "I've been thinking there's nothing I want more than to be a part of this family, a real part of it, legally and everything. You're practically my dad." His voice broke.

He pulled away from Cassie and stomped the few feet to stand over the man he'd called uncle as long as he could remember. "I already have a family who lies. If this is the kind of behavior your family engages in, I don't want any part of it."

Uncle Willie stood and tried to put his hand on Danny's arm. "I'm sorry, son. I—"

Danny pulled away. "Don't call me that." He hurried out the door and pounded down the steps, slamming his truck door before anyone could see his tears. He peeled out of the parking lot, heading for Jax's place.

He thought he'd found everything he wanted, that he'd finally made good choices, that he'd finally been able to put the past in the past. But it was clear to him now — *everyone lied*.

His mother and brother lied.

Lily lied.

Uncle Willie lied.

Cassie... He thought for a moment. Maybe Cassie was still the only person who hadn't lied to him about something important. As always, she was the one person he could count on.

But that didn't matter now. He needed to get back to Lansing, get back to work. Think later, drive now.

He grabbed his things and left Jax a note. He didn't want to talk to him or text with him now. He needed to drive. Thank goodness, Lansing was a couple hundred miles away.

He was lucky, and he knew it, that he didn't get pulled over on the way to Grayling. He passed every car, truck, and RV he could on the hilly two-lane road. Once he got on the freeway, he flew south, drinking the Mountain Dew he'd picked up at the gas station, and playing the radio as loud as he could stand it.

He turned off I-75 onto US 127. It was a straight shot from here. Not having to think about driving allowed other thoughts to creep in.

Uncle Willie wasn't going to die.

Relief hit him like a sledgehammer. His truck weaved in his lane and someone honked. His hand shook as he put his pop can in the drink holder. He wiped his eyes so he could see clearly, and put both hands on the wheel.

Thank you, God.

But where did that leave him? After the last few weeks in Loon Lake, he didn't know how to be satisfied with his life in Lansing. He felt like a dog without a home, just wandering, trying to survive.

His phone buzzed. Jax was calling for the third time. On the last ring, Danny hit the Accept button and put the phone on speaker. He cleared his throat and tried to pull himself together.

"Hey, brother." Jax said.

"Hey." His voice sounded almost normal when he spoke in single syllables.

"What's up?"

Danny knew the question was the umbrella for all the questions his friend wanted to ask.

"I'm on my way back to Lansing." That was kind of the answer to all the questions.

Except there was a niggling doubt that maybe Lansing *wasn't* the answer to his problems anymore.

"And when you get there?"

Danny hadn't thought that far. He'd needed to run, so he'd run. Seemed like he thought better when he was driving and he'd needed a destination.

"He lied, Jax. I thought he was going to die."

"Yup."

Danny drove in silence. "I didn't tell him I'm glad he's not dying."

"You can still tell him." After a moment, Jax said, "I'd feel better if you weren't driving while we talk."

After a moment, Danny turned on his blinker and pulled over to the side of the road. He turned off the engine and hit the switch for the hazard lights. He hit the button to cancel the speaker function and held the phone to his ear.

"Cassie called you?" he asked.

"Yup."

"How is she?"

"Not as good as you."

Danny rubbed his eyes. What a jerk he was. She'd just had a major shock and he'd left her all alone. Out loud, he said something very unkind about himself in relation to a donkey's cousin.

"Yup."

That brought out a grunt and half a smile. "You're a good friend."

Jax sighed. "Not that good."

Danny let his head fall back on the seat's headrest. "How many people knew?" His anger was dissipating. A part of him wanted to hang onto it, wrap it around himself like a shield. But a better part of him worked hard to let it evaporate.

"Willie, Dr. Dillon, me, and Tabitha. That's it. You know why he did it?"

"He wanted me to come home."

Jax repeated Danny's earlier unkind remarks. "I swear, you've got a doughnut-brain. There's a hole in the middle. Think about it, Danny. Think about the last few weeks. Who's been happy and why? Why would Willie go to such lengths? You think he thought this was funny?"

Of course Uncle Willie wouldn't think this was funny. So why would he do it? If not to get Danny home, then...

Right.

He said a few more stupid words about himself. "You're right, I do have a doughnut-brain." He sighed.

"Will you forgive me, brother?"

"Yeah. But don't do it again."

"I promise. So...what now? You gonna leave Cassie crying up here all by herself?"

What should he do? What his heart urged him to do meant taking a huge risk. *Huge*. He could fail. Again. And if he failed, he'd hurt way more than he hurt now.

Or he could try to live a life of safety. A boring, unhappy, safe existence.

"Why are you encouraging me to do something you won't do?" he asked his friend.

Jax chuckled. "I got issues, man. You know that."

"And I don't?"

"Hey, maybe if I see that it works out for you, I'll take a chance. Who knows?"

Danny snorted. "History says I'm not the best role model."

"That was a mistake. This wouldn't be." Jax sounded so sure of himself. "You know it, too, brother. It wouldn't be a mistake. It may not be easy but..."

Uncle Willie had said something like that, about marriage not being easy but being worth it with the right person.

Who could be more right than Cassie? There was no one he got along with better. She made him laugh. She made him feel strong. She even made him feel safe.

And he'd left her.

"I'm going to have to crawl back over broken glass to get her to take me back."

"You know she'd never make you do that." Jax's voice had an odd quality to it. Was he thinking about Cassie, or about Tabitha?

"She should," Danny said. "I deserve it."

"There should be a word for that," Jax mused, "for not getting the punishment you deserve."

"There is," Danny murmured, thinking again about Uncle Willie's advice. "Mercy."

He and Jax sat silently, miles apart, thinking their own thoughts. It occurred to him mercy was something his mom needed, too. Maybe it was something Cassie and his friends could encourage him to give her. He'd thought he couldn't live in the same town as his broken mother, but...maybe he could find a happy medium between totally ignoring her and being her emotional punching bag.

Mercy.

He'd need practice to get any good at it.

A sense of peace stole over Danny's heart, something he hadn't fully felt in a long time. Now that the dark cloud of imminent death wasn't hanging over him, he felt he could breathe again, think clearly once more.

"Listen, brother," he said to Jax, "can you watch over things for a few days? I gotta take care of business down here."

"You notice that you haven't said 'home' in relation to Lansing for a while?"

Danny grinned. "Huh. Interesting."

"Interesting," Jax agreed.

Feeling lighter, he looked around to see how far he'd

driven. "You wanna guess where your doughnut-brained friend is sitting?"

"Where?"

"Near the billboard for Cops & Doughnuts Bakery in Clare."

Jax laughed. "Well, go get yourself one, doughnut-brain, finish your business downstate, and get back home. People are waiting on you."

"I'm on it."

Danny hung up and pulled back onto the freeway, exited to get a doughnut the size of a salad plate, and tried not to speed too much as he continued south. He didn't want to be slowed down by getting pulled over.

He made lists in his head of everything he had to do, placed a couple of phone calls, and finally pulled into his apartment complex off Grand Avenue. If only he could snap his fingers and be done quick.

He needed to get back home to his girl.

CHAPTER 23

*C*assie's tears turned to sobs as she heard the front door slam shut. A moment later, an engine gunned and tires squealed. And then there was silence.

Her emotions were so tangled. She knew she needed to focus on relief that Uncle Willie was healthy and well. But she kind of wanted to throttle him.

She understood Danny's need to run away to think, but she wanted that option, too. Instead, she was sitting here dealing with the situation alone.

She was so angry, it came out as a roar of frustration. "*Why?* Why this? Couldn't you have found another way to interfere? What if he doesn't come back?" That was the fear she hadn't meant to voice. "What if he never talks to either of us again?"

Her body shook as her fears threatened to overwhelm her. Then the couch sagged next to her and Uncle Willie's strong arms held her tight.

"I'm sorry, darlin'. I'm so sorry."

She hugged him back, hard. Then she pulled away. "Are

you sure you're okay? Maybe the stress is...could..." She glanced at Dr. Dillon.

He rose and stood fidgeting. "He's fine, really. Probably outlive us all. I'm sorry, Cassie, for leading you to believe..." He looked to Uncle Willie and sighed.

"No, it's my fault, it was all my idea," Uncle Willie said next to her. "I didn't think it would get this far. I only wanted to make sure you two really *saw* each other again, clearly. You belong together and..."

"I feel like punching you right now," Cassie said into his shoulder.

Dr. Dillon must've heard her because he said, "Go ahead, he can take it. He's perfectly fit."

Uncle Willie growled, "Dill," and the doctor left. After the door closed, he said, "You probably should punch me. I deserve it." He let go of her with one arm and pointed to the bulge of his bicep where it met his shoulder. "Right there. Hard as you can."

Cassie choked out a half laugh. "Uncle Willie, I'm not going to hit you."

"Come on, didn't I teach you to punch properly when you were in elementary school?"

"No, you taught Danny to punch and you told us never to hit first." She was trying not to laugh, but it was easing the pressure inside.

"Well...I hurt you first, so you owe me one." His voice sounded broken at the end.

"Oh, Uncle Willie, I forgive you." Cassie hugged him hard. "Don't get upset. I don't want anything to happen to you."

He hugged her hard back. "If Velma were here, she'd be skinning me six ways from Sunday."

"If Aunt Velma were here, you wouldn't have gotten this far."

Uncle Willie nodded. He pulled back and held her shoulders. "You're right, you know why? Because she was a strong woman who knew how to handle me. You know how to handle Danny. He needs your strength. And you need him. You know that, right?"

Cassie bit her lip and nodded.

"Well, then..." He waited, his expression hopeful. "Go after him. We'll fix this." At her stern expression, he amended, "*You'll* fix this. By yourself. No more interfering from me."

She kissed his cheek and stood. "I'm going to wash my face and go find him."

She grabbed her keys and her purse and headed in the direction she thought the truck had gone. He wasn't in the first three places she'd checked. She stopped at Jax's but neither of the guys' trucks were in the driveway. Hoping her hunch was wrong, she knocked and tried the front door. It was open.

She walked in, looking for Danny's suitcase. It wasn't in the living room, the bedroom, or either of the closets. Her stomach filled with lead. She leaned against a wall, holding herself, trying not to cry, trying to think of what to do.

Danny had left.

He'd left her.

After a minute, she caught her breath and drove to Tabitha's. She had two customers, one getting a cut and one under a dryer, but a glance at Cassie's face and Tabitha hurried over.

"What happened?" she asked, taking Cassie's arm.

Cassie gave her the highlights, ending with, "He left."

She stared at Tabitha, unable to process the events of the last hour. "I don't know what to do."

Tabitha enveloped her in a hug. "I'm so sorry," she said, "this is my fault, too. Uncle Willie asked us to help him get you two together. I'm sorry it went so far. I hope you'll forgive me."

"I will if you help me figure out what to do."

Tabitha pulled two tissues from an embroidered canister on the counter and handed one to Cassie. They both blotted their eyes and cheeks. "What do you want to do?"

"I want to run after him," Cassie said immediately.

"And then what?"

Something in Tabitha's tone, in her expression, caused Cassie to stop and think. What *would* she do? Twist his arm to come back to Loon Lake? And then what? What if he said no? Worse, what if he said yes and regretted it the rest of his life?

It hit her that no matter how clear she'd been to men she'd dated that she had every intention of staying in Loon Lake, it was, in the end, her selfishness that ended those relationships. She refused to yield, to give up the one thing she wanted. When it came to where they would live, her boyfriends had always known it was her way or the highway.

Danny had just hit the highway.

Was that really what she wanted?

"What should I pack?"

Tabitha shrieked and hugged her. "I'm going to miss you!"

"ARE YOU SURE YOU HAVE EVERYTHING YOU NEED? DO YOU have enough money? I filled up your tank while you were packing." Uncle Willie held Pirate while he watched Cassie stack the last box next to the door.

She hugged him again. It felt so good to have no worries about his health. But the last few weeks had taught her not to take anyone for granted. Anything could happen. So she hugged him long and hard.

"I've got everything I need for now. I'll call you when I get there so you know I'm safe." She knew that was important to him.

"Tell him I'm sorry. Tell him I'll wait as long as he needs, he doesn't have to forgive me now."

Cassie couldn't hold onto her anger when she saw how badly Uncle Willie was beating himself up over his foolish plan. "He'll come around, don't worry."

They loaded her car, and clipped Pirate into the safety harness in the front seat. Cassie put the cooler of drinks and snacks on the floor on the passenger side so she could reach them easily, and slid her insulated water bottle into the drink holder between the seats.

Uncle Willie tried to give her more money, succeeded in giving her driving advice she didn't need, and finally kissed her and told her to get on the road so she wasn't driving in the dark. She chuckled and kissed him and waved as she turned toward Grayling and the freeway.

"Say goodbye, Pirate," she said, only a little bit wistful, "we may not be back again until the next holiday."

She honked and waved as she passed Tabitha's house with the beauty shop out front. A minute later, her phone beeped.

Go get him, girl.

Cassie grinned, hit the thumbs up emoticon, and put her phone down. The last thing she needed was to get in an accident on the way to the rest of her life.

She expected to feel sad, but she what she felt was fidgety. She wanted to hit the freeway and gun it. She wanted to knock on his door five minutes from now. She wanted to tell him about all her new decisions.

But she didn't want to call him. He'd try to convince her to turn around. She couldn't take another emotional meltdown right now, so she drove, choosing to believe it would all work out.

Somehow.

It was getting dark by the time she pulled into Danny's apartment complex. Pirate had needed a lot of bathroom breaks. Or at least he acted like it, and Cassie hadn't wanted to take a chance.

Sitting in her car in the gathering dusk, she stared at the light in Danny's apartment. He was home. Thank goodness. She wouldn't have to sit in her locked car for hours waiting for him, wondering how much of what she'd seen on TV crime dramas came from real life.

She took a deep breath and focused on what was important: proving to Danny that she loved him, not just saying it.

She looked around the apartment complex. She could get used to this. People moved to the city all the time. Her sisters would be thrilled.

Cutting off her thoughts, she unhooked Pirate from his harness and led him out to a grassy spot. "One more time, buddy, just to be sure," she said encouragingly.

Then she picked him up and headed up the stairs. She could do this.

She knocked. And waited.

The door opened, and there he stood, tall and stunning — and stunned.

"Cassie." He didn't move. "You remembered where I live."

Pirate yipped and wagged his butt.

Danny reached over and patted him, his eyes never leaving Cassie. She'd dressed for success tonight, and he noticed. His gaze swept over the button-down blue shirt with the deep V in front that he'd complimented her on last week, taking in the newer jeans that hugged her shape perfectly, coming back up over the soft pink sweater she wore on special occasions, and back to her face.

"Can I come in?" She tried to speak with authority, but even she heard the hesitation in her voice.

"Of course, sure, come in," he said, pulling the door wide and stepping back.

Pirate wiggled to get down and set about sniffing everything he could reach while still on his leash.

The apartment didn't look much different from the only other time Cassie had been here, a few years ago. She looked around, but pushed away the old memory. Danny had turned her down then, turned her away. It had been the last real conversation they'd had until Uncle Willie called them together a few weeks ago.

"Can I ask…" Danny hesitated. "Why…are you here?"

Cassie took a deep breath. She'd been practicing this speech for the last few hours and she was pretty sure she could nail it.

"Danny, I've been selfish. I didn't really realize it until

today, but now that I have, I'm going to change. I promise. I used to think that the most important thing in the world to me was making a life in Loon Lake, continuing to work with Uncle Willie, living in one of the greatest little towns I know. But it's not the most important thing in my life."

She took a deep breath and moved half a step closer, nervous and trying not to be. "You are. You're my best friend, you're the man I love, and I'm not going to lose you just because we want to live in different places. So…I packed my suitcase and I moved to Lansing."

"Oh, baby, no." Danny said.

That wasn't even close to what Cassie had thought he might say. She knew he might say no, but not like that.

He put a hand on her shoulder. "Uncle Willie did something stupid, really stupid, but you've got to forgive him. Don't quit and move away. I'm still a little ticked at him, too, but we'll get over it. It took me awhile to calm down and think about it, but your sisters helped me figure it out."

Now she was really confused. "You spoke to my sisters?"

He chuckled. "No, no. I mean, I was thinking about you and your family and how your sisters do so many irritating things because they love you. You get mad at them pretty frequently, but you always forgive them. And I realized, that's just life with people you love. Who am I to not forgive someone for doing something stupid? Huh?"

"I'm glad you feel that way because Uncle Willie feels just terrible. He said to tell you to take your time, forgive him when you're ready, no pressure."

Danny looked away and mumbled something like, "That old man."

"I don't want you to drive back in the dark," he said, "but

promise me you'll go back in the morning. Don't throw away your whole life because of a stupid mistake."

Cassie frowned, trying to figure out where her speech had gone wrong. "I'm not going back. I'm staying here with you. Not *here* here. But I'm going to get an apartment and a job and we'll continue our relationship and..." She couldn't exactly say, *and then we'll get married.* After all, he should ask her, not the other way around.

Danny was the one frowning now, still not understanding.

She tried to be crystal clear. "Danny, I didn't quit and leave because I'm angry at Uncle Willie. I left because I love you, and I want to be wherever you are, even if it's not Loon Lake." She swallowed, trying not to let her nerves show.

His eyes widened. "Oh." That's all he said. He stood there for a moment staring down at her. Then he moved a step closer and cupped her cheek in his hand. "But it's too late."

Cassie felt the breath leave her lungs. When Pirate pulled on his leash, her numb fingers let go. It was all she could do to stay standing.

Fight for him. Chase after him. Make him understand.

All the advice and encouragement Tabitha and Uncle Willie and even a text on the road from Jax — it all rushed into her mind and forced her to keep talking, try to convince him.

"No, it's not too late." She finally inhaled a good breath and the oxygen helped her brain to focus. "We're good together. We love each other, we have fun together, and we're just plain good for each other. You need me. You know you do, and I need you." She felt herself talking faster as she tried to make him understand. "This is the right decision. Even if it's hard, we can do this. Lansing's not Chicago or Ann Arbor. It's not a concrete jungle. I can be happy here."

"Not as happy as in Loon Lake," Danny said.

She could feel his breath against her cheek. His lips were telling her no, but his body seemed to be saying yes. The fight wasn't over yet.

"It's too late for us to live here." Danny took another step forward.

Cassie took a step back so she could focus without getting a crick in her neck. "Danny, you're not listening to me."

"Oh, I am, I'm listening to every word you're saying. You're not listening to me. When I left home this morning, I was angry and hurt and confused. But I got over it. I knew I had to make a decision. Either accept the love and friendship of a bunch of wonderful but flawed people, or hide out in a lonely, 'safe' half-life, not allowing anyone to get close enough to hurt me."

Cassie felt the wall at her back. Danny hadn't seemed to be moving, but his presence was overwhelming. The sound of his voice, the smell of his skin, the warmth of his hand on her cheek — they were mesmerizing. She desperately wanted to kiss him. But he was still talking.

"I may be slow, but I'm not stupid," he continued, his voice smooth and slow and thick like maple syrup. "I didn't get halfway before I realized my mistake."

"Mistake?" If leaving her had been a mistake, that was a good thing. She tried to focus, tried to stop thinking about kissing him.

"So for the rest of the trip, I worked on fixing my mistake. And I did. The wheels are in motion. So, yes, it *is* too late for you to think about moving down here. You see, I quit my job and gave notice on my apartment today."

Cassie gasped, her eyes widening as they met his. "You quit your job? Why?" She wanted to hear him say it.

He grinned and pressed his forehead to hers. "Because there's a girl up north I've been in love with for years, and I'm going back up there to win her back just as soon as I can get packed."

Joy washed over her like a flood. It poured over her mind and washed over her heart and settled into every part of her being. "Really?"

"Yup." He closed that last inch of space and kissed her. Not *just* a kiss. It was an *I love you and I'm never letting you go* kiss.

Cassie kissed him back with all the love and longing she had inside. She poured all the joy he'd given her back into that kiss, wanting him to feel what she felt. She kissed him in a way that she hoped God Himself would understand how grateful she was.

A few moments later, Danny backed up half a step and let go of her, resting his hands on the wall on either side of her head.

Cassie felt safe and secure there, giddy and yet with a river of peace running under her feet.

"Now," he said, his voice deep and rough, "we need to get you to a hotel."

"Why?"

Danny let out half a chuckle but it sounded pained. "Remember that kiss at lunch in the woods?"

Did she ever.

"Remember where it was headed?"

Cassie felt the heat rise in her face. Oh yeah, she

remembered. She remembered that she was embarrassed that she wasn't embarrassed to want to take all her clothes off right then and there.

"If you stay here tonight, Uncle Willie is definitely coming after us with a shotgun. And that's not how I want to start out my new life with you."

Cassie felt the joy bubbling up in her again, this time like a volcano about to blow. "You said, 'my new life with you.'" It was all she could do not to jump up and down and clap her hands with glee.

Danny grinned. "Yup," he drawled.

"So..." Cassie gazed into his eyes, never wanting to leave his side. "Do you have...any questions for me? Or anything?"

He leaned in slowly and kissed her. Against her lips, he whispered, "That's for me to know"—he kissed her again—"and for you to find out."

CHAPTER 24

*I*t was all Cassie could do to let Danny go. First, they got some dinner at a diner he knew that served great steaks. Then Danny called around and booked a room for her at a nearby Holiday Inn. Cassie tried to convince him that a Motel 6 was perfectly fine, but he insisted she sleep in a place where the room doors opened into the building, not the parking lot.

The Holiday Inn had a strict no-pets policy so he took Pirate back to his apartment. The next morning, they met for breakfast, spent too short a time kissing goodbye and, before she knew it, Cassie was back on the freeway headed north.

She grinned the whole way home.

Danny Kessler loved her.

Danny Kessler was moving back to Loon Lake to woo her.

After a lifetime of waiting, someday soon she was going to be Mrs. Danny Kessler.

She about swooned. A horn sounded, and she jerked the wheel.

Pirate cocked his head at her.

"I know, I know, pay attention to the road." She rubbed his head. "But Pirate, you don't understand how amazing this is!" She laughed and kept driving.

She'd promised Danny not to text or talk on the drive home. The way she'd been acting since last night, he must've figured out that she wouldn't be able to focus on anything else if she were telling someone about her and Danny.

The drive seemed to take forever, but daydreaming about Danny the whole time made the trip feel about five minutes long. Soon she was pulling into her driveway in front of the Fluff and Fold. She grabbed Pirate and bounced up the stairs. "Uncle Willie," she called. But he wasn't home.

She jogged across the street to The Laughing Loon. "Uncle Willie!" She hurried behind the counter, glad there were no customers waiting to be served.

"What are you doing here? What happened?" He hugged her and stepped back. His initial worried expression gave way to one of tender bemusement.

"He's coming back! Danny quit his job and gave notice on his apartment and he's coming back." Cassie bounced on her toes and Pirate yipped happily at her shoulder.

"What did you say to convince him to do that?"

"It wasn't me," Cassie insisted. Her uncle was looking at her like she'd gone off-plan and twisted Danny's arm to come back. "I told him I was moving to Lansing, and he said it was too late, that he'd already done those things when *he* was driving down there. He's packing and coming back as soon as it's all taken care of."

Uncle Willie looked the happiest he had in years. "And?"

Cassie sighed and let her eyes fall closed as she leaned

against the counter. "He said there's a girl up here he has to win back."

Her uncle gave her a great big hug and kiss. "I'm so happy for you, darlin'."

Cassie bounced toward the door. "I gotta run. I have to tell Tabitha, and we have to decide what to do with my hair, and I should go to Traverse and get some new clothes, and then—"

"Go, go," Uncle Willie laughed and waved her away.

"Bye!" She laughed as she pulled open the door. The tinkling bell sounded like every wish coming true.

"I love you," she heard her uncle call.

"I love you," she shouted as she ran for her car.

WATCHING CASSIE BOUNCE FROM ONE PLACE TO THE NEXT over the next several days was making him dizzy. When she wasn't texting Danny, she was talking to him on the phone late at night, her voice all dreamy and soft.

But Willie could hardly be unhappy about it. This was what he wanted, what he knew they'd all wanted deep inside. He'd gone about pushing them together in the wrong way — he still regretted how he'd hurt them both — but he was thrilled that it was all working out. The Lord and His mercy.

Danny had texted him last night and asked if they could meet this afternoon down at Sandy Beach Park. He wanted to talk privately before he saw Cassie again.

Willie hoped his guess was correct regarding the topic. But he braced himself just in case the conversation went sideways. Cassie made it sound like Danny had forgiven him, but they hadn't actually spoken yet.

He sat on the edge of a picnic table waiting, hoping, and praying that all would be well. Half an hour of that and he saw Danny's truck pulling a bright orange rental trailer through the twisting driveway of the park. Willie stood and raised his arm.

As he watched Danny park and walk over, he held onto the words he needed to say. When he was close enough, he said, "Danny, I—"

Danny pulled him into a bear hug. Willie felt his heart rise to his throat as he held onto the younger man. After a few moments, they pounded each other on the back and stepped back.

"I'm sorry," Willie said, forcing himself to meet Danny's eyes.

"Forgiven. I'm sorry for leaving like that, and I'm really sorry for the terrible things I said." Danny held his gaze, but it looked like it was equally hard for him.

"Forgiven." Uncle Willie held out his hand and they shook, gripping each other's shoulder and letting go.

After a semi-awkward pause, Willie asked, "How was the trip?"

"Easy. Jax and I loaded up the two trailers by mid-morning. He was right behind me, probably home now. I'm lucky to have a friend like him."

Danny gestured for them to sit at the picnic table. "I'm lucky with all the friends I have. Blessed, in fact."

"Same here. Good friends change your life." Willie thought about what he'd asked his best friend to do. "Or they go along with you when you screw things up."

"Well, that's probably good," Danny said. "I'd hate to have been alone all the times I screwed up."

Willie nodded and smiled. Danny really was going to forgive and forget. Thank God.

Danny cleared his throat and sat up a little straighter. "So, I wanted to talk to you privately for a minute."

Willie tried to keep his expression neutral. "Sure." He hoped he knew what was coming next, though he hadn't thought about it or expected it until Danny had asked to meet.

The younger man rubbed his hands on his jeans, then folded them in front of him on the picnic table. "Sir," he said, his eyes meeting Willie's, "I'd like your permission to marry Cassie, and I'd like you to give us your blessing."

Hard as he tried to match Danny's serious expression, Willie found a grin nearly breaking his face in half. "You have my permission and my blessing."

Danny wilted for a moment, then looked up through his eyelashes. "I was pretty sure you were going to say that, but I was still really nervous all the way up here."

They laughed together and Danny relaxed. "I know Cassie and I have a lot to talk about. We have to decide where to live, what we can afford, what kind of wedding she wants and where and how much that will cost, and a hundred other questions. So I guess the first thing you and I need to do is figure out what my job is, how much I should really get paid — because I think you've been paying me too much — and how I fit into your retirement plan. You know I'm willing to work hard, sir, but I'd like to know what you expect of the man marrying your niece so we don't disappoint each other."

Willie was glad he didn't have a heart problem because right now his heart was about to burst with love and pride for the young man in front of him. He couldn't speak for a moment, so he patted Danny's hand and looked out at the lake.

"Why don't you go kiss that girl of yours hello before she explodes, and we'll go fishing tonight, just you and me, son."

CHAPTER 25

From the moment Danny kissed Cassie goodbye in Lansing to the moment he kissed her hello again in Loon Lake, he'd been thinking about the perfect way to propose to her. He wanted to do it in a way that meant something special to the two of them. He'd thought up and discarded a hundred ideas, but one of them kept tickling his mind as something Cassie would like.

He finally asked Jax, who agreed they should ask Tabitha. She said the plan was incredibly juvenile and undeniably sweet.

Perfect.

Danny grinned at his friends. "She's going to love it, isn't she?"

The three of them started brainstorming what needed to be done. Jax suggested Danny buy flowers. Tabitha insisted no, it would clue Cassie in as to what was about to happen.

Danny watched them argue, really seeing them for once. They danced around their attraction to each other, Jax saying something immature just to get a reaction from her, Tabitha putting up a bossy shield to keep from laughing. How could they not see they were perfect for each other?

But then, who was he to talk?

He texted Uncle Willie to say he'd swing by to pick them up for church on Sunday. Uncle Willie texted back that he shouldn't change their routine so that Cassie wouldn't become suspicious.

Lying on Jax's couch Saturday night, Danny wondered why he'd let so many people get involved in his proposal in the first place. Everyone had an opinion about what he should do and how he should do it. Sheesh.

Then he grinned in the dark. This was what he was buying into. Family. They were all so interfering because they loved him and they loved Cassie, and this was their way of showing it.

It took him forever to fall asleep that night. He wanted to text Cassie, ask her if she was thinking of him, ask her if she'd seen the moon tonight, brilliant and full.

He wanted to ask her to marry him right this minute.

But he controlled himself. Just barely. He wanted to give her something special to remember forever, even when they were old and gray and couldn't remember much of anything.

Old and gray. He felt himself smile even as he finally drifted to sleep.

He woke suddenly the next morning, afraid he'd overslept. He calmed down when he saw it was just after seven. He pulled back the curtain to see an overcast sky hinting at rain. Good thing his plans were for indoors.

Half an hour before church, Cassie texted.

Might rain. Want to pick us up for church?

"Ha!" Danny shouted triumphantly. Having so many cooks in the kitchen made him feel vindicated when something went his way.

> Sure. Be there in a few. P.S. It'll cost you.

They texted back and forth a couple more times, determining how many kisses were required for taxi service. Danny finally looked up to see Jax rolling his eyes.

Danny just grinned at him. "You about ready?"

"I'll wait a few minutes until I know you're all inside," Jax said, "then I'll bring the flowers over to Tabitha and meet you after. Got everything?"

Danny patted his pockets for the fourth time. "Yup. See you soon."

Above the Fluff and Fold, he knocked and walked in. A fleeting image crossed his mind of Cassie walking toward him, then presenting her back and asking him to zip up her dress. It seemed like ages ago, but it was only a few weeks. Soon, he'd be doing that every day.

Though he hoped he'd be *un*dressing her more than helping her dress.

The thought made him grin just as the woman on his mind exited her bedroom. She looked absolutely kissable in a red dress and red shoes.

"Morning," she sang out.

They walked to each other and stood staring and grinning and looking foolish, Danny was sure.

"Payment, please."

She took a step closer. "I believe we agreed on three kisses for a ride."

She put her hands on his chest and leaned into him. She kissed him sweetly on the lips. "One."

Danny tried to stand still and take it but he couldn't do it. The second kiss lasted longer and made him want more. He moved his hands to her waist.

"Two," she said when she pulled away.

He leaned forward, capturing her lips with his. Every movement of her mouth and hands made him want more. He pressed forward, one hand moving down her back, down to—

Uncle Willie cleared his throat.

Danny jumped, his hands moving to her elbows as he eased her away.

"Three," she whispered with a giggle.

Danny shook his head at her. She was going to get him in trouble before he could even propose.

"Good morning, Uncle Willie," he said, trying to sound casual and not like he'd just been breathing heavily.

"Morning," Uncle Willie replied with a nod. "You ready?"

Danny tried to act natural. "I think so. Yes. Yes, I'm ready." Now that Uncle Willie had asked, though, he began to feel his nerves kick in. If only he could pop the question now and get it over with.

Cassie giggled again. "Come on, then," she said, grabbing his hand and heading for the door.

"Get used to it," Uncle Willie said from behind him. "You'll be on her schedule from now on."

THE LAST TEN DAYS HAD SEEMED SURREAL, EVEN MORE THAN those first days a few weeks ago after Danny had first kissed her.

Now she knew that he not only loved her, but was intent on pursuing her. She wanted to tell him, *you have me, just ask me*. But his words kept repeating themselves in her head: *That's for me to know and for you to find out.*

Every day she wondered how he would propose. And every day that went by, she wondered how much longer she'd have to wait. She kept her patience by reminding herself that every day drew her closer to the day he'd ask the big question.

But sometimes a niggling doubt would get in through a crack and she'd wonder if it was all in her head, if she'd misunderstood him, if there would be no marriage proposal.

Then they'd talk on the phone until midnight about a hundred inconsequential things. More than once he'd started a sentence with "I can't wait until..." and her fears would abate. At the end when they both hung up, Cassie was sure again that he loved her.

This morning when she woke up, the sun was hiding, the clouds hovered steel gray, the air had a bite to it — but her heart was singing before she was fully awake. She said thank you to God about a hundred times before she even got out of bed. Someday soon, Danny would decide how he wanted to propose. And Cassie could begin planning the rest of her life.

Just like when he needed time to think during an important discussion, Cassie reminded herself that he needed time now to do things his own way. No matter that she wanted to ring up the church and ask what days were free for weddings this summer. No matter that she had to bite her tongue when she saw Pastor Nick and his wife, Sarah, at the grocery store on Thursday and she wanted to ask about marriage counseling and how long she'd have to wait to get married.

If it killed her, she'd wait for Danny to do what he was going to do in his own time. This was his moment as much as it was hers and she wouldn't ruin it for him. She already knew what she was going to say — *Yes!* — and what she was going to do — throw her arms around him and hug him and kiss him until neither one could breathe. She just didn't know what he was going to do or when.

Would it be something as wild as skywriting? Probably not practical with so many tall trees around Loon Lake. It would be difficult to see a big enough patch of the sky to get the question out.

Would it be something as quiet and sweet as sitting at the end of the dock together, talking and holding hands, and then he'd hand her a ring box? She loved that idea, but she'd thought about it often enough to already be terrified she'd drop the ring into the lake.

Maybe it'd be something traditional like over dinner at a fancy restaurant. That didn't sound much like Danny, but if that's what he chose, she'd enjoy every moment of it.

When he picked up her and Uncle Willie for church this morning, Cassie felt so full of joy and life that she didn't even care about when he'd ask. She was just thrilled to see him, to kiss him, to hold his hand, to sit next to him in church and catch him watching her when he should be paying attention.

They made it through the whole service without embarrassing themselves, though Cassie did let her mind wander during The Lord's Prayer and she had to peek at the screen at the front to get the words right.

She sighed happily when Pastor Nick gave the benediction and the organist played the leaving-church music. She squeezed Danny's hand and looked up at him, knowing her heart was showing all over her face. "So what do you want to do today?"

"Well, uh, I thought maybe we'd ask Jax and Tabitha if they want to have lunch with us." Danny's voice sounded strained.

"Everything okay?"

"Oh, yeah, yeah, sure, no problem. Uncle Willie, want to have lunch with us?"

"Sure, if you kids don't mind my company." Uncle Willie smiled benignly when Cassie glanced at him.

"Of course we don't mind," she said with a smile.

Danny took her hand and pulled her through the church sanctuary and into the lobby.

"Danny," she said with a laugh as she almost bumped into the third person in as many minutes, "it'll take awhile for Tabitha to be free. She can't leave until all the parents collect their children. Slow down, will you?"

Just then, one of Willie's friends stopped them. Cassie and Danny paused to say hi, then started inching away. "We'll find you after we get Tabitha," Cassie said to her uncle.

"No, no, I'm coming," Uncle Willie said. "Sorry, Frank, off to lunch with the kids. I'll talk to you later."

Cassie turned back to see Frank's surprised expression. "Uncle Willie, it's okay, we'll wait for you."

"It's fine, I'll talk to him tomorrow." When Cassie started to argue, he continued, "It looks like it's going to rain and I don't want us to be caught in it. Rather get to the restaurant before a cloud bursts."

Cassie nodded as if that made perfect sense, but she couldn't shake the feeling that Uncle Willie was keeping something from her again. The last secret had been a horrendous idea, so one would think he'd learn. She hoped he wasn't about to do something stupid again.

They turned a corner and slowed to get through the wall of people. Kids ran around and through groups of adults, laughing and yelling. Cassie smiled and patted the head of Tabitha's adorable daughter, Summer, who backed into her, eyes fixed on the construction paper roses attached to her black Mary Janes.

Danny's grip on her hand tightened as they approached the first and second graders' room where Tabitha taught Sunday School every other week. They waited for a dad to sign for his son, the sticker on the boy's back reading "Junior." Cassie hoped Danny was fine with her vetoing "Junior" as a name for any of their children.

She walked up to the half door and greeted her friend. "Hey, wanna have lunch with us? We're making a party of it."

"Sounds fun," Tabitha said. "I've just got a few more kids here and then I'm free."

Cassie counted four kids left. "Wow, how did you get rid of so many so fast?" She laughed. "And is there some kind of parent convention in the hall? I haven't seen the Sunday School area this jammed up since Christmas."

"Must be something going on," Tabitha said with a shrug. She grinned at Danny. "How you doing? You feeling all right?"

Cassie looked more closely at Danny's face. "You do look a little pale. Are you okay?"

Danny sent Tabitha a sour look. "I'm fine. I was just

looking at something. Cassie, remember the felt board they used to explain Bible stories when we were kids? They've still got one. Come here."

He opened the half door and walked in the room, heading for an easel with a felt-covered board on it sitting in the corner.

Cassie asked Tabitha, "Is it okay if we come in?"

Tabitha grinned and nodded her head. Cassie looked at her strangely, but followed Danny. Tabitha sure was in a good mood today.

"Check this out," Danny said, pulling some felt cut-outs from a pouch on the back of the board. "Remember when we used to play with these?"

Cassie chuckled. "What I remember is you getting in trouble for some of the stories you told with the Bible characters. Like when you had Jesus standing next to a table piled with fish and you said he was selling them so he could take the apostles to Disney World."

Danny grinned. "It could've happened — if Disney World had existed back then."

"And then you convinced me to try to help you catch enough fish to sell them and go to Disney World ourselves," Cassie reminded him. They'd made it about three days before they got bored and decided to use their money and ask Uncle Willie and Aunt Velma to take them to the movies. That was a fun day. Cassie had almost forgotten about it.

Danny sorted through some of the felt figures. "We had a lot of good times here. Hard to believe it was twenty years ago, huh? Who'd have thought we'd be standing in the same room in front of this felt board today?"

Cassie thought for a moment. "Twenty-one, I think. I

hadn't turned five yet. We met the Christmas before I went to kindergarten."

"The chairs look so tiny now," Danny mused. "They seemed perfect at the time. Sit down." He lowered his voice. "I'll make up another story for you."

She laughed. "I'm afraid my dress would hike up." She looked over to Tabitha who was signing out the second to last of her charges. "And I don't want to get in trouble."

"Come on, sit," Danny said. He held out a little red chair for her. "It goes with your dress."

She rolled her eyes and played along, trying to keep her dress from embarrassing her. "It feels like I'm sitting on the floor." She laughed. "You try it."

Danny started placing felt figures on the board. "Once upon a time, there was a boy and a girl who became best friends." He put a cutout of a group of children on the board.

"Until the boy did something stupid." He put a cutout of a man in a Bible-era robe on the board, followed by a big yellow diamond-shaped star.

Danny made a face as if the Bible man was an idiot. Obviously, the star of Bethlehem was standing in for Bright Shiny. Cassie laughed.

"One day, the boy finally figured out that the Bible story stuff really worked, the girl had really forgiven him and still loved him."

The star was replaced by a smiling Bible-era woman in robes.

Cassie's heart picked up its pace. Could today be the day? She tried to act normal in case Danny was just playing around, but she felt herself breathing faster.

Danny caught Cassie's gaze and winked at her, mischief written all over his face. "Then they kissed." He moved the two adult figures so that their heads touched, and turned and waggled his eyebrows at her. "Good ending, huh?"

Cassie shook her head and rolled her eyes. Goofy Danny, just playing around. She couldn't help but grin at him. He certainly could make her laugh. It was one of the things she loved most about him. She'd have to be patient a while longer.

Danny pulled a blue chair from around the little table and sat down. "You're right, these are too small to be comfortable." He kneeled in front of her.

On one knee.

Cassie felt her mouth open as she watched him. Was he going to…?

Danny grinned his wicked handsome grin at her.

Yes!

She turned to see if Tabitha was watching. Her mouth dropped open more. Tabitha, Jax, and Uncle Willie huddled a few feet away, all three of them with grins almost as big as Danny's. Behind them, a dozen or more people were crowded around the open door, everyone trying to see in, everyone grinning.

Danny cleared his throat.

Cassie's head whipped back to focus on him.

He took both of her hands in his, staring into her eyes with all seriousness. "The first day I met you, we were playing in this room. I thought you had the sweetest smile I'd ever seen, and I couldn't believe how smart you were, especially since you were younger than me."

Cassie felt her throat closing. She didn't want to cry now, she wanted to enjoy this.

"I don't know who started following who, all I remember is that we became friends forever that day. Best friends.

You're the one I wanted to tell my secrets to. You're the one I wanted to share my successes — such as they were — with."

Cassie wanted to interrupt and remind him of all the wonderful things he'd done so far in his life. But since she was pretty sure she couldn't speak, she let him continue.

Danny leaned closer. "I even remember the first day I started wondering what it would be like to kiss you."

"What?" Cassie heard someone call out in a stage whisper.

"He wants to kiss her," someone else whispered loudly.

"No, he wanted to kiss her in kindergarten."

"No, he said—"

"Shh!"

Cassie tried to hold it in, but a giggle burst out. Danny chuckled and shook his head. He looked down at his shoe, probably trying to get his thoughts straight again.

Cassie whispered, "Welcome home to your family."

Danny chuckled again. "Yay," he said with uneven enthusiasm, making Cassie giggle some more.

Danny cleared his throat and looked serious again. "I've made some mistakes over the last twenty years, a lot of mistakes. And I can guarantee that I'll make far more than I want to in the next sixty years. But if you'd be willing to walk this path with me, I promise to do everything I can to make you proud, to love you more than anyone else ever could, and to never, ever leave you."

Cassie's lower lip quivered. She pressed her lips together, trying not to cry. Her eyes filled with tears, but they didn't spill over. As much as she'd looked forward to this moment, her heart was moved more deeply than she could have imagined.

Danny reached into the front pocket of his khaki trousers and pulled out a sapphire blue ring box.

He opened the top so that the beautiful ring faced her. Cassie felt more than heard a whimpering noise in the back of her throat. The ring was perfect. A simple gold band with a medium-sized diamond in the center and a tiny diamond on either side. It was so *her*.

Danny held the ring box in one hand and grasped her left hand in the other. Cassie could feel the strength of emotion running through his tight, somewhat-clammy grip.

"Cassiopeia Michelle Lane, would you do me the great honor of becoming my wife? Will you marry me?"

The last thing Cassie saw clearly over the next few minutes was that beautiful, hopeful, loving look on Danny's face as he asked her that life-changing question. Then all the tears she'd been holding in fell like rain and she couldn't see.

"Yes," she cried. "I'll marry you, Danny Kessler." And she fell into his arms.

Literally.

The child's chair couldn't have been more than six inches off the ground and was not made for the weight of an adult. When she leaned forward, the chair went flying backward, hitting the bookcase. She pitched forward into Danny's arms. He managed to keep them both from falling all the way over only because his right knee was still planted firmly on the carpet.

But between the kissing and falling and catching and laughing and more kissing, Cassie also heard the cheering and clapping and hooting. She and Danny held onto each other tightly while she wet his shirt with happy tears.

Tabitha put a box of tissues on the tiny kids' table next to the bucket of Lego bricks, and Cassie wiped her face enough to see again.

Danny pulled the ring out of the box and slipped it on her left ring finger. It fit perfectly. They grinned at each other and kissed again. Then Danny pulled her to her feet and presented her be-ringed hand to their audience.

Pastor Nick and his wife had pushed their way in to stand next to Uncle Willie. They clapped and cheered, and Tabitha and Sarah wiped their eyes with more tissues.

With such an audience, Danny flashed Cassie a mischievous wink and bowed. She curtsied to more applause and cheers, and they both laughed. For a moment, she thought she knew a bit of what it must be like to be Princess Kate, even better than Cinderella.

Danny leaned in and whispered, "I wanted to give you a Ring Pop candy ring, but Tabitha insisted I keep the immaturity to a minimum today."

Cassie laughed. "I still would've said yes," she whispered back, "but I really like *this* ring."

Uncle Willie stepped forward and hugged Cassie hard, then kissed both of her cheeks. "Your mother and aunt are so happy right now," he said. "I know it."

A few new tears slipped out, and Cassie held him tight. "I love you, Uncle Willie."

"I love you more."

Then it was Tabitha's turn, and Jax's, and Nick and Sarah's, and a dozen more friends.

Eventually, Danny pulled her back into his arms. As people filed out of the Sunday School room, Danny spoke quietly in her ear. "Did you like this? Was it good enough?"

"Oh, Danny, it was perfect. I loved it!" She ran her hand over his cheek. "I love you so much. I would've said yes no matter how you asked." She leaned in and kissed his cheek three or four times, trying to control herself.

He gave her his lopsided grin. "I thought about proposing in the Fluff and Fold since we spent more time there than anyplace else growing up. I was going to tell you it was a clean start."

Cassie laughed. "I like it."

"But then I thought about how this was where we actually met, and this is a foundation we can build on. It's kind of a permanent, unlimited-use restart button."

Cassie was sure her joyful heart was not only on her sleeve, but written all over her face and radiating out from every cell. "It's the best marriage proposal ever."

And the start of the next and absolutely best part of her life.

A PEEK AT LITTLE MISS LOVESICK

AVAILABLE NOW AT MAJOR ONLINE RETAILERS

We were all going to die.

My great escape into the wilderness of Michigan's Upper Peninsula to vanquish Heartbreak from my life was going to end in my early demise. And here I thought it was my broken heart that was killing me.

We'd been driving for over seven hours. The last town snuck past us an hour ago when we'd turned off the paved road. Pavement became gravel, then dirt, then two-tracks. The wooden hand-painted signs with arrows and mileage that marked our way made it feel like we were driving through another world. Like the kids through the wardrobe in the Narnia books. Okay, that part sounded kind of nice, actually.

Dirk would hate it here. No tennis courts in the forest. No skim lattes with soy milk and a sprinkle of cinnamon. And he certainly wouldn't drive his BMW down a two-track through the woods with the top down.

I sighed. This was harder than I thought it'd be, getting Dirk out of my head. If I could exorcise him from my head, I'm sure my heart would heal faster. I was so tired of crying, of whining, of wishing life was different. All I wanted was to settle down with a husband and a house and a dog and 2.4 kids. I knew exactly how I wanted to decorate our home. I'd planned the kinds of parties we would have. We'd be part of the Neighborhood Watch team, and we'd plan block parties for 4th of July. We were going to have the perfect life together.

Then it all ended. Abruptly. Without warning. And I thought I was going to die. But that was four months ago. I had to find a way to get my life back again. Hence the trip into the wilderness.

Then I remembered we were *all* going to die. Who knew there was this much wilderness out there?

"How much gas do we have?" I called from the back of the fifteen-passenger van. I could just see the obituary.

Ten city girls who should have known better died last

*week when they drove a van through the wilderness without
gassing up in the last town.*

Yeah, that's the way I can see my life ending right now.
Great.

"There's plenty of gas, don't worry," said Patty.

Patty McEntyre had organized this fly-fishing trip — an
idea I'd loved before I became convinced of our imminent
deaths. Patty had become my Mom-away-from-home since
I'd moved to Traverse City two years ago. My mom and I
talk, but we don't communicate. Patty's the one I trust to
listen and give me good advice. Mom's advice...well, she
means well, but she's a big Dirk fan.

See, I met Dirk — Frederick Wayne Schneider III —
when we both worked for the same company in Lansing,
Michigan, where we're both from. All the girls lusted after
him, but I was the lucky one who got to sigh into the mirror
and say, "He picked *me*." Naturally, when he moved north to
Traverse City, I came with him.

Well, I followed him. Looking back, I see the difference.
On the one hand, he didn't want us to move in together to
"protect my reputation." On the other hand, he had no
compunctions about sleeping with me. Silly me, I thought
that if I saved myself for the man I'd marry, he'd actually
marry me! Instead, after four years of promises, he dumped
me. Said he was in love with someone else.

So there I was in Traverse City with a job I loved (turns
out I'm a *great* residential realtor), an apartment I'd assumed
would be temporary, and a naked ring finger. Completely
heartbroken. After four months of tears, I'd decided I needed
an escape. Well, Patty suggested it, and my best friend Emily
signed us up. A girls-only fishing trip into the wilds of the
Upper Peninsula with the Harbor View Nature Club.

Though if we didn't find some kind of civilization soon, I had my doubts that we'd ever be seen or heard from again.

"Only fifteen miles to go," Shelley said from behind the wheel.

"Fifteen miles?" Emily cried. "At five miles an hour, that's three more hours!"

Emily Dodson, my best friend in the whole universe, had been unnaturally excited about this trip. I wanted her to come because she's my best friend and I didn't want to go alone. But I wasn't prepared for her — well, *exuberance*. Emily's a city girl. Well, as city as you can get where we live. She's all about malls and looking great and having beautifully painted nails. She's more *Sex in the City* than *Northern Exposure*. Emily had never even gone hiking with me. In a healthier state of mind, I would've seriously questioned her newfound desire to kill and cook her own dinner.

Patty smiled soothingly at us from the front passenger seat. "She's teasing you. We're almost there. Half an hour at the most."

"That'll make us look even more intelligent in our obituary," I said. "'Ten women died twenty minutes from civilization. It's rumored that they drove in circles saying, 'Just a few more minutes, a few more minutes.'"

Emily grunted. My pseudofascination with how I would die usually amused her. The fact that she wasn't laughing meant she wasn't so sure I was wrong this time.

She waved her cell phone. "It's impossible to die in the wilderness if you're anywhere near civilization in this day and age." She sounded like she was trying to convince herself more than the rest of us.

I looked at her phone and quirked an eyebrow. "Oh yeah?

How much longer do you think it'll say, 'Searching for signal'?"

Emily looked at her phone. "Panic" would aptly describe her expression. "Are you sure you know where we are, Patty?"

But twenty-eight minutes later (I looked at my watch so I could gauge time of death), the two-track suddenly opened into a huge yard of sorts, a meadow really. Obviously it was used as a parking lot because there were half a dozen vehicles there.

But wherever tire tracks hadn't crushed them, the lively color of wildflowers sprang from the ground. The pine, birch, and maple trees joined together to form a harmony of forest around us. To the left as we pulled in was a two-story building with a quaint painted sign, "Abundance Creek Lodge and Store," nailed above the door.

Next to the store stood what appeared to be the bunkhouse. Two, no, three little cottages peeked out from the woods on one side of the meadow. The first thing that came to mind when I saw them was *The Three Little Pigs*. It made me smile. So long as the Big Bad Wolf and all of his real life brothers stayed far away. Yikes. I'd forgotten the U.P. (Michigan-speak for the Upper Peninsula) had actual wolves. I tried not to think about it.

Thing is, I expected all of the buildings to be rugged, wooden structures, hardly a step up from tree forts. Wooden they were, but there was a sense of artistry here. Nothing like what I assumed men would build in the wilderness — or even what I figured men would choose if it were this pretty place or a more earthy, flea-infested fishing lodge.

But hey, I'm single, so what I know about men is obviously in question here.

I don't know where I went wrong, sighed Little Miss Lovesick. *I was so close to having it all.*

Ignore her. I'm not Sybil or Eve or anything, but…well, you know those voices in your head? I named them. Not all of them, just the obnoxious ones. I mean, it's nothing weird or anything. Okay, it *is* weird, but it's better than talking out loud, right? Then *everyone* knows you're crazy. Oh, forget it. *Anyway…*

Shelley parked the van and we all spilled out, groaning and stretching. The feel of real, not-planted-by-human-hands grass under my feet made me take off my sandals. I sighed with pleasure as the long grass enveloped my feet. This trip was a great idea.

"I hope they sell fudge," said Tracey, a marketing consultant I remembered from a previous Nature Club excursion.

"Why?" I asked. "We just drove here from the fudge capital of the world."

She laughed. "But now *we're* the ones on vacation. We can act like Fudgies and the locals can wish we'd spend our money and leave."

It's true. That's what we call tourists in Traverse City — Fudgies. They're always backing up traffic when they try to turn into a fudge shop unexpectedly. Very annoying when you're trying to get somewhere. On the other hand, you have to be grateful for the economic boost. Me especially, since sometimes it's a "Fudgie" buying a vacation home that helps me make rent.

Of course, the fact that you pay rent and not a mortgage is Dirk's fault, said Pride (Sergeant Pride, I call him). *You give the man love, loyalty, sex(!), and what do you get? The old kick in the caboose. Jerk.*

Turns out Mom was right about the milk and the cow, sighed another Voice.

Whatever. I mentally stuck my tongue out at myself. I would be institutionalized — or medicated at the very least — if anyone ever found out about all the voices in my head.

Everyone followed Patty into the store. Everyone but me. I waved Emily off, deciding I needed to breathe in some soothing, wilderness air. The sugar blues that follow a sugar buzz wasn't helping my roller coaster of emotions. I decided to self-medicate. I opened another candy bar and a can of Sprite from our stash.

Starting today, I would force my broken heart to heal if it was the last thing I did. Then maybe I'd lock it away someplace safe.

Don't say that, said Little Miss Lovesick. *Love is the most wonderful thing in the world. You just need to find* true *love.*

True love. That's what I wanted, but if I thought I had it once and I was wrong, how was I ever going to know how to find it for real?

I walked through the grass, trying unsuccessfully not to tread on the flowers. Closing my eyes, I savored the feel of the breeze on my face. Ahh, heaven. Feeling calmer, I folded the empty candy wrapper and stuck it in my pocket. I took a swallow of ice cold Sprite as I climbed the porch steps—

And ran smack into an opening screen door. Which wouldn't have been so bad except the body moving through the door was moving in my direction and crashed into me. Cold Sprite sloshed down my shirt, making me gasp.

"Damn! Are you all right?" A hand cupped my cheek and moved the screen door away from my face. Cold Sprite dripped all down my front. I took a step backward in an awkward attempt to get away. I felt my balance wobble. The hand firmly gripped my elbow, moving me away from the danger of the stairs.

Sputtering from the pop up my nose and in one eye, I wiped at my eyes and squinted to see what had just happened.

It's The Diet Coke Man, Little Miss Lovesick choked out.

I know I watch too many YouTube videos, but Lovesick may have been right. The Diet Coke Man from the "11:30" commercials was standing right in front of me. A flash of the commercial where the office women ogle the construction worker across the street blew through my brain. Dark hair and piercing eyes, built like a Viking. The way his black T-shirt outlined his muscular form did nothing to remind me that Heartbreak was the reason I had to get away.

Luscious, said Lovesick.

Holy… I tried to squeegee the liquid from my eye. Yeah, he looked equally fabulous with both eyes open. He stared at me in a concerned way that made my stomach flutter. I kind of liked men who looked at a woman this way. Like all you had to do was say the word and they'd fix whatever was broken.

The Diet Coke Man brushed drops of Sprite from my cheek and chin and I immediately sprang back, which only caused him to grasp my elbow tighter as I fell onto a lower step. Theoretically, I liked that kind of man. Realistically, I needed to keep my distance.

"Excuse me!" I found my footing and backed out of reach. He let go when I grabbed the handrail on the stairs.

"Sorry, sorry." He wiped his damp hand on his jeans, and had the grace to look embarrassed. "Are you all right?" He was dangerously appealing standing there trying to help, looking both embarrassed and amused.

I shook my wet right hand, not really wanting to wipe it on my shorts (like a guy), and wiped my face with my left hand. My cold chest caught my gaze and I gasped, pulling the fabric away from my body.

"Fine!" Did I *look* fine? My shirt was white and wet. My bra was black and lacey. I glared at him so he knew I was lying about being fine. He couldn't have noticed my glare, however, because he was staring at—

Look for a ring, Lovesick murmured.

You're not looking for a wedding ring on a stranger who knocked you down and is now ogling your breasts, declared Sergeant Pride.

"Uh, wait right here," said The Diet Coke Man, and he rushed back inside. As he opened the door, my eyes followed his left hand — but *accidentally*. Didn't matter. Couldn't tell. A moment later he was back, ripping a wad of napkins from a plastic package.

I swear, if he started dabbing at my chest with them like Hugh Grant did to Julia Roberts in *Notting Hill*, I'd pour the rest of my pop over his head.

"Here, I'll trade you," he said as he took the can and handed me the napkins.

"Thanks." I tried to blot my shirt without making a peep show out of the black lace. I turned slightly to my right for a bit of privacy. Why did I wear this on a *camping* trip?

I glanced up to see if he was watching. He smiled. My hand paused while blotting my shirt. This man's smile was so — so *gorgeous*. His eyes were an amazing shade of blue. I wanted to offer him the smallest of smiles back. After all, he did look fairly innocent and embarrassed. Instead, I stopped giving him the evil eye. That was as accommodating as I was willing to be.

A Rescuing Hero if I ever saw one, sighed Lovesick.

I tried to think of something to say, something funny to diffuse the tension. Something smart so I wouldn't look like such a dork.

"I, uh..."

"I'm really sorry," he said. He took my damp napkins and handed me back my pop can. With his left hand.

No ring! Lovesick squealed.

"Let me buy you another shirt," he said, nodding at my wet chest. He was trying to pretend he wasn't still staring. Rather gentlemanly for the backwoods.

He was already halfway through the door when I mumbled something that was supposed to be, "Don't worry about it, I'll get a fresh one from my suitcase," but came out as, "No, I-I..."

A moment later he pressed a blue plaid button-down flannel shirt into my hands. I stared at it trying to remember a time I had ever worn a flannel shirt. Before I could think about it further, he grabbed it, ripped the tag off with his teeth, and handed the shirt back to me.

I blinked at him. He was so not Dirk. I liked that about him.

"Sorry again," he said. "If you'll excuse me, I've got to get a few things done before we get started." He trotted off the porch to a nearby pickup (which he'd left unlocked in a decidedly small town way) and started rummaging around.

Before we what? I stood there staring stupidly after him, a flannel shirt in one hand and a forgotten pop can in the other. A fly buzzed past my nose and I snapped out of my trance.

You could go over and talk to him, suggested Lovesick.

Of all the things I might do on this trip, I was *not* going to flirt with some handsome stranger. No freaking way. My plan was to get over men, not rebound like a basketball.

He wasn't even that handsome. Honestly. His hair was too long, well past his collar. And his hands were too rough, as I remembered from when he wiped the Sprite from my cheek. And...and he smiled too much. Yeah. Seriously annoying.

Before I could think about it much more, I hurried into the store. Girls only. This is a girls-only fishing trip. Say it like a mantra. No boys allowed.

Okay. Deep breath. Close your eyes. Calm. Calm. Girls-only fishing trip. That means nature, which means tranquility, which means peace.

I opened my eyes. The inside of the store was as much a surprise as the outside had been. I expected more of what was in the general store in the last town — tourist trinkets and junk food and fluorescent lighting. The Abundance Creek Store had windows on three sides, letting the sunshine bounce off the polished wood beams in the ceiling and walls, and the well-worn but polished hardwood floor. One full wall held nothing but fishing tackle, most of which I knew was fishing tackle only because this was a fishing lodge.

As I walked around, I noticed fishing poles in a huge wooden barrel, a magazine and book rack, two full aisles of canned and boxed food, even a few kitchen utensils. I walked past a refrigerated unit with a sliding glass top and looked in hoping for a frozen Snickers bar. At first I thought the little tubs might be homemade ice cream or something since they had no labels. Then I saw something move under the plastic lid.

I jumped back, gasping and wrinkling my nose. The sign above the fridge read — Night Crawlers, Fresh Water

Shrimp, Black Flies. Ugh! I looked back at the wall of *artificial* lures gratefully. That's where I'd be shopping, if necessary.

I smiled as I passed Janice and Shelley, and walked over to the book and magazine rack. There was one copy each of some novels that had been on the *New York Times* bestseller list at some point. Some of the hunting and fishing magazines were special editions. The rest were either May, June, or July issues. I'd hazard a guess that these constituted the entire summer inventory. But still, it was a nice touch. You can never have too much reading material on vacation.

I picked up a copy of *Fisherman's Weekly* and flipped through it.

"If I can help you with anything, let me know."

Startled, I whirled around, bumping my elbow into the person behind me. "Oh, sor—"

I stopped in mid-apology. It was him, The Diet Coke Man. I tried to move away, but my back was against the bookshelf. I felt a little shock, like when you were a kid and put a 9-volt battery on your tongue. It scared me at the same time that it made my heart race.

It's the sugar. I ate enough to throw an entire kindergarten class into a coma. He's not making my heart race; it's the sugar. I slowly turned away and put the magazine down. Don't look at him. Just nod and smile, then pretend he's not there.

A muscular arm reached around me and moved the magazine back to its original spot. I realized I'd put *Fisherman's Weekly* in front of a stack of *Bow & Arrow Hunting* magazines. I felt the heat from his body and got a whiff of his aftershave or deodorant or something. I grabbed one of the books and read the back cover. Safe to be reading. People don't talk to you when you're reading.

His presence sent tickles up my back. Which was stupid. My shirt was still wet and sticky from him spilling pop on me. That was the cause of the ticklish feeling. I couldn't focus on reading the book so I put it back. The arm reached around me again with more magazines, arranging them on the shelf in front of me.

I got the feeling I was invading his precious orderly wilderness. It's wild. That's the point of calling it *wild*erness. What was he doing anyway? He must work here, I guess. But Patty said this place was owned and operated by a friend of hers.

I turned back to him. "Am I in your way?"

Ooo, attitude girlfriend, said a Voice.

Crap, I hadn't meant to sound so rude. But he was unnerving me.

He looked up from straightening candy bars in the snack rack behind us. I watched as a dimple appeared to anchor one corner of his grin. What is it everyone loves about dimples, anyway? They're just big vertical wrinkles.

"No, not at all." He picked up an empty candy box from the floor and broke down the ends, folding it into a neat square.

"Listen, I'm really sorry about spilling your drink." His gaze dropped to my shirt for a second, then popped back up. I folded my arms across my chest and scowled.

His eyes were that shade of bright blue that surely only comes from colored contacts. No one aside from Paul Newman has eyes that blue.

"Do you need any help with the shirt?" He pointed to the one he'd given me earlier, still in my hand.

I knew it! He's some kind of redneck gigolo. "I don't know what you think I came up here for, but it wasn't to be hit on by you. I'm just here to fish, okay?"

I saw his eyebrows raise before I turned on my heel and stalked away. There. That should show *him*. I gave myself a mental high-five.

"I was only going to tell you where the bathroom is," I heard him say.

Little Miss Lovesick sighed. *It's a pretty bad day when you confuse a gentleman with a gigolo.*

ALSO BY KITTY BUCHOLTZ

The Strays of Loon Lake

Welcome to Loon Lake

Love at the Fluff and Fold

Traverse City in Love

Cherry on Top (free short story)

Little Miss Lovesick

Death and Tacos (coming soon!)

Adventures of Lewis and Clarke

Superhero in Disguise

A Very Merry Superhero Wedding

Unexpected Superhero

My Bullheaded Superhero Valentine

Also…

Adventures of Lewis and Clarke: The Beginning (the first three
books)

A NOTE FROM KITTY

One of the things I want to do as a writer and a person is to bring more love and laughter into the world. The Strays of Loon Lake series has made me laugh and sigh (and occasionally cry) as I've written it. I hope it has done the same for you!

If you're curious about how I created it...

Loon Lake is a combination of Manistee Lake, Michigan, where I grew up, Kalkaska, Michigan, where I went to school kindergarten through twelfth grade, and the best parts of my imagination. It's full of wonderful, quirky people, beautiful countryside, and lots of adorable pets. (I wish Pirate was my puppy!)

The idea for Danny and Cassie was pulled directly from my childhood. One of my best friends from about second grade was a boy named Danny, and there was a moment when it looked like we would turn a high school romance into a life together.

I actually had an Uncle Wilfred, and he and my aunt owned several businesses not dissimilar from Uncle Willie's businesses. I have fond memories of eating Superman ice cream when I was about five at their ice cream shop with all the family.

The rest of the characters in Loon Lake are combinations of the best parts of people I've known — Tabitha is similar to a young woman I met on a writing retreat in Las Vegas — combined with whimsical ideas of people I'd like to meet.

When I was a teenager, my mother despaired of me dating the kind of boy who had it all together. I kept bringing home strays, as they were sometimes referred to by Mom. I kept telling her I could see lots of potential in the underdog. But she's a mom and she wanted to make sure I lived up to *my* potential! Haha!

"I understand that you want to help them, but why do you have to date them? You can't save them all," she said.

And that's where I got the idea for The Strays of Loon Lake! It's all about lost men and stray dogs and the women who love them.

I hope you enjoyed reading *Love at the Fluff and Fold*. More books are coming in this series! Until then, be sure to read the short story prequel, *Welcome to Loon Lake,* where Chip, the border collie, finds his forever home.

My books are available as ebooks and in print at most online retailers. *Unexpected Superhero* and *Little Miss Lovesick* are also available as audiobooks. All the ebooks, print books, and audiobooks will be added to my own web store over the course of 2024. Purchases there support me and my work in a significantly greater way so I'd love it if you'd like to buy from me directly (kittybucholtz.com/books)!

You can also join my free or paid membership community over on Patreon (links at the end of About the Author). Read chapters early before the books even come out, discuss the stories with other readers, see fun art about the settings of the books, and more!

Would you like to read *Cherry on Top* for free? It's set in the same town as *Little Miss Lovesick* during the famous

National Cherry Festival. It's my gift to you when you join my reader newsletter at kittybucholtz.com/freebook. Enjoy!

If you really want to make my day, I'd love for you to post your thoughts about the book in a review. Thanks so much!

And just so you know, I rebranded all my books in 2024 to be "sweet" — so no swear words or overt sex scenes. I hope you enjoy the change.

Happy Reading!

ABOUT THE AUTHOR

Kitty Bucholtz writes sweet romantic comedy and superhero urban fantasy, often with an inspirational element woven in. Her stories feature women whose sense of humor and nervous gutsiness get them into and out of all kinds of trouble. She grew up forty miles east of Traverse City, Michigan—where she loves to set her books. She went to college there, met and married the love of her life, and waved goodbye to everything she knew when she and her husband, John, struck out for parts unknown.

Their romantic adventures have included a scolding at Parliament House in Belfast for canoodling, three trips Down Under where her handsome hubby made animated movie animals look real, and a delicious taste of European life living in Sweden. After earning her M.A. in Creative Writing in Sydney, she formed Daydreamer Entertainment and began self-publishing. Founder of Write Now! Workshop and Write Now! Workshop Podcast, she loves to teach and coach writers.

Only God knows where they'll wind up next – but they're pretty sure it will be another cool chapter in their adventure!

If you enjoyed this or any of Kitty's books, please leave a review—they are a tremendous help to both writers and readers!

Connect with Kitty today!
kittybucholtz.com
kitty@kittybucholtz.com

Get your copy of the free short story *Cherry on Top* at kittybucholtz.com/freebook today!

patreon.com/kittybucholtz

tiktok.com/@kitty_bucholtz

facebook.com/kittybucholtzauthor

bookbub.com/profile/kitty-bucholtz

amazon.com/author/kittybucholtz

x.com/KittyBucholtz

instagram.com/kittybucholtz

goodreads.com/kittybucholtz

youtube.com/kittybucholtz